Murder in Bridal Lane

Miss Hayward and the Detective series

By Helen Goltz

Atlas Productions

Murder in Bridal Lane
First published in 2022
Copyright © Helen Goltz 2022

This book is written in British - Australian English.

Atlas Productions
Greenslopes QLD 4102
Web: www.atlasproductions.com.au
This book is a work of fiction. Names, characters, places and incidents are either the product of the author's imagination or are used fictitiously. Any resemblance to actual persons, living or dead, or to actual events or locales is entirely coincidental. Any medical experiments or results cited in this novel have been fictionalised and any slight of specific people, experiments, research or organisations is unintentional.

Proofread by: Penny Clarkson
Cover images: Bride – Syrotkin Studio; Bouquet – Syrotkin Studio; Background – RenataP; Shutterstock.
Cover design by Atlas Productions.

NATIONAL LIBRARY OF AUSTRALIA

A catalogue record for this book is available from the National Library of Australia

Dedicated to my nieces who are just like Miss Matilda Hayward – smart and beautiful.

The future is in good hands.

Emma, Chloe, Sienna, Isabella, Angela and Peyton.

Author's note:

This is a book of fiction but I try to be as accurate to the era as possible, in this case – 1889. Set in Brisbane, Australia, you will find at the back of this volume, more information about some of the happenings and historical references that I use, should you be interested.

You can be assured that Matilda, her family, and friends have a happy ending and even though it will no longer be 'Miss Matilda Hayward & the Detective'—after all, she will be Mrs Thomas Ashdown—I hope you might enjoy the pending series featuring the mortician, Miss Phoebe Astin from the previous volume, and yes, she is still dating Gideon Hayward. Read on fair reader.

Chapter 1

Brisbane, Australia, 1889

The tarot reader saw the pretty young lady consulting a slip of paper and looking up at the address at the crossroad to the lane. The young woman—whom she would later learn was Miss Matilda Hayward—appeared to ask for directions, but the tarot reader knew the young miss was on her way to the neighbouring florist shop, *Blooming Blossoms*. Gerta Schneider, or Madam Gerta as she was known, saw all the comings and goings in the street, but not much else despite her promises and assurances of seeing and knowing all. She sat at the small round table that faced the street, looking out through the glass panels of her store; her clients, when in her company, sat with their back to the street for their privacy and to ensure people passing saw how busy Madam Gerta was with customers. Surely, she must be successful then.

Madam Gerta shuffled a worn pack of cards and placed them down on the table, then cut the deck into three piles – the past, the present and the future for the young woman in the blue dress. Madam Gerta drew a card from the first deck and placed it down on the table. It represented the past. She looked at the card, then at her subject. Madam Gerta inhaled and released a long breath.

'Three of Wands. You are a very curious young woman, perhaps to your detriment,' Madam Gerta said out loud, as if the subject were sitting opposite for a reading. Little did she know Miss Matilda Hayward did not believe in fortune-telling and would not waste her time or limited earnings on something so frivolous. Madam Gerta tapped on the card. 'Your need for discovery is constant, and your lover will never tire of you. But curiosity will not serve you well in our laneway, miss.'

Madam Gerta drew from the second pack which represented the present and nodded her head as if the card made perfect sense.

'The lovers,' she announced. 'You have a deep connection and you have made the right choice for tender affection and admiration.' She glanced at the florist shop nearby. 'On your way to order wedding flowers, no doubt.'

Turning the last card in the deck that represented the future, Madam Gerta smiled. 'Ah yes, the Ace of Swords, just as I predicted. You are at great risk because you are an impulsive young lady. Too impulsive for your own good.'

*****

Miss Matilda Hayward glanced up at the sign over the awning, then back to her note. She had the correct address, but the florist shop appeared to be a fruit and vegetable grocer. Boxes of fruit replaced the familiar buckets of flowers she was expecting, and while the apples looked enticing, she was on a mission and did not want to be distracted.

Today Matilda intended to organise the flower order for her wedding, cross that off her list, and let Aunt Audrey relax that it was in hand. As well-intentioned as her dear aunt was towards the looming marital event between Matilda and her childhood friend, now fiancé, Detective Thomas Ashdown, one would think it was a royal wedding for the planning and budget that Aunt Audrey had allocated to it. Still, Matilda was her only niece and the only girl in a family of four boys, so she could not begrudge her aunt's enthusiasm, and her generosity had been overwhelmingly kind.

A deep voice from behind made Matilda look up with a start from her jotted-down notes.

'Vincent Sebastian at your service.' A middle-aged man with a full head of dark hair, wearing a distinctive black and white apron over his shirt and pants, gave a small bow. 'You look like a young lady who needs a bunch of grapes or some plums.'

'Goodness, do I?' Matilda asked, surprised. 'And here I was, looking for a florist.'

He laughed. 'A young bride to be?'

'How can you tell, Mr Sebastian?' Matilda said, with a smile. She ran a hand down her pale blue dress, conscious of the large diamond ring on her finger.

'Young, beautiful and with a glow about you. He's a lucky man, that fiancé of yours,' he said and gave her a wink.

Matilda laughed. 'I am not sure he would agree with you every day of the week. But yes, I am looking for *Blooming Blossoms*.'

'You are not the first to lose them, I assure you, miss,' Mr Sebastian said. 'I have the good fortune of meeting many young ladies, and many confused young gentlemen on some occasions in search of the very same shop.' He nodded behind her. 'You'll see a laneway there. They moved a few years ago into Bridal Lane. It seemed like a good fit, according to the owner, but the other bridal stores are gone now. There used to be a very good cake store in the lane and a dressmaker, or so the wife says, but they've both gone.'

'Ah, thank you, Mr Sebastian. How fortunate you are a man of good humour as the mistake might become quite annoying.'

'But see now you have found *Vincent's Fruit and Vegetable Grocers*,' he said, waving his hands around as if introducing Matilda personally to his stock on hand. 'I live in hope that one day, a bride might say, "forget the flowers, I am going to have a bouquet of berries!" and I will fulfil the order for her.'

Matilda laughed at his theatrics, as did several other customers.

'I shall give it some thought, Mr Sebastian. It is certainly a novel idea. But in the interim, I will take an apple and two of your plums, please.'

'Good girl,' he said with a grin, and selected what he claimed to be the best on show, placing them in tissue paper for her, and accepting the coin with thanks. 'Be careful now, lass,' he said, with a nod to the small laneway.

Matilda looked over her shoulder and back at him, wide-eyed with surprise. 'Why is that, Mr Sebastian?' She narrowed her eyes. 'You are not going to warn me that the roses have thorns?' she joked.

Vincent Sebastian laughed a hearty laugh. 'No, but well done, young lady.' He sobered. 'It's not the nicest of lanes. I can have one of my delivery boys escort you if you like?'

'You are too kind, Mr Sebastian, thank you,' she said. 'But as it is only just nearing midday and hopefully any shady characters are still recovering from the night before. I shall do my business and not dally. But I thank you for the warning.'

'Right you are then. Enjoy your fruit and do come again,' he said, with a smile and a small bow.

Matilda thanked him and on reaching the corner, she glanced back to see him applying his charm on another victim. Still, she would enjoy the apple on her walk home. She waited to safely cross the busy road and glanced down the small laneway.

'*It's not the nicest of lanes*', she heard Vincent Sebastian's words in her head and hurried her step, all the time looking out for the *Blooming Blossoms* sign and debating whether she should seek another florist, despite the fact they advertised with the *Women's Journal* where Matilda worked, and the ladies were encouraged to support the magazine's sponsors.

She slowed her step and relaxed as several other ladies and couples came into sight; there was safety in numbers. Mr Sebastian was right; it was an odd little laneway with a strange mixture of shops and it felt a little tired and dirty.

On her left was a small gift store filled with trinkets from little music boxes to figures; next was a costume store with a suit of armour in the window and a costume that appeared to be some sort of angel, except it was a little wilted and worse for wear. Above it was a sign for bridal dresses, now faded, and the store gone. Across the lane was a lady offering tarot reading, and a private loan business was next to that. Right in the middle was *Blooming Blossoms*. Matilda could hear music down the end of the laneway and from the small crowd that gathered around the venue, it appeared to be a saloon.

Pushing open the glass door that led into *Blooming Blossoms*, Matilda entered, taking in the scent and beauty of the little shop as the bell above her head announced her arrival.

Chapter 2

T he young boy ran up to the two detectives and studied their shoes.

'Mister, you could use a clean,' he said, looking up at Detective Thomas Ashdown.

'I cleaned them last night,' Thomas said, sounding offended and looking down at his very shiny shoes, as his partner, Detective Harry Dart chuckled.

'I'd get them cleaner,' the boy boasted, holding up a scuffed rag and a tin of shoe polish.

Thomas took his measure. He was a confident child with a handsome face and an attitude as a consequence of both. But his clothes looked like they hadn't left his body for a long time. He wore no shoes, and a jaunty cap donned his head. He had the air of a rascal.

'How can I trust a young man with no shoes of his own to show his shining prowess?' Thomas teased him. 'If your shoes were really shiny, then I might be convinced.'

The boy looked at his bare feet. 'Ma says we haven't got money to waste on shoes. Anyway, it's too hot to wear them.'

'That it is, young man,' Detective Harry Dart said. 'What's your name then?'

'Charles Doyle, but everyone calls me Charlie because Da's name is also Charles.'

'Right then, young fellow,' Harry said, 'well we're detectives and I know you wouldn't be trying to swindle us, so how about if I give you a coin today just because your surname is Irish and it's the luck of the Irish?'

Charlie Doyle grinned. 'Every time Da says that, Ma says we left that luck behind in Ireland.' He happily accepted the coin and pocketed it before Harry had a chance to change his mind. 'Thanks, mister.' He turned to Thomas. 'If I can keep this coin and you want to part with one too, I could tell you where a crime has happened? Since you're a detective and all.'

Thomas smiled. 'You're an enterprising businessman, young Charlie.' He reached into his pocket and pulled out a coin. 'I'm prepared to pay for your street wisdom, but not until I hear about the crime first.' He wrapped his fingers around the coin and raised his eyebrow at the boy with expectation.

'Fair enough,' Charlie said with a nod; he was no stranger to business arrangements. 'It's a woman; she's dead, lying up there in the alley. I'll take you.'

Harry stopped him. 'Charlie, have you seen her with your own eyes?'

'Yes, mister. She's not looking pretty.'

Thomas frowned. 'You don't need to be seeing things like that, Charlie. You should be out playing with your mates. Having a bit of fun.'

'I've got to make some dough first, then I'm allowed out to play. I have responsibilities,' he said, no doubt repeating a conversation often bestowed on him by his parents.

'Did you see who brought about this harm to the lady?' Thomas asked.

Charlie shook his head. 'I just came upon her. I don't think anyone else has… I was chasing a cat,' he said, looking sheepish as if he should have been working.

Thomas got out a few extra coins and once Charlie had pointed to the lane in question, he gave them to the young boy.

'Gees, mister, that's great, thanks.' He tore off.

'I hope he hasn't told you a fib now,' Harry chuckled.

'I almost hope he has,' Thomas said, with a sigh as they ventured up towards the laneway in question.

*****

Matilda brightened at the beautiful surroundings of the little shop, *Blooming Blossoms*. Unlike the laneway in which it resided, it was much prettier on the inside, a virtual escape from the town and its crowds. The theme was pink and white, with silver trimmings. The two ladies serving both wore pink and white aprons over their pale gowns. Buckets full of flowers adorned one side of the shop, while a large desk with ribbons and paper was on the other side. A woman who looked to be no more than five-and-ten was busy preparing a bouquet for some lucky recipient. Her name badge read 'Rose'. She glanced up at Matilda.

'Good afternoon, miss, we will be with you shortly.'

'Thank you, do not rush. I am content to stop and admire the flowers,' Matilda said. She looked enviously at the bouquet being prepared. 'Some lucky lady.'

'Indeed,' Rose agreed. 'We've been very busy today. Must be something in the water.'

Matilda laughed as Rose continued tying ribbons through the flowers. Behind the counter, a very presentable woman, most likely in her fourth decade, wore a name badge that said 'Mrs Celia Dalton, Manageress'. She served what could only be a mother and daughter from their similarity.

'I shall be with you shortly,' Mrs Dalton called to Matilda.

'I am in no hurry, please do take your time,' Matilda assured her and wandered off to sniff the bouquets in the buckets.

A young man hurried in, startling the customers and earned himself a glare from Mrs Dalton behind the counter.

'Forgive our delivery boy, Jacob, he must do everything at an exhausting speed,' she offered the clients in store, as Jacob tipped his hat with a grin and disappeared behind the counter to the back of the store.

'I'll have another bunch for you shortly, Jacob,' Rose called after him. She glanced at Matilda. 'He does quite well with the tips if the ladies remember before they get overwrought by the bouquet.'

'Goodness, I confess to having forgotten to tip myself.'

'That's quite alright. We always include a little extra for delivery with each order. Jacob does alright for himself,' Rose assured her.

Mrs Dalton's face expressed relief as the door behind Matilda opened and another woman, similar in age to Rose, entered. She donned a pink and white apron and her name badge as she walked to join the manageress behind the counter.

'Just in time, Esther,' Mrs Dalton said. 'Could you please help this young lady?'

'May I help you, miss?' she asked, with a glance at Matilda's ring finger to ensure she was still a miss, while pinning on her own name badge.

'I have come about a bridal bouquet. I work for the *Women's Journal* and saw your advertisement,' Matilda said. 'I am seeking a bouquet for myself and my three bridesmaids.'

'It would be an honour to provide for your day,' Esther said, the words not sounding practised despite her youth; a credit to the training imparted by the manageress, Mrs Dalton. 'If you have a flower or colour in mind, Rose can prepare some flowers in a sample bouquet for you to take home to consider before making your decision?'

'Oh, that sounds like a wonderful idea,' Matilda said, pleased. 'My bridesmaids are wearing white embroidered muslin dresses, blue sashes, and white sailor hats.'

'Delightful,' Esther said, and looked at Mrs Dalton, who was now free, having given her clients some prices to consider. 'Forget-me-nots?' Esther asked the manageress.

'An excellent idea, Esther,' Mrs Dalton said, and Matilda looked keen to accept their suggestion.

'Forget-me-not wreaths are very popular at the moment,

miss,' Esther said, returning her attention to Matilda. 'They would go perfectly with the bridesmaids' sashes. Now, would you be so kind as to describe your dress please, miss?'

'White satin, a silk net veil and lace.'

'So romantic,' Esther said as if inspired if not by the fabric but the extravagance, bumping the price to be charged for the bouquets higher. 'May I suggest a bouquet for you of white roses, white chrysanthemums, and delicate forget-me-nots woven in between, with white and blue satin ribbon?'

'That sounds better than anything I could have imagined,' Matilda said, delighted.

Esther looked pleased with Matilda's praise and looked at Rose.

'I am free now,' Rose said. 'I shall give this bouquet to Jacob to deliver and make your samples now, miss,' she said to Matilda. On securing Matilda's agreement, Rose departed for the backroom. Matilda heard more voices as Rose gave instructions.

The timing was perfect, Matilda mused. Tonight was Daniel's birthday and everyone would be in attendance at the Hayward family home, including their lady partners and Aunt Audrey. She could get everyone's thoughts on the sample bouquets.

She watched Rose through the doorway selecting flowers and congratulated herself on having done a chore so successfully. Another young lady entered and Esther moved to serve her, assuring Matilda that her sample would be ready post haste.

Five minutes later, Matilda accepted the two beautiful, small bouquet samples—at no charge—with great delight and headed home to show the Hayward's life-long housekeeper, Harriet, before the rest of the family gathered.

Matilda was yet to find the message hidden amongst the flowers of one of the bouquets.

Chapter 3

'Dead alright,' Harry said, pushing his hat back off his head and studying the woman lying prone in front of them at the end of the alley.

'And for a while, I'd say,' Thomas said. His nose was sensitive to smells at the best of times and the smell of death was one scent he was most familiar with, despite only being eight-and-twenty. But he and Harry had been on enough cases to have seen bodies in all states of disrepair. This one, however, surprised him.

'She looks most respectable,' Thomas added, as he gingerly made his way around the corpse in the dark alley.

'That she does,' Harry agreed. 'Ignoring her flesh, of course, that has decayed and suffered the indignities of small rodents in the alley, her hair is secured, her dress and shoes are fashionable. Theft perhaps? She is wearing no jewellery, which is most unusual for a lady.'

'Perhaps it is theft. She has a faded mark on her wedding finger, so she must normally wear a ring,' Thomas agreed.

'Why would she have business around here? Most likely she was dumped here.'

'I'd say. Young Charlie's right, she's not easy to see from the entranceway. Doesn't even have a name this alley, by the looks of it, it is just a service strip for the shops.'

Thomas saw a faded sign on the wall of the building and pointed at it. 'Looks like it does have a name – Tea Lane. The stores out the front might have once been in the tea and coffee trade.'

'Most likely,' Harry agreed.

The men noted the bins and several doors opening out into the alley. Thomas tried a few, found them locked and mentally made a note to ask the shop owners in the front street if they'd seen anyone and how often they use the lane adjoining their shops.

'Give me a minute and I'll call for backup and the coroner,' Harry said, walking back down the alley as Thomas surveyed the scene. He could not recall anyone being reported missing in the last few days, so either no one was expecting this lady home or friends have not yet noticed her absence. In light of the limited family he had remaining, it made him grateful for his friends. In a matter of a month, however, Matilda would always be at home waiting for him. The thought made him smile before a frown took over… she was just as likely to be on some investigation for the *Women's Journal* and he would be at home waiting for her.

He returned to the job at hand and walked up and down the alleyway, looking for anything that may have been dropped or disturbed. There was nothing. Who was she, and why was such a respectable woman murdered and dumped in this part of town? Then he saw a small fabric bag protruding from underneath the lady's elbow. He wheedled it out and opened the bag.

'Found something then?' Harry asked, coming up the alley and rejoining him. 'Backup is on its way.'

'Yes, a small bag underneath her arm. But look at this... most peculiar,' Thomas said, taking out a fine lace handkerchief and a small card that read *Louise's Fine Lace, 42 George Street.*'

'Is this Louise then?' Harry asked. 'Was she a lacemaker or did she frequent *Louise's Fine Lace,* I wonder.'

'The coroner will be able to tell from her fingers, I imagine. Regular needlepoint will harden the calluses,' Thomas said and looked up to see Harry smiling at him. Thomas rolled his eyes. 'I look and learn.'

'You do indeed, most impressive, Thom,' Harry said with a chuckle. 'What was peculiar about the card and handkerchief?'

'That's all that's in her possession. Someone has most likely robbed her of her coins and keys, along with her wedding band and perhaps an engagement ring. I've never met a lady who did not have more than they need in their handbags.' He smiled and explained to Harry. 'Last year, Matilda was carrying around a salve, just in case.'

'I like a young woman who is prepared,' Harry said with a laugh.

They were interrupted by the sound of two junior constables arriving and not long after, the hansom delivering the coroner, Dr Patrick Nevins, and a wagon with two burly men to remove the body.

'I'll need some light up here please,' Dr Nevins said, issuing orders to the men with him. One of them fetched a lamp. It was only early afternoon, but the laneway was narrow and a dead-end; evidence could be hard to spot in the shadows.

'Gentlemen,' Dr Nevins addressed the two detectives, as his cane made a thumping sound each time it hit the dirt floor of the alleyway. 'I appreciate you choosing a death site with a flat surface for a change.'

'We thought you were due one, Patrick,' Harry said in jest. 'But don't get used to it.'

The coroner and Detective Harry Dart were not dissimilar in look – both distinguished, with greying hair and a slim build, but Patrick was some years younger than Harry and began greying early... perhaps the corpses across his worktable had something to do with it.

As expected, the sight of the constables and the wagon brought a crowd of onlookers who gathered around the mouth of the alleyway to peer up and see what manner of crime was afoot. The young constables prevented them from coming any further.

'Goodness, I know this lady,' Patrick declared, stepping back from the corpse.

'I am sorry for that,' Harry said.

'Would her name be Louise, by any chance?' Thomas asked.

'Indeed. This is Mrs Louise Greenwood. She is a member

of my church and a fine lace maker; that is her profession. Her husband passed away many years ago leaving her with two young children, who are adults themselves now, but she was able to support her family with her lacework. She has quite a reputation for it, I believe. Goodness me.'

'Patrick, would you prefer we call for your assistant?' Thomas asked.

'No, no,' Dr Nevins said, standing straighter. 'I am but an acquaintance… it was just a surprise, a shock. Bring the lamp over here, please.' He directed the man holding the lamp and suggested he put it down for now and return to the wagon. 'Right then, what have we got?'

'Our next case, I'd say,' Harry said.

Chapter 4

T o ensure all was well in the kitchen, Aunt Audrey—Mrs Samuel Bloomfield—arrived at the Hayward household well before the Hayward family birthday celebration was due to begin. Things were always under control; Harriet, the family's housekeeper, had been in the role since the children were born, and Mary, the Irish cook, for just as long. But as the family matriarch in the absence of Mrs Hayward, long since deceased, Aunt Audrey felt it her duty. She usually arrived an hour earlier but had been delayed with her community work.

'Always a roast for Daniel, Mrs Bloomfield,' Mary told her, flushed with the heat of the kitchen as she held the trays out for Aunt Audrey to inspect. 'It's his favourite and he requests the same thing every birthday.'

'And yet again, it is cooked to perfection,' Aunt Audrey said and sighed. She straightened, reached for her handkerchief nestled discretely between her bosoms, and dabbed the perspiration from her forehead.

'I shall be so pleased when the summer is over,' she said.

'Rest easy, Mary, I shall not try to convince you to come and cook for me and my guests again. But allow me to say that if you change your mind…'

Mary chuckled. 'Aye, I assure you, you will be the first to know, Mrs Bloomfield, and I am flattered by your offer, truly I am.'

Aunt Audrey smiled and watched as Mary returned the roasts to the heat.

'What has the birthday boy requested for dessert? Let me guess, bread-and-butter pudding and jam roly-poly,' Aunt Audrey said, making Mary and Harriet laugh, as Harriet gathered the place settings to set the table.

'That's the ticket,' Mary said. 'They are prepared and soon to be baked.'

'Thank you, Mary, and Harriet. I shall join the family then and be on hand to meet and greet.'

'Right you are, Mrs Bloomfield,' Mary said, and as she left, Mary turned to Harriet. 'Can yer believe Daniel is seven-and-twenty? I can remember the day Mrs Hayward brought him into this world like it was yesterday.'

'As can I,' Harriet said and smiled at the memory. 'The second born, and so different from Amos.'

'Always in awe of everything, wasn't he?' Mary said, and smiled.

'And always into everything, what a handful,' Harriet said with a chuckle.

'Ah, he was a grand lad, and now he has that lovely English lass. Let's hope there's another wedding soon.'

'I think we might be enjoying more than two weddings

this year if Elijah and Miss Urry continue their fascination with each other,' Harriet said. 'I'm off to set the table,' she said and headed to the dining room. The new conservatory was finished but best suited to lunch when no lighting was needed. Everyone would just have to squeeze in, Harriet thought with a smile as she made the settings work as best she could.

*****

In the drawing-room, Daniel almost choked on his brandy, prompting his sister, Matilda, to give him a firm hit on the back.

Once he recovered, he narrowed his eyes with suspicion: 'You enjoyed that,' he said.

'Don't be ridiculous,' Matilda said and grinned.

'I can't believe you went into Bridal Lane by yourself,' Daniel remonstrated. 'Don't tell Pa or Aunt Audrey, they'll have something to say about it and Pa might never let you out of the house again, even if you are married.'

'It's where the florist shop is located,' Matilda defended herself. 'How bad can it be?'

'Bad. There's a saloon at the end of that lane that has been the site of many a fight and several deaths for that matter. I have seen the cases come through the court while I've been illustrating.'

Matilda frowned. 'I do have to return to order my bouquets, though. I only have a sample. Best you don't tell them,' she said, a hint of begging in her voice.

'I won't if you tell me when you are next to go there and I shall accompany you.'

'Will you?' she said, giving him an affectionate smile. 'Thank you, Daniel.'

'Only because we both won't hear the end of it if Thomas hears you have been there as well.'

'Been where?' Thomas said, entering the room.

'Ah, you are here and on time,' Matilda said, brightening at the sight of her fiancé and aiming to distract him from the topic at hand. Thomas moved to her, and taking her hand, planted a kiss on it.

Behind Thomas were Mr Hayward and his guest, the widowed Mrs Betty Purcell. Like Georgina and Alice, Betty met Matilda at the *Women's Journal* and after some clever match-making on Matilda's behalf, her father and Betty found themselves to be enjoying each other's company considerably.

'Hello birthday boy, and Tillie dear,' Mr Hayward said, accepting a kiss from Matilda and greeting Daniel. 'Well, you've got to the ripe old age of seven-and-twenty, Daniel. You have a responsible job, a beautiful lady in your life; I couldn't want anything more from you... except maybe a wedding and grandchildren.'

Daniel laughed. 'Right, I'll get onto that then,' he said, 'and here's the lady who could make it happen,' he added, as Alice walked into the room with Elijah and Georgina.

'Cutting it fine,' Daniel said, after accepting their birthday wishes. Cook was a stickler for eating on time. She never minded how many came to dine, but Mary insisted they eat the food when it was ready and at its best.

Aunt Audrey entered the room with Amos, his wife, Minnie, and their baby girl. She pressed an envelope into Daniel's hand, accepting a kiss on the cheek from him.

'What is this then, Aunt? A list of your hopes for me in the coming year,' he teased his aunt.

'It is exactly that,' Aunt Audrey joined in his joke. 'Open it later, just a small gift.'

'Thank you,' he said sincerely, and she gave a small nod of her head. 'I am yet to sponsor you, Daniel.'

'For what, Aunt?' he asked, confused.

She lowered her voice to speak with him alone. 'For your future. I have had the pleasure of sponsoring Amos to study law and Elijah medicine, purchasing a share of a gallery for Gideon, and gifting Matilda her wedding. Do think about what you might like… perhaps a honeymoon abroad, especially if your beloved is from the mother country?' she said with a raised eyebrow, making him smile and shake his head at her persistence to see her niece and nephews betrothed.

'Thank you,' he said quickly, as Amos and Minnie joined them. Daniel reached out his hands to have a hold of his niece, which Minnie agreed to, given he was the birthday boy. She was rather protective.

'Come to your favourite uncle,' he said, kissing the baby's head.

The front door opened and slammed closed and Gideon, the last of the Hayward boys, rushed in.

'One minute to spare,' he proclaimed and grinned.

'And dinner is ready,' Harriet announced, seeing Gideon and giving him a wink.

'Happy birthday, Dan,' he said and cooed at the baby girl. 'Come to your favourite uncle,' he said, trying to take the baby from Daniel.

'She is currently with him,' Daniel assured his younger brother.

'So paternal you boys, who would have thought?' Matilda said as Minnie reclaimed her daughter. 'Since you boys are so sensitive, I wish to have your advice on my flower bouquets for the wedding. I have put them on the sideboard in our dining room so we can discuss them over dinner.'

'How exciting,' Alice said, her eyes alive with interest.

The group glanced at Thomas who realised he was meant to react with some enthusiasm. 'Oh, yes, good,' he added late.

Matilda rolled her eyes and everyone laughed.

'Sorry, it is not my specialty,' he said, flushed. The idea of ordering flowers, even the groomsmen's button-hole flowers, had never crossed his mind.

'I am sorry we couldn't come with you,' Georgina said. 'It was rather busy at work today.'

'That is quite alright,' Matilda assured her as the group made their way into the dining room. 'Alice had her meeting and I know your illustrating work does not end until the *Women's Journal* goes to print. Whereas, I am ahead of the deadline for this issue and thought I would take advantage of that.'

'When the time comes,' Alice said, with a glance to Daniel as they seated, 'I am going to have pink peonies in my bouquet. I love them.'

'I will have wildflowers,' Georgina said. 'Lovely bunches of them, with plenty of green.'

'From your family farm?' Matilda asked.

'Yes, fortunately, the cows don't much like the flowers, so there should be some on hand to pick,' Georgina said.

'Sounds wonderfully economical too, Georgina,' Betty Purcell said.

'That's very true, Betty,' Georgina said and smiled. 'But I'm sure my mother will find somewhere to spend the savings.'

'Or the savings could go towards the honeymoon,' Elijah suggested.

'A much better idea,' Georgina said, and they smiled at each other as if they had a hidden secret.

Matilda diverted the family's attention to the two bouquets and accepted the compliments on her choices. Teasing, and with a glance at the girls who understood her motives, she began:

'What do you think, Daniel, as you are the birthday boy, your opinion today is the most important?' she asked, as Daniel looked stricken and Alice, sitting beside him, hid a smile. He studied the two bouquets momentarily, scrambling for something sincere to say given the gravity of the pending nuptials of Matilda and his best friend, Thomas.

'The one with the blue forget-me-nots will be the bridesmaids' bouquet and the white roses with the blue forget-me-nots are for the bridal bouquet,' Matilda informed him.

'Ah, yes, well, they are very pretty,' he said with a nod.

Matilda waited a moment and when Daniel commented no further, she turned to her next brother.

'Elijah?' she pressed on.

Elijah gave Daniel a look as if he had stolen the only word he knew to say, and looked to Georgina, then back at the flowers and cleared his throat.

'I think you have chosen well, very well,' he said, with a nod and then a look of relief swept his face. His turn was over.

'Thank you, Elijah,' Matilda said with a smile.

'Gideon? What do you think?' Minnie asked, getting into the spirit of Matilda's game.

'Me? Well, yes, I think they will do nicely. Pa?' he said, quickly moving the attention from himself.

'Oh,' Mr Hayward said, surprised to be asked. 'I can't say I have much experience despite being wed. I was not asked for my thoughts on the flowers back then. But you've always had good taste, Tillie dear. I am sure they are perfect for the occasion.'

'What do you think, Amos?' Alice asked, with an encouraging look from Matilda.

'Yes, Amos?' Matilda asked. 'I don't want to leave anyone out...' she said, hiding a smile and noting Aunt Audrey's amused look.

'Well, as we are not privy to seeing the bridal or bridesmaids' gowns to compare how well they suit, I can only say that they are most attractive bouquets and will look lovely in the hands of the beautiful ladies at this table,' he said, and Aunt Audrey patted his arm, he was her favourite after all. Minnie looked at her husband as if he should be a diplomatic ambassador, and Amos's brothers gave him an expression that said they were not impressed by being upstaged.

The ladies around the table laughed and the men looked less than amused as Harriet entered the room with platters of roast and vegetables.

'I believe we are being mercilessly teased,' Daniel said, 'and on my birthday!'

'Outrageous,' Matilda agreed.

'They will match our dresses beautifully,' Minnie said, 'well done, Matilda.'

'Thank you, sister,' she said to her sister-in-law. 'But the most important question is for Thomas, of course.'

Thomas jumped beside her, having been congratulating himself on not being asked. He groaned and inspired another round of chortles around the table.

Matilda turned to him, studying his handsome face and knowing that in one month she would be Mrs Matilda Ashdown, and asked: 'Do you fancy a white rose or a white chrysanthemum for you and your groomsmen's button-holes?'

'Good question. What do you think, Thom?' his best friend, Daniel, stirred from the other side of the table.

For a moment, he looked as if he were a startled deer. He gave Daniel a quick look that said he would pay for that later, and then he gathered himself, and with a glance to Mr Hayward, took Matilda's hand and said: 'As your beautiful mother did before you, I am sure I best leave the decision to you with all your poise and wisdom.'

Matilda beamed widely and the men at the table groaned. Thomas chuckled.

'Most charmingly said, young man,' Aunt Audrey congratulated him, and Mr Hayward gave him a wink. He was learning.

Chapter 5

After the guests had left for the evening, Matilda returned to the dining room to retrieve the two bouquets. She felt a little emotional saying goodbye to Thomas this evening; maybe as the time was drawing nearer to them being together forever, she was frightened something might prevent it. Matilda hurried the thought from her mind, not willing to give it credence. She buried her nose in the bridal flowers and inhaled. Something scratched her nose. Matilda pulled away and stepped back, studying the flowers. In between the roses was a folded piece of paper. Retrieving it, Matilda opened it and read:

11pm, Fig Tree, BG. PAID.

'Goodness,' she said aloud. 'What could that mean?' She turned after hearing a noise behind her and Daniel entered the room.

'It was a good night,' he said with a grin. 'I was just thanking Mary for making my favourites.'

'She knows them without asking,' Matilda said with a smirk. 'You do have the same thing every year.' She waved the piece of paper at him. 'Look what I just found in my flowers.'

Daniel joined his sister and read the note. 'Is it meant for you?'

'I don't know. I don't know why it would be,' she said. 'I've never been to that flower shop before and I only dealt with a girl on the front counter, no one who would leave me such a cloak-and-dagger note.' Matilda's eyes widened. 'Do you think they mixed up the flowers, or maybe the note was put in the wrong bunch and there was to be a romantic liaison tonight?'

'Could well be,' Daniel said, handing her back the note. 'But how did the mix-up occur?'

'There was a young delivery boy in the back room as well. Perhaps he is the carrier of the note for another party and got it wrong. We have to work out where the liaison is to be and go there.'

Daniel stopped filling his glass with port and wheeled around to look at his sister.

'Why? No. Not at 11 at night! Definitely not.'

'BG… BG…' Matilda mused. 'It's a fig tree, and I imagine it is somewhere in public or they'd most likely not need to be so clandestine. I wonder what the "PAID" means. Where are there fig trees?'

'In parks,' Daniel answered drily.

'B-G – it must stand for the Botanic Gardens!'

'It could be a man's initials,' Daniel said.

'No. It is so obvious – *11pm, Fig Tree, BG. PAID.*' Matilda ignored him. 'It is only one hour until then; we must go Daniel.'

'Why must we?' he said and returned the stopper to the decanter of port wine.

'If we don't go, whoever is waiting for their lover will think they have not arrived and it could be heartbreaking. Imagine if you were waiting for Alice and she never got the note, and you thought she was not interested in you? It could mean the end of a love affair.'

'I wouldn't be meeting her at 11pm or asking a young lady to come out unattended at that hour,' he said. 'Besides, what if it is not? What if it is a couple that should not be meeting or some crime in the making?'

'A crime that begins with a small note in a bouquet? Hardly,' Matilda scoffed. 'Then I shall go and tell whoever is waiting that I received the note by mistake.'

Daniel rolled his eyes in frustration. 'We shall both go now, and you best come up with something to explain to Pa where we are going at this hour if he should ask.'

'He is not yet returned from seeing Betty home. But if he should see us or realise we are not home before he turns in, I will tell him we went for a walk post-birthday dinner. A very late walk,' she said, 'which is somewhat true. We'll walk to the corner and hail a hansom to get us there quicker.'

'I have one condition,' Daniel said, following her from the room and grabbing his hat from the hallway hat stand.

'What is that?' Matilda asked impatiently, lowering her voice as she quietly opened the front door and slipped out, despite only Gideon being home upstairs.

'We observe out of sight. If it looks like a jilted lover, we'll let them know about the mix-up. But if it looks like something more sinister, we shall stay put until they depart and we return straight home.' He caught up with her.

'Agreed,' Matilda said, as they hurried down the path, Matilda going as fast as she could with her fitted skirt to match Daniel's long strides. 'We could go via Thomas's house and tell him if it turns out to be something nefarious.'

'I'm sure you are keen to see Thomas in his bed shirt, but I'm sure it can wait until the morning,' Daniel teased her, and Matilda laughed.

'As soon as you become engaged to lovely Alice, you can expect my teasing to begin in earnest since you have done such a fine job of delivering in kind to me.'

'I look forward to it,' he said with a grin, and hailed a hansom as it came into sight.

Chapter 6

Alaric Osbourne waited, pleased that the large fig tree provided shelter for hiding. The Botanic Gardens at that time of the night was not a place he liked to dwell for fear of thieves, pickpockets, drunkards and thugs, all of which he imagined were lurking around every turn. He was not a small man by any means, rather tall and agile, but he was not a fighter and was keen on self-preservation.

Osbourne made a point of arriving right on time to avoid waiting; Miss Pettyfore was late. She was never late. He would give her five minutes in case something untoward had hindered her journey, and then he would depart. Osbourne hoped they had not been found out and her plan, with all its widespread reaches, had not come to an end.

It was then that Osbourne saw them. A young couple walking quickly toward him but trying to also look nonchalant. In his years of practising subterfuge, he had become very adept at reading people and there was no doubt in his mind these two looked like they were up to mischief.

The man—who from a distance looked to be closer to his third decade than his second—was tall, quite strikingly handsome with dark wavy hair, and was well dressed. He looked as if he came from money. The lady beside him was beautiful indeed. Petite, slim with blonde hair swept up, and a fashionable fitted skirt and a white blouse; like Miss Pettyfore chooses to wear.

Could they be eloping? he wondered before realising they were heading his way. What a nuisance; he would have to move. But then they stopped and hid behind a bank of bushes. He gave a smile. Desperate for privacy, he thought; he knew the feeling. If he could have five minutes alone with Miss Pettyfore, he would be the happiest of men. Speaking of which, he thought, where is she? He had money to give her and required some information, and Miss Pettyfore was now officially late.

*****

Matilda pulled Daniel beside her and peeked around the corner of the shrubbery to study the man waiting in the shadows.

'That must be him,' she whispered. 'He is alone and appears to be waiting for someone... the lady who was meant to get my note, I imagine.'

Daniel looked over her head and around the bushes.

'It does appear as if he is waiting for someone,' he agreed. 'He looks respectable enough.'

'He does. He is well-groomed and well-dressed. A lovers' meeting, I am sure of it,' Matilda said.

'We'll see, let's wait a little longer,' Daniel said, observing the man, who now appeared to be pacing and looking quite agitated.

'But we can't wait, because no one is coming as they did not receive the note. We have to tell him.'

'I will tell him,' Daniel said, pushing her back behind him. 'You shall stay safely here.'

'Daniel, you will scare him off if he is expecting a lover. He might think you are a suitor or jealous beau. I must tell him.'

'We will tell him,' Daniel concluded, and they stepped out from behind the trees and caught the man's eye.

He began to walk away quickly.

'Sir, please wait,' Matilda called. 'I received a note, an invitation that was not meant for me.'

Daniel went to catch him up and the man took off hurriedly, running fast now, too fast for Daniel to care to chase him. He returned to Matilda, a little breathless.

'What do you make of that?'

'Most odd,' she said. 'Did you get a good look at his face?'

'I did and I suspect he of mine. Can we go now?' he asked, and turned to walk back to the road upon which they arrived.

Matilda sighed and followed. 'I am saddened by the thought he believes himself to be jilted.'

'Well, it is not for lack of trying,' Daniel said and shook his head. 'The things I let you lead me into... and on my birthday.'

Matilda laughed and looped her arm through his.

'You were always the brother most willing to explore my brilliant ideas.'

'The silliest brother and silliest of ideas, don't you mean?' he asked and raised an eyebrow.

'No, many of them have been good,' she said haughtily, defending herself.

'Name one.'

'Let me think,' which she did as they walked at leisure towards the road. 'Despite the hour, it is a delightful time in the evening for a stroll.'

'Can't think of anything, huh?' he teased.

'I have it! What about the time I suggested we build a dam for the boats that you and Thomas made? Gideon and Elijah helped, and it was brilliant.'

'Yes,' Daniel agreed. 'Until we flooded Pa's shed.'

'Until then,' she said. 'He was only cranky for a little while.'

'I think he quite admired our work,' Daniel said, raising his hand to hail a hansom as several loud men who had imbibed far too much alcoholic beverage approached them.

'Spare some change, mister?' one of them slurred as he got nearer, his breath nearly knocking them over.

'Here you go,' Daniel said and fished a coin out of his waistcoat. He hurriedly pushed Matilda up into the hansom that had drawn up and followed her in. 'Let's get out of here.'

Matilda gave the driver the address, and then, in the corner of the Botanic Gardens, exiting out onto Albert Street, was the man they had seen waiting near the fig tree.

'Look, Daniel,' she said, pointing.

But again, the man took off at a fast pace, scurrying up the street, and before the hansom cab had drawn near him, the man had disappeared from their sight into a laneway.

In the early afternoon of the next day, Thomas would find him.

Chapter 7

As much as Detective Thomas Ashdown hated the smell of the coroner's room, it had made for a welcome change to be in the cooler surrounds in the months of summer, which were coming to an end. He stood at the end of the table, as his partner, Harry, and the coroner, Dr Patrick Nevins, stood on each side of the recently deceased mature lady.

'There is evidence of strangulation, but death was delivered by a blow to the back of the head,' Dr Nevins said, showing Harry, who stood nearest. 'It is by an instrument similar to the round end of a bottle or a police baton of sorts. Same size indent, applied to the skull several times with severe force.'

'Was she caught unaware, do you believe?' Harry asked.

'No, there had been a struggle. The blow did not initially fell her. I would say the killer tried to strangle her first as the welts on her hand indicate she attempted to pull whatever was placed around her neck away from her. It may have been a ribbon or tie.'

'So, Mrs Greenwood resisted her attacker,' Thomas said, more to himself than to the gentlemen present.

'Yes. I can't imagine what Mrs Greenwood was doing in that area,' Dr Nevins said with a shake of his head. 'There are no dirt marks on her clothes other than where she had fallen. I'd suggest she was forced up that alley to meet her end or carried there.'

'That would require a man of some strength, as she is not a small lady,' Thomas suggested.

'Indeed,' Dr Nevins agreed, 'a dreadful end for a kind, homely lady.'

'Why there?' Harry mused. 'The shopfronts nearby are not related to lacework or ladies' fashion. The address on her business card is not near the lane either.'

'Nothing untoward that might tip us off to the nature of the assailant then, Patrick?' Thomas asked.

'I am sorry to have so little for you to work with, gentlemen. She had been lying there some time, I'd say since late the evening prior, but that is the best I can offer you.'

'What can you tell us of her nature?' Harry asked.

'She was active in the community. I believe Mrs Greenwood taught lace-making and as mentioned at the scene of her demise, is quite renowned for her work. My wife was telling me last evening when we spoke of Mrs Greenwood's untimely death, that her lacework fetched quite impressive sums. She was a lady of great virtue, I am told, and God-fearing.'

'Hmm,' Thomas mused, and they both looked at him. He gave a small shrug and stored the information away. Given the less than salubrious area in which Mrs Greenwood's body was found, had she interfered in something she should not have in the name of virtue or righting a wrong? Or was she assisting someone in need?

*****

Thomas and Harry allowed the sergeant and his constable to deliver the news to the widowed Mrs Louise Greenwood's next of kin – two adult children and their respective families. Meanwhile, Thomas and Harry got to the business of detecting. Thomas glanced at the card that read *Louise's Fine Lace, 42 George Street,* and at the address before him.

'This is it then.'

Harry frowned and looked at the neat house in front of him and then at Thomas. A sign on the door read '*Louise's Lace, formerly of Bridal Lane, has closed.*'

'Well, that will be that then,' Harry said.

'Bridal Lane. Can't say I know it,' Thomas frowned.

'And you, in the bridal way,' Harry teased him.

Thomas chuckled as they walked up the small path, took the steps, and knocked on the door of the premises even though it appeared deserted – best to check.

'I've already been stretched this week having to comment on bridal flowers,' he told Harry. 'Good Lord, how am I supposed to know what would make a good bouquet?'

Harry grinned. 'Thank goodness for the ladies, or we'd all be married at the registry, followed by lunch at the pub.'

'That sounds rather appealing,' Thomas agreed, not letting on how much he was looking forward to seeing Matilda walk down the aisle towards him on her father's arm. Mr Hayward had been a father to him for many years of his childhood in the absence, and on many occasions, lack of interest by his much older father in the activities of his son.

'So, Mrs Greenwood lived here but no longer sold her lace from her premises,' Thomas stepped back and looked up at the windows above. 'Perhaps she just took commissions.' The curtains were open but no-one was in attendance. 'To Bridal Lane?'

'Next best bet,' Harry agreed. 'I have an idea where it is.' Harry started walking.

'That so?' Thomas said with a grin as he caught up with his partner. 'How would you know that? Bit tender-hearted in your old age?'

'A poet at heart,' Harry joined in the joke. 'It is very near Tea Lane, just off Albert Street. It's a rough part of town now, but it wasn't always.'

'So, the uniform squad would be well acquainted with it?' Thomas asked.

'Without a doubt.'

They headed towards Albert Street, eventually passing by Mr Sebastian's fruit and vegetable store.

'This is it then,' Harry announced and started down the lane; he watched Thomas taking in his surroundings. Some rowdy men sat around outside a saloon at the end of the lane and the shops on either side of the alley had their doors open and wares on show.

'A tarot reader, bet she saw something,' Thomas muttered under his breath and glanced in the window of the little shop, seeing a mature lady sitting at a table playing with a deck of cards.

'In the here and now, or spook world?' Harry asked and laughed as Thomas huffed.

The men strode down both sides of the alley and found nothing resembling a former lace shop. Some old signage from former bridal stores had faded or been half painted over, but nothing bearing Louise's name. They stopped out the front of the floristry.

'This is the best of it, by the looks of it,' Harry said, and Thomas agreed. They entered the building, a small bell announcing them and the faces of five ladies turning to observe the newcomers. Three were customers and two were behind the counter – a mature lady and a young girl. The men removed their hats.

'Gentlemen, I will be with you shortly,' the mature lady said, as she finished decorating a bouquet and her young assistant offered a sample of ribbons to the two ladies who were enjoying every moment of their preparation.

Thomas ran a finger around his collar and grimaced, then realising he was looking uncomfortable, adopted a neutral position.

'Got cold feet, Thom?' Harry asked quietly, observing him.

'Never,' Thomas said. 'Just realising all the traps that are in here for unwary fellows.'

Harry laughed.

'We don't see too many gentlemen in here,' the mature lady said, moving towards them as her young assistant finished up with the ladies, who were eyeing Thomas with interest. A man in a bridal store must be the easiest of catches, and he was not wearing a wedding ring.

'Mrs Celia Dalton at your service, gentlemen,' she said, clasping her hands in front of her and looking from Thomas to Harry. 'Now which one of you is getting married and what in particular are you seeking? It is normally the bride-to-be that we see, but we like a man with a keen interest in his future.'

Harry smiled. 'Mrs Dalton, our apologies for the intrusion. We are not here on bridal business, although Thomas is getting married in a matter of weeks.'

One of the ladies groaned with disappointment, which made Thomas colour slightly, and the young lady behind the counter giggled.

'A great loss to the ladies of our town, apparently,' Mrs Dalton said with a sly grin to her right at the customers. 'What flowers will you be having at your wedding, young man?' she asked.

Thomas's expression conveyed his ill-preparedness at the question. 'Ah, I believe my fiancée has that in order, Madam. Cream and white flowers, and some blue ones in the bridesmaids' bouquets,' he said, giving his best answer.

Mrs Dalton smiled. 'Well, that does sound lovely.' She bid the customers goodbye and Thomas hurriedly began.

'Before any more customers arrive, Mrs Dalton, we are here on police business. Detectives Thomas Ashdown and Harry Dart,' he said, indicating his partner.

Mrs Dalton's hand went to her heart. 'This is about the death of our dear lacemaker, isn't it? Mrs Greenwood, God rest her soul.'

'Yes, the very same, Mrs Louise Greenwood,' Harry confirmed.

'I heard last evening of her demise. Mrs Greenwood used to have the small store next to us but then decided to take commissions and work from home. We ordered a great deal of lace work from her, didn't we, Rose?' she said, involving the young girl behind the counter.

'We did, Mrs Dalton. Our delivery boy, Jacob, would go to her house to collect our orders once a week,' Rose said.

'So, she did not come into the shop?' Thomas asked.

'No. Only on the rare occasion when we had an urgent order, then she might drop it in herself,' Mrs Dalton said. 'I always offered to send Jacob, but she said that she enjoyed the opportunity to get out and to visit now and then.'

'Can you tell me if she was visiting in the last two days?' Harry asked.

'Yes, in fact, she was. Louise did a rushed order for us… a bride had torn her dress at her final fitting and Louise was able to make some lacework to cover the tear and provide a matching strip for the bouquet,' Mrs Dalton explained, no doubt wishing every client was as extravagant. She added: 'Louise dropped in with the lace for us mid-afternoon.'

'Were you here when she came by?' Harry asked.

'No, I wasn't, unfortunately. I had an order to take… some ladies like to book appointments and I see them at their residences. As you can see, this is no longer the most salubrious of streets.'

'But you remain here?' Thomas asked. 'It can't be the safest environment for yourself or the young ladies in your employ.'

Mrs Dalton nodded. 'Perhaps so, but we are not too

far from the Albert Street entrance and my husband has a business upstairs. He is an accountant and manages the books of many of the city businesses. He has two in his employ.'

'Excellent, so you have men on the premises should you need to call on them,' Harry said. 'Were you here that afternoon, young lady?' he turned to the girl behind the counter and enquired in a kindly voice.

'Yes. Rose is my name, sir, and I was here. I accepted the lace from Mrs Greenwood, took her invoice and thanked her. She purchased a bouquet for her home and departed after a short chat.'

Thomas frowned. *We found no flowers in the alleyway. Had she gone home first and come back or were they stolen, or thrown away by the killer?*

'Was she frightened or concerned about any matter?' Harry persisted.

'No, sir,' Rose said in all sincerity. 'She was friendly and happy like she was every time we saw her.'

'What time did she depart and did she say she was heading anywhere in particular?' Thomas asked.

'It was just after 3 o'clock and I remember that because Jacob was meant to do his last delivery run of the day at three, but he was running a little late and I had just given him a hurry on,' Rose said. 'But Mrs Greenwood did not say she was going anywhere in particular, and she had bought the flowers for her home, so she would want to get them in water before too long.'

The bell rang as three ladies entered the small shop.

'Ladies, you have been most helpful, our thanks,' Harry said with a small bow.

'I am glad we have been able to assist, Detectives,' Mrs Dalton said. 'We shall miss Mrs Greenwood and not just because of her lace. She was a solid worker and a considerate lady.'

Thomas gave his thanks and followed Harry from the store. Before they left the lane, he glanced at the tarot reader, who now had a client with her.

'We'll come back and see who in the street might have seen our lady,' Harry said. 'For now, perhaps a visit to her home again, and this time we might have to force entry.'

'Yes. Let's see if the missing flowers are there,' Thomas agreed.

Chapter 8

$\mathbf{M}$rs Dora Lawson—editor of the *Women's Journal*
that employed Matilda and her dearest friends, Miss Alice
Doran and Miss Georgina Urry—looked excited; her lips
were pursed, her breathing heightened, and she sat down
with great expediency. The young writers and illustrators
around the table at her weekly meeting were keen to know
the source of her enthusiasm.

Mrs Lawson cut a most striking figure with her silver-
white hair pinned atop her head with military precision and
a modest navy-fitted dress befitting her station in life. She
was a firm but kindly lady with a no-nonsense approach
to life, widowed and, despite not needing to provide for
herself, she could not abide idle hands and felt women
needed a voice. Thus, the *Women's Journal* was born and
employed an all-female workforce, including Matilda, now
in her second year of writing for the magazine. Even Aunt
Audrey approved and subscribed.

Mrs Lawson cleared her throat for attention, but need not have, as every lady present had hushed on seeing her earnest countenance.

'What a week for news, ladies, goodness there is much to report and it will be all hands to the pumps,' she said with as much agitation as the ladies had ever seen of their editor. 'First up, I would love to see a story encouraging women to undertake medical training!'

There were several gasps and great enthusiasm amongst the ladies for the notion. Mrs Lawson continued, and the chatter ceased immediately.

'It is 1889 after all and university degrees in medicine and surgery are open to women at the Royal University of Ireland and the University of London, the latter has been open to women for 10 years!'

'But is there anyone studying such a thing here in Australia, Mrs Lawson?' Alice asked.

'Well, that is the story, Alice. Two sisters, in fact. Constance and Clara Stone, but Constance had to travel overseas for her degree and graduated last year. Clara has successfully petitioned her way into the University of Melbourne's medical school and is studying as we speak,' Mrs Lawson said, looking inspired. 'Thoughts?'

Several hands shot up, suggesting angles for the story, and Mrs Lawson chose one of the writers. Then she discussed a less inspiring story. 'The words of Mr Grant Allen that appear in today's newspaper, reproduced from the *Pall Mall Gazette,* are most aggravating and we shall write a counter article,' she said with lips thinned in distaste. 'Mr Allen claims to be a biologist and is concerned that as women seek to be emancipated, it will distract us from the primary duty of reproducing and thus our society may become a survival of the fittest. Did anyone read the article?'

Several hands were raised and there were nods, muttered comments and even some smiles at the ridiculousness of his words.

Mrs Lawson continued. 'Mr Allen's analogy referred to the queen bee who bore the task of all reproduction, and stated we should not be looking to model ourselves in such a fashion by allowing a few to shoulder the burden of reproduction while the rest of us seek education and careers.'

'Goodness me,' Ursula, the typesetter exclaimed, with hand to heart.

Mrs Lawson's lips twitched in a smile at the absurdity of it. She looked at the newspaper clipping in her file. 'He warns men and I quote: "Adopt a system of female education, which enfeebles your women for maternal functions, and you lose in the next generation." Is there anyone here who agrees with Mr Allen, and please, do not be afraid to speak, everyone is entitled to their opinion in this office?'

Georgina raised her hand slightly; the young illustrator and country girl, now courting Matilda's brother, Elijah, was a rough diamond and most independent. Several faces expressed surprise at her raised hand.

'I do not agree with his aggressive sentiment,' she began, 'but I do agree that the family is the most important element of our society. It is that way on the farm too when you see

49

the cattle caring for their young. But I believe he is very much off wandering in a paddock if he thinks the entire female population wants to work, or that granting us an education or independence means we might wish to be without children or a family.'

Mrs Lawson smiled, pleased with Georgina's interpretation. 'Bravely said and well-articulated, Georgina. I agree with you as I'm sure many of the ladies around the table do. I will pen an unemotional, practical and family-centric reply to Mr Allen and send it post haste to the newspaper for printing tomorrow. Betty, I believe you have a lighter topic?' Mrs Lawson quipped and handed the meeting over to her deputy editor.

Betty smiled. 'Yes, I do. In my community baking group, there has been some talk—especially from the younger ladies—about women having the right, and courage, to propose!'

Many of the ladies smiled, several giggled, and Matilda looked at Betty in astonishment. Was Betty intending to propose to her father?

'Fear not, Matilda,' Betty said hurriedly, 'I will not be putting your dear father on the spot,' which got another round of laughs.

'I think I am all for it,' Matilda said with enthusiasm making Betty smile and give her a look of fondness.

Betty continued: 'Why should a woman wait for the feeble excuse of a leap year to propose? Rather than be at the mercy of a man in these days of almost equal rights, let us have the same dignity. We are not a bargaining tool after all. Shall we canvas opinion, including that of the clergy who perform the ceremony?'

'Excellent, assign it please Betty,' Mrs Lawson said, pleased. 'One more thing which I did have on my list...' she cleared her throat at the emotional subject she was about to share. 'It is coming up to my wedding anniversary – it would have been 35 years with Harold, God rest his soul, and I have been thinking about marriage. We have three young ladies in our presence who will be married this year, so far,' she said and smiled, as a few of the ladies giggled in hopeful anticipation of receiving a proposal. 'You may have read of the death of Mrs Louise Greenwood, a bridal lacemaker. Was anyone familiar with Mrs Greenwood?'

Several ladies around the table spoke up.

'—she is a member of our church group.'

'—Mrs Greenwood does community work with my mother.'

'—she made the lace for my wedding dress.'

'Good, I see she is a woman who impacted her community,' Mrs Lawson said. She looked down the table at Matilda, who had been thoroughly enjoying the discussion. 'I thought as the next bride-to-be in our office—to be wed in less than a month—Matilda, perhaps you could write a tribute piece on Mrs Greenwood for the lady readers?'

Surprised, Matilda responded enthusiastically. 'Yes, Mrs Lawson, I would be delighted to do so, thank you.'

Betty made a note of the story allocation and added: 'It is quite a skill to make such beautiful lace. I believe Mrs Greenwood was widowed young and supported her family from her lace earnings.'

'Admirable indeed,' Mrs Lawson said. 'Include if you will, Matilda, the names of any prominent brides that wore her lace.'

'I will seek them out, Mrs Lawson,' Matilda responded. 'Should I conclude with the details of her untimely death?'

'I think you must in order to portray the genuine sense of loss and the injustice of her life cut short,' Mrs Lawson agreed. 'A quote or two from your detective on the progress of the investigation would not go astray either if he would permit it.'

'Absolutely, Mrs Lawson,' Matilda said with a small smile, keen for an excuse to work with Thomas, even if he was not quite as enthusiastic about working with her.

'Georgina, if you have the fortitude to view the deceased, will you accompany Matilda when she speaks with the family and request the opportunity to illustrate Mrs Greenwood? Of course, if there is an existing portrait, you may be able to reproduce Mrs Greenwood's likeness from that.'

'Ooh, I'd love to,' Georgina said, with a glance at Matilda. 'Fear not, Mrs Lawson, I am quite good with the dead.'

Mrs Lawson laughed. 'Well done, Georgina.'

'I shall alert our Sales Manageress,' Betty said. 'There may be bridal stores who would like to advertise in that issue given we will discuss lacework and bridal matters.'

'Good thought,' Mrs Lawson said moving on.

Matilda made notes, excited by her project. She wondered if brides had changed much from Mrs Lawson's time. After all, Mrs Lawson was a working woman, but was she before being widowed? The thought made Matilda fearful of how long she might have with Thomas. They had known each other since they were children, and he had promised to marry her several times in their younger years. Now it was happening, and she hoped and prayed they would have many years together.

She mused on her handsome fiancé, who despaired of her involvement in his cases, and wondered how he would respond to her article. Yet again, she had somehow managed to immerse herself in a current investigation. The thought made her smile again.

Chapter 9

The two detectives walked back the way that the now deceased Mrs Louise Greenwood may have walked after leaving the *Blooming Blossoms* flower shop.

'Tea Lane to Bridal Lane, then,' Thomas said, studying the area around him and heading in the direction of Tea Lane. 'Assuming Mrs Greenwood did not make a dozen more stops on the way.'

'If she departed the flower shop to get to the laneway in which we found her, she could have taken two routes,' Harry said.

'But if she had no reason to be in Tea Lane, which we know is most likely, then she must have had business in the adjoining shops or street, or encountered someone who drew her down that alley,' Thomas mused. He glanced towards the tarot reader's window as they departed, and she raised her hand and beckoned him.

'Here we go,' he said.

'What's that?' Harry asked, looking around expectantly for the clue that Thomas must have discovered.

'The soothsayer has requested our company. Shall we?' Thomas asked, hesitating.

'Good a time as any,' Harry said. 'Her client appears to have left.'

'We are the next to be duped then,' Thomas said under his breath, as they pushed open the door to her small shop. The smell of a sweet incense struck his particularly sensitive nose, and Thomas decided he preferred the smell of death and that was a revelation. In the corner sat the small pot with the coil of smoke rising from it, the scent wafting over the room. The room was painted a dull red that once may have looked brighter, and the fabrics and cloth draped around for effect appeared tired and musty. As did the fortune teller in a loose blue and gold dress with a matching turban.

'Gentlemen,' she said, rising, 'I am Madam Gerta, and I believe you need my assistance.'

'Madam,' Harry said, politely. 'Detectives Harry Dart and Thomas Ashdown.'

'But you knew that,' Thomas said with a wry smile and she returned his smile.

'I am a tarot reader and fortune teller, Detective. I read what the cards tell me; I am not a psychic,' she clarified. 'Although I am very astute at sensing things around me and on seeing both of you, I sense there is trouble afoot.'

She waved to the two seats in front of her table and both gentlemen declined to sit; Madam Gerta sat. The room was stuffy and warm, and Thomas was already edging his way to the door.

'We must keep going,' he explained, 'but as you have a

prime view to the street, can you tell us if you are acquainted with Mrs Louise Greenwood or saw her coming and going?'

'Both, Detective,' she said, and picked up the pack of cards and started shuffling it, not taking her eyes off the two men. 'Mrs Greenwood had a store in this street for many years so I recognised her, although she is still a frequent visitor to *Blooming Blossoms*.'

'Ah yes, of course,' Harry said, 'bridal lace.'

'Yes, this street was once so respectable,' she said, with a sigh. 'It was lovely to have the bridal stores, flower shop, milliners, and dressmakers here, and so fittingly named Bridal Lane.'

'When did all that begin to change?' Harry asked.

'Well, I have been here a good ten years now and when the owner of the tea shop at the end of the lane died, his grandson took up the lease and opened a saloon.' She shook her head. 'So ill-fitting, it's a disgrace.'

'I'm surprised he didn't sell it,' Thomas said. 'Did he think the grooms would wander down the lane for a quick tipple while the brides fussed with their gowns and flowers?'

'That's exactly what he thought, Detective, but unfortunately it became a place where the shady characters of our city could drink and no doubt do illegal business without being in sight of passing trade and the constabulary.'

'You have not thought to leave yourself?' Harry asked.

'I still do very well from the trade that enters the street and the saloon's clientele leave me largely alone.' She gave a little shrug. 'I cannot afford the luxury of moving elsewhere.'

Thomas brought the subject back on track. 'Did you see Mrs Greenwood coming and going on Tuesday?' he asked.

'I most certainly did. As I recall, she arrived well after 3pm and stayed a little while to talk with Rose behind the counter. The manageress, Mrs Dalton, was out on errands, I believe. Mrs Greenwood left before 4pm and went the same way in which she came.' Madam Gerta dramatically pointed in the direction of Mrs Greenwood's departure, despite there only being one entry and exit to the lane.

'Did you see anyone following her?' Harry asked, 'or anyone who was loitering near *Blooming Blossoms*?'

'No, but not long after she had left, maybe five minutes or so, the young delivery boy tore out of the store and raced in the direction in which she had departed,' Madam Gerta said. 'I thought at the time that perhaps she had delivered the wrong lace or there was a problem with the order, but she did not return and neither did the young boy... well, not before I left at five o'clock.'

'Why do you believe there is trouble afoot, Madam?' Thomas asked.

Theatrically, Madam Gerta put her tarot cards down on the table and cut the pack in half. She explained: 'Every time I see a bride-to-be entering *Blooming Blossoms*, I study them from afar and, if I don't have a client, I draw a card for them. I was idle when Mrs Greenwood came by the other day and I drew a card for her. It was the *Tower*,' she pronounced.

Thomas had little interest and patience for her theatrics, but Harry was prepared to play the game.

'Pray tell, what does that card mean?'

'The *Tower* can mean danger, a crisis, a sudden change... even destruction. Fitting, was it not?'

'Madam Gerta, thank you for your time,' Thomas said, his hand upon the door to exit. 'Should you think of anything that might assist us, please ask for Detective Ashdown or Dart at the station or alert a constable to fetch us.'

'I will, Detectives. Go carefully now and I hope the delivery boy can provide some more information for you. He may, of course, not have been pursuing Mrs Greenwood at all,' she said.

'Thank you, Madam Gerta,' Harry said. 'We will definitely speak to the young man.'

With that, the men donned their hats and departed, Thomas well ahead of Harry in his haste to depart. He did not see Madam Gerta watching him and turning the card on the top of her deck for him, or the surprised look upon her face when she saw the *Knight of Cups* – the card of loyalty and romance. Not one she would have picked for the young detective on face value.

Chapter 10

Matilda skipped out at lunchtime to return to *Blooming Blossoms* and order her wedding flowers. She had left the detail to the last minute and wished she had been more organised, but there were just so many more things to do than think about flowers. It was one of the small tasks that Aunt Audrey had left in Matilda's capable hands and had reminded her about it every day since. But Matilda rationalised that as flowers were supposed to be fresh, surely the later you ordered them the more accurate your choice of flower in bloom. Daniel had promised to accompany her on her return visit, but he wasn't sure he could get a lunch break given the court case in session that he was illustrating, so Georgina happily came along.

'Safety in numbers,' she said as they approached the alley. 'I can see why Daniel did not want you to go alone. Goodness gracious, what a forlorn-looking alley.'

'It appears to have passed its heyday,' Matilda agreed, and they both lifted their skirts a little as the alley became dustier and dirtier.

'Ooh, watch out,' Georgina said, and they moved out of the way as a young man ran past them with another in pursuit. The smell of alcohol was notable on both of them. 'Right then, shall we?'

Matilda stopped. 'Are you sure you want to accompany me?' she asked. 'I seem to be constantly leading you into trouble.'

'I wouldn't miss it for the world,' Georgina said with a smile. They waited as a couple of mature women entered the lane and followed them. The ladies deviated into the fortune teller's room.

'What do you think of tarot readers?' Matilda asked, with a glance at the quirky little shop with its faded signage.

'I confess they scare me a little,' Georgina said. 'I don't want to know anything bad that is going to happen and if they tell me something good, it has ruined the surprise.'

Matilda laughed. 'Yes, good point. I have a friend whose mother attended one weekly. I suspect she became quite dependent.'

They were about to enter *Blooming Blossoms* when Matilda heard her name called and winced, recognising the voice. In a moment, Thomas and Harry were at her side.

'What on earth are you doing in this disreputable street?' Thomas asked, shocked, forgetting his manners.

'Miss Hayward, Miss Urry,' Harry said, removing his hat and the ladies greeted him.

'Forgive me, Georgina,' Thomas said informally, given they had become quite familiar with each other at the Hayward events.

'Not at all, Detective, I can imagine ten places you would prefer to meet us than here.' She smiled and glanced down the laneway as a fight broke out.

'I am ordering my flowers, Thomas, the very flowers you all gave an opinion on last night,' Matilda said.

'From here? From this street?' Thomas asked, an incredulous look on his face. 'Why? Why did you not ask me to escort you?'

'You are so very busy,' she said.

'Never that busy,' he told her, holding her gaze. 'So, you came here once before to get the samples?'

Matilda took a breath for fortitude before answering. 'Yes.'

'Did you come alone?' he persisted.

'Well, yes, the first time, but I did not know it would be so… well, awful.'

'I am sure you are determined to put me in an early grave, Matilda.' He shook his head and they stared at each other for a moment.

'It is very warm today, isn't it, Detective Dart?' Georgina said.

'Most warm indeed, Miss Urry, but you would be used to that on the land, no doubt,' he said, smiling at the young woman fondly.

'Yes, but it is different when you are working out in nature rather than trapped in the heat of the town.' She glanced at Matilda and Thomas, who appeared to be stuck in an impasse.

'Well then, we could accompany you on your business, surely,' Harry said. 'We have fifteen minutes up our sleeve, do we not, Thom?'

'Thank you, Detective Dart,' Matilda said, with a smile his way. 'But we would hate to keep you from police business for something as trivial as bridal flowers. What business are you on?' she asked, with a raised eyebrow and saw Harry repress a grin as Thomas's eyes narrowed.

'Important business that does not concern the *Women's Journal*,' Thomas answered.

'Is that so?' she said, brightly. 'I suspect it is concerning the death of the lacemaker that I read about in the newspaper.'

'Come, we will accompany you to the florist,' Thomas said, nipping her interrogation in the bud. 'We need to speak to the delivery boy, anyway.'

'Ah, is that so?' Matilda asked, and Georgina laughed.

'Unless you have ordered a bouquet, Thomas, you have given us a hint of your investigation,' Georgina said.

Thomas sighed. 'You two are far too clever for your own good.'

Matilda scolded Thomas. 'Really? You are just realising that now?'

Harry interrupted. 'What day were you here, Miss Hayward, getting your samples?'

'Wednesday, Detective Dart, in the morning.'

'Good,' Thomas said with a satisfied smile. 'The lace lady, Mrs Greenwood, was here on Tuesday, so there is no chance you saw anything.'

Matilda saw him straighten, pleased she could not involve herself in his case for a change.

'Oh, but I did notice something strange, or rather, Daniel and I did. But you are right, Detectives... let's get to the business of flowers and then we can relieve you of your obligation and return you to your duties,' Matilda said brightly and stood aside as Detective Dart opened the door for her.

'You were here with Daniel?' Thomas asked, following her into *Blooming Blossoms*. 'I thought you said you came here alone?'

'I did, but there was a mystery accompanying my flowers and Daniel and I acted upon it that very evening. But to flower business first. Perhaps if you have time to drop by this evening, Daniel and I could discuss what we witnessed with you. It may not be relevant, of course.'

Thomas shook his head, and muttered: 'You are the most exasperating woman sometimes, Matilda.'

She smiled up at him. 'Only sometimes, Thomas?'

'You are right. Most times,' he concurred.

'No, *you* are the most exasperating person in the world, Thomas.'

He chuckled. '*You* are the most exasperating person in the whole universe.'

They both laughed at the childhood memory of exaggerating until one of them won or ran out of hyperboles.

'But you have come to my rescue again,' she said and smiled up at him.

'Let's order our bridal flowers then,' he said drily.

She placed her arm through his and they approached the counter, leaving Georgina and Harry to discuss matters unrelated to crime and flowers.

✳✳✳✳✳

Then…

Eight-year-old Matilda hid behind the large copse of trees at the back of the Hayward property. Next to her, 11-year-old Thomas, her brother's best friend, huddled beside her. From their hideout, they could see if Daniel and Amos, or Elijah and Gideon, approached. Or rather, they would if Thomas did not spend half his time watching Matilda and acting the hero in her company.

Matilda stuck her head gingerly around the tree trunk to spy. They were playing *Castle*, and Amos and Daniel were the champions. In their possession was the castle, which the other two teams wanted to take back. An old and battered tin trophy Amos had won in a running race at school some years back served as the castle to be won.

'No sign of them yet,' she said, eyes narrowed and studying the surroundings. Thomas stayed nearby, ready to defend her and only too pleased to be partnered with Daniel's little sister.

'Shh, you'll give away our position,' he said, holding the stick shaped to be a play sword as Matilda brandished hers beside him. Her cotton dress and boots were covered in mud and Aunt Audrey, upon seeing her earlier, had already exclaimed she was a most exasperating girl and it was time to start acting like a young lady.

'But the boys have mud on their trousers and boots!' she proclaimed, pointing out their short trousers and muddy shoes.

'As to be expected from young lads,' Aunt Audrey told her, and Matilda smirked at her brothers' expression.

'I promise I will, Aunt Audrey, soon,' she said, with a very firm nod that she hoped would satisfy her departing aunt. No sooner had the carriage departed the property, than Matilda gave a shrug to Thomas and her brothers, and the game continued.

'We need to sneak up on them and get the advantage,' Thomas said, looking around. 'I know Dan's tricks; he'll be waiting in ambush near the creek trying to lure us out. This way,' he said with a nod, and started, staying close to the trees and checking back to make sure Matilda was following.

'Why can't I take the lead?' she asked.

'Because you are a girl and I need to protect you.'

'Phooey. I could protect you.'

'I doubt it. I'm much stronger. There they are!' he whispered hurriedly. 'There's Dan and Amos, come on.'

Thomas dropped low as he and Matilda stalked the enemy through the line of trees. Amos and Dan were behind the rocks near the creek. Dan's stick weapon was only just visible, but Amos's surveillance had given them away.

As Thomas rose to lead, Matilda grabbed at his arm and pulled him down. 'Look over there! Eli and Gids are sneaking up on them just like we are… it's going to be an ambush!'

'We need a plan,' Thomas said. 'We can do this, we can win.'

'I know,' she beamed up at him. 'I say while Amos and Dan fight Eli and Gids, we sneak in and steal the castle, run to the rock and stand upon it, declaring victory!' she said, her eyes alive.

'But then we don't get to fight them,' Thomas said, and he wanted to fight and win, to defend her.

'But we will have won, which is the aim of the game,' she said, keeping the prize in sight.

He thought about it. 'Okay, how about this plan... we do what you suggested but I shall join the fight and distract them while you grab the castle and run to the rock, stand upon it and holding it high, proclaim us the winners.'

'But if you are going to fight, I want to fight too,' Matilda declared, her face determined and her eyes studying him with great attention.

He rolled his eyes. 'You are the most exasperating girl, Matilda!' he said, emulating Aunt Audrey in all his 11-year-old importance.

'No, Thomas, you are the most exasperating boy in the whole world,' she shot back at him and straightening behind the tree, put her hands on her hips.

He looked affronted. '*You* are the most exasperating girl in the whole universe.'

'Charge!' Gideon yelled and Thomas and Matilda turned in surprise! While they had been fighting, they had not noticed the advance upon them. The team of Matilda and Thomas eventually surrendered, although Thomas went down fighting as expected of the young hero and Matilda gave her best, but still believed her plan was better.

Chapter 11

Proudly standing beside Matilda as she ordered the flowers for their wedding, Thomas studied his beautiful bride-to-be, who was taking pleasure in the task at hand. He concluded that despite her beauty, her ability to hasten his heart rate and often completely undo him with one gaze, she was still exasperating. He dutifully answered questions with no idea if he was saying the correct thing – a flower was a flower after all, but some coaching from Georgina over Matilda's shoulder was most appreciated and he would be sure to thank her next time Matilda could not overhear their conversation. Soon after, the detectives saw Matilda and Georgina safely onto the omnibus.

'Sorry about that deviation,' Thomas said, turning to Harry as they returned their hats to their heads and watched the ladies depart.

'It was a lovely break to a day of crime,' Harry said, 'and fortunate timing.'

'I cannot believe she came here alone the first time.' Thomas shook his head as he studied the dingy and dangerous alley.

'I gathered that,' Harry said with a chuckle. 'Well, see what Miss Hayward and Daniel have to say for themselves tonight and fetch me if you need to act upon it.'

'I doubt that will be necessary given Matilda has kept it to herself for two days. But I shall bear it in mind, thank you.'

The detectives resumed their task of talking with the delivery boy from *Blooming Blossoms*.

'You'd be after Jacob then,' Rose said and went behind the curtain to fetch him. A young boy followed her out and agreed to talk with the detectives outside so as not to disturb the business Mrs Dalton was conducting.

'I know her,' Jacob said, after Thomas explained their query, 'but I wasn't chasing after her that day.' He glanced across the alley at the tarot card reader. 'That old woman is a tittle-tattle, always nosing into other people's business.'

'Ease up, lad,' Harry said. 'Madam Gerta was acquainted with Mrs Greenwood, and like all of us, wants to get justice for her.'

'So, where or what were you running to in such a hurry?' Thomas asked.

Jacob shuffled. 'I can't remember; it was days ago.'

'Righto young man, this is how it is going to go,' Harry said, reading the delivery boy's body language and guessing he knew more than what he was saying. 'You can try your best to remember and tell us now, or we can go to the station and we can give you a quiet room to sit in so you can think about it without being interrupted.'

Thomas did his best not to smile, and Jacob scowled.

'I thought I gave Mrs Greenwood the wrong bouquet, so I ran after her to get it back and swap it over, but then I couldn't find her. I don't know where she went, she'd only left a few minutes earlier and I'm much faster.'

'Why would it matter if she had the wrong bouquet?' Thomas asked.

'Because Mrs Dalton and Rose spend ages making them and filling the orders. If I got the orders wrong, I'd be in big trouble. Might even have my pay docked.'

'Did it turn out to be the wrong bouquet?' Harry asked.

'Nuh, it was all good in the end.'

The two men studied him and Thomas eventually said: 'Righto, Jacob, back to work then but if you think of anything that might help us find Mrs Greenwood's killer, come find us.'

'I will,' Jacob said and hurried away like a boy with a secret.

The detectives watched him leave and rush back into the florist shop.

'We've got nothing,' Thomas said and sighed.

No sooner had they stepped away from the florist than the detectives heard a youthful voice calling for them.

'Mister!' Both of the detectives turned around to find the young street lad, Charlie Doyle, running towards them.

'Hello Charlie, how's business today?' Harry asked him, as the enterprising boy pulled up beside them, breathless.

'Good, sir, thank you.'

'Do my shoes look like they need a shine today?' Thomas teased him, and Charlie looked at both of the detectives' shoes and grinned.

'No, they are both alright, I guess, but I'd have them shinier.'

'Have you eaten today, lad?' Harry asked the thin, dusty boy.

'Aye. My Ma makes me eat porridge every morning. When I grow up, I'm never eating porridge ever again.' He put his hands on his hips as if declaring that to be a fact, and there was to be no debate on the subject. The men chuckled.

'I agree,' Thomas said. 'Awful stuff.'

'I've got another body for you,' Charlie said.

'Dead?' Harry asked surprised, eyes wide.

'Dead as a doornail as my Pa says,' Charlie said, with a grin.

Thomas groaned. 'Okay, Charlie, lead the way, and let's not tell anyone about it on the way.'

'I never tell in case someone gets there before I can come back. There could be a reward or something,' he said, with enthusiasm, not at all affected by the sighting of a dead body.

'Can we walk there from here?' Harry asked, as an afterthought.

'Sure, it's in the same place as the last one.'

Thomas and Harry exchanged looks and hurried to catch up with the young boy.

*****

Matilda and Georgina arrived at the largest fabric supplier in town, *Edwards and Chapman Drapery Store*, where Mrs Greenwood was commissioned to provide lace to the ladies' mercantile department. Matilda hoped to gain

Mrs Greenwood's address and next of kin's information to conduct interviews for her story. Had she known that Mrs Greenwood supplied lace to *Blooming Blossoms*, she might have secured the address earlier, not that either lady was complaining about visiting a drapery as part of their working day.

'Goodness, it is enormous,' Georgina said, as they entered the building.

'Do you have many stores in your hometown?' Matilda asked.

'A few. A grocer, a hotel, and several large stores for farming products. We have several very good dressmakers in town, but not much use for lace.' Georgina chuckled and nudged Matilda. 'If we follow the ladies in front, I suspect we'll get to the right area.'

'Good thinking,' Matilda said and found them to be heading straight to the fabrics, ribbons, and millinery section of the store. 'Will you use a local dressmaker to make your wedding dress?' Matilda teased.

Georgina smiled. 'If that happy day ever comes, my mother would like me to wear her dress. Goodness knows how… she was a dainty little thing and no one has ever used that word to describe me! Were you not inclined to wear your mother's dress?' Georgina asked.

'I did think about it, but… I know this may sound silly, but as she died not long into the marriage, but seven years, I did not want to tempt the same fate.'

'I understand,' Georgina said. 'Besides, I suspect your aunt was rather keen to spoil you and see you in a new dress.'

'Dear Aunt Audrey,' Matilda said and sighed. 'It is probably the first time in my entire life she can enjoy me not being a tomboy.'

'Here we are then,' Georgina proclaimed, finding an entire counter of lacework. Moments later, they were looking at the work produced by the late Mrs Louise Greenwood. Matilda touched it, tracing its delicacy. It was quite exquisite.

'Isn't it beautiful and delicate?' A woman wearing a badge reading *Sales Manager, Miss June Johnson*, said in a melancholy voice. 'Mrs Greenwood only ever provided pure white lace and only the best work. I don't know what we will do without her.'

'Did she supply exclusively to your fine store?' Georgina asked.

'No, she was much in demand. I know of at least four places she supplied, and I believe she also provided pieces to private dressmakers,' Miss Johnson said. She leaned in as if to share a great secret. 'She also supplied to a florist shop in a lane near where she was murdered.'

'*Blooming Blossoms*!' Matilda exclaimed.

'I believe that is the very one,' Miss Johnson said, surprised. 'I don't know why they needed lace, but I only recall that detail because Mrs Greenwood was going there on one occasion after dropping some samples here, and we were both aghast at the decline in the area.'

'It's rather awful,' Matilda agreed.

'I could not do it,' Georgina proclaimed, looking at the lacework and changing the subject. 'My mother has tried several times to get me to sit with her and work on a sampler with decorative embroidery, she even organised an instructor. Neither the sampler nor I got on at all.'

Matilda laughed and Miss Johnson smiled and nodded her head.

'It requires a great deal of patience,' Miss Johnson agreed. 'I have never been idle enough to finish one.'

'Nor have I,' Matilda added, thinking how she would have been teased mercilessly by her brothers had she sat around stitching.

'I think it is lovely that you wish to write a profile on Mrs Greenwood, and as the manageress of the ladies' department, I would be only too willing to contribute my thoughts,' she said, and Matilda eagerly reached for her pad and pen. 'But I must warn you...'

'Yes?' Matilda leaned forward slightly, intrigued.

'Mrs Greenwood was very... how shall I say... clear cut in her views and she did offend some with her strictness. She was a woman of great virtue.'

'I understand,' Matilda said, a little disappointed that the lady she had painted in her imagination was actually quite unyielding. She acquired some information and useable quotes while Georgina looked at the bridal section with renewed interest – an interest Matilda guessed Georgina did not share before meeting Elijah; things were changing. Then Matilda gained from Miss Johnson's files the address of Mrs Louise Greenwood.

The two ladies thanked her for her time and departed, agreeing to leave the visit to Mrs Greenwood's home until the morning.

'I hope they will welcome us,' Georgina said. 'People react in different ways to grief and they may not want a profile piece on their beloved. I remember when a neighbouring farmer's wife died and the local paper tried to write a tribute, her husband would not allow it.'

'Why ever not? It would flatter me to have my loved one remembered in such a way,' Matilda said, as they walked through town towards the omnibus.

'I am sure I would feel the same. We were all surprised that her husband would turn it down,' Georgina said. 'But then it turned out she hadn't died but deserted him and he just told everyone that story to save face.'

Matilda laughed before realising how sad the story truly was; she stopped at the omnibus shelter. 'Well, that is a better outcome for his wife, but still quite sad for the poor man. I just hope there is someone in the Greenwood family who can speak on behalf of Mrs Greenwood. I wonder what Thomas knows of the case so far,' she mused.

'More than he is telling us, I imagine,' Georgina said, and the ladies exchanged a smile as they boarded the omnibus to head back to the *Women's Journal*. In the morning they would venture to Mrs Greenwood's former place of abode.

Chapter 12

Y oung Charlie stopped at the entrance to the alley and glanced towards the darkened end. A satisfied smirk lit his face; the dead body was still there. He pointed to it as Detectives Ashdown and Dart arrived behind him.

'That's him, the dead man,' Charlie announced, as if introducing the detectives to the deceased. 'Told ya.'

Thomas reached into his pocket and gave the boy several coins. 'Here you go, Charlie, well done.'

'Wow, thanks, mister,' he said, pocketing them straight away.

'Think you could spend one of those on a pair of shoes?' Thomas asked.

'Ma wouldn't like that when it can buy food,' he said.

'Of course. Next time we see you, we're going to get you some shoes and a coin for your Ma, alright?' Thomas asked.

Charlie shrugged. 'My brothers will just take my shoes, but if you like.'

Thomas sighed and gave up.

'I've got another coin for you if you do us a favour, Charlie,' Harry said.

'Sure. I'm available to do any work,' he said, importantly.

'Can you go find a police officer, and tell him Harry Dart wants him to come to Tea Lane, please?' Harry said.

'I can.' He repeated the instructions. 'Get a policeman and bring him here.'

'Yes, tell him Detective Dart said so. It's an easy name to remember, isn't it?'

Charlie nodded and ran off.

'Righto then, let's see what we've got,' Thomas said, shrugging off his jacket as the laneway became more stifling on entry. They arrived at the body at the end of the alley to find a well-dressed man curled up in a fetal position lying on the paved and dusty surface.

'He's only a young man by the looks of it, about your age I'd say,' Harry said in a flat tone, saddened by the deathly outcome. 'What have you done to earn this, sir?'

Thomas moved closer to the body and reeled back with surprise; the body sat up and stumbled to his feet, fists up to defend himself.

'Steady, we're police,' Harry said, blocking him from running down the alley.

'Police!' he said, and exhaled with apparent relief. He leaned against the back wall for support, and rubbed his hands along his trouser pants, before placing his hands on his hips, all the time breathing heavily and glancing around.

'Do you need medical attention?' Thomas asked.

'No, definitely not, no,' he panted. 'Just a minute to recover. Are you really the police?' he eyed them suspiciously.

'Detective Thomas Ashdown and this is my partner, Detective Harry Dart, from Roma Street Police Station.'

The man nodded, satisfied. He ran a hand through his wavy brown hair, removing dust and a spider web. Charlie and a constable appeared at the end of the laneway.

'He's not dead?' Charlie exclaimed, running up the lane to the detectives. 'But he looked dead. I even touched him.'

'Doesn't matter young man, I think it's a good thing he is still alive,' Harry said. 'We're glad you alerted us, and here's that coin. Try not to find too many more of the city's dead, hey?'

'It's easy work,' Charlie said with a shrug and pocketed the coin. 'I'll see you again then, misters.' Looking satisfied with his day's work, Charlie took off back down the lane as fast as his legs could take him.

'You want me, sirs?' The constable asked.

'No, I think we can manage this now. Thank you, Constable, resume your patrol,' Harry said.

'Want to tell us how you ended up lying there looking dead?' Thomas asked.

'I wish I could. I don't remember.' He ran a hand over his face. 'I was on my lunch break… maybe I was meeting someone, but I can't remember who, what, or why.' He shook his head as if to clear it.

'Your name then? Do you remember that?' Thomas asked.

The man looked at the two detectives. 'Alaric Osbourne.' He stood and patted down his jacket and trouser pockets. 'I think I've been robbed.'

'I doubt it,' Thomas said, and Harry and Alaric Osbourne looked at him, surprised.

Thomas pointed to a bundle of goods in the corner – a timepiece, wallet, and hat.

'They're mine!' Osbourne said, surprised.

'I think it is best you remember what business you had in this shady area, Mr Osbourne, as clearly it did not go well,' Harry said.

'Trust me, I would never be meeting someone in this lane,' he said, looking around. 'But I was with someone.' Then his eyes widened, and he remembered.

'Who?' Thomas asked, studying him.

'A lady, just a friend,' he said, suddenly looking very awkward.

'We are not going to find her lying in a laneway too, are we?' Harry frowned.

'God no, well, I hope not. She didn't arrive, and I left, and that's all I remember. Perhaps I was attacked and before they could steal from me, they were startled and ran away.'

'Perhaps,' Thomas said, unconvinced. 'I suggest we go to the station and take your statement if you feel up to it, and then you may return home.'

Osbourne stood straighter and nodded.

'What do you do for an occupation, Mr Osbourne?' Harry asked.

'I am a bookkeeper, assistant to Mr Dalton, accountant of Bridal Lane,' he said, with a nod to the end of the laneway, which went someway to explaining why he was in this part of town.

Thomas noted the man's hand went to his jacket pocket and patted it several times.

'Is something else missing? Something important?' Thomas asked.

Osbourne gave an uncomfortable chuckle. 'No, nothing. That's all I had on me,' he said, as he moved to his possessions, picked them up and dusted them off before putting them back in his pockets.

Thomas wasn't convinced. Alaric Osbourne was hiding something that he had in his possession or was meant to deliver to the person meeting him, and he looked fearful of its outcome.

Chapter 13

It was an unconventional night at the Hayward family residence. Head of the household and father to the brood, Mr James Hayward, was out at dinner and a show with Betty; Harriett had been given an early mark; Cook was told to take the night off and despite her desire to feed "her boys", she agreed and left the cold meats and salads, along with a few desserts and instructions that were not needed. The "children" were fending for themselves, and it was a cheery group that all pitched in and sat around the dining table to eat.

However, Matilda anticipated there was tension to come as Thomas had specifically come around to hear about her misadventure with Daniel the evening prior. She wished she had not mentioned it now, but at the time she was trying to get information from him and offered it as a hook.

Thomas sat next to her, opposite sat Elijah and Georgina, and Daniel and Alice. Matilda glanced at Thomas several times during the evening, knowing full well that he would be displeased with her when he found out what she did.

The group spoke of their day, of work, of Gideon's next exhibition – his first as the owner of the *Gallery of Fine Art*, and his burgeoning romance with the mortician, Miss Phoebe Astin. They spoke of Aunt Audrey's new friendship with a church-going man, and their father's happy liaison with the widowed Mrs Betty Purcell. The conversation turned to Alice and Georgina's family before it could no longer be avoided. When everyone was served and well into the meal, Thomas broached the subject.

'I am not going to forget, so best you get on with the tale,' he said, with a glance to Daniel and then to Matilda.

'Ooh, this is the dangerous liaison story?' Georgina asked enthusiastically, and Elijah looked up with interest.

'Hopefully not,' Thomas said. 'Matilda?'

Matilda grimaced. 'Let me just begin by saying we were never really in any danger.'

'That's correct,' Daniel confirmed, giving his best friend, Thomas, the sincerest look he could muster. He turned to Matilda. 'Why did you tell him?'

'Because I thought it might be related to the death of the lady who made lace,' Matilda said.

'I am sitting here,' Thomas said, reminding them.

Elijah laughed softly. 'Do forge on, Matilda, and put us out of our misery,' he said. 'What have you done this time?'

Alice and Georgina smiled and exchanged looks. Their dear friend was a beacon for trouble.

'More potato salad?' Daniel asked, offering it across to Matilda.

'Why thank you, Daniel,' she said, and placing it on the

table served herself and offered it to Thomas who declined, before passing it on to Elijah.

'Matilda, you're delaying the inevitable,' Thomas said, and Matilda sighed.

'Fine then. Last night you saw my bouquet samples I collected from Bridal Lane...'

'That awful lane that you should not have risked entering unaccompanied,' Thomas said.

'It is hellishly dangerous,' Daniel agreed. 'We have cases through the court that herald from that lane all the time,' he said, for the benefit of Alice, Georgina, and Elijah.

'We visited today to place the flower orders and it is quite rough indeed,' Georgina agreed.

'How odd that a flower store would be in such a location,' Alice commented. 'Surely not many ladies would venture there if it was so frightening.'

'Exactly,' Thomas agreed.

'None of you is helping my situation at all,' Matilda moaned, frowning at them.

'Sorry,' Georgina and Alice offered apologetically, setting Elijah off again with another round of chuckles.

Matilda cleared her throat. 'I did not realise at the time that Bridal Lane and *Blooming Blossoms* would be such a colourful area, so to speak. Anyway...'

'I offered to go with Matilda on her return visit,' Daniel said, to Thomas, 'even though it was your job.'

'And I would have happily fulfilled it if I had known,' he said, with a look at Matilda.

'It comes back to me again,' she said accepting the blame.

'Can we just hear the story?' Elijah asked. 'You are all like my patients, starting a story somewhere in the middle and going around in circles.'

'Hardly surprising,' Thomas said. 'Matilda is sending me to the asylum.' He gave her a wry look. 'Please begin, from the top.'

'From the top,' she agreed. 'I picked up the sample bouquets and safely made it home,' she said, looking pointedly at Thomas. 'And then, I found a small note tucked into my bridal bouquet requesting a liaison at 11pm, near the fig tree at BG, which Daniel and I decided was the Botanic Gardens. And we were right!'

Thomas's eyes widened and he sat upright, holding up his hand for Matilda to stop. 'Pray pause while I grasp this.'

Alice bit her lower lip as Georgina hid a smile behind her napkin. Elijah was not as subtle and laughed at Thomas's theatrics; Thomas was prone to melodramatics where Matilda was concerned.

'Please do not tell me you both went there?' he said.

'If you prefer. Let's talk of something else then,' Matilda suggested, happily.

'You went there?' he demanded of Daniel.

'Well, at the time we—that is—Matilda, thought that some poor man would be meeting his belle and she would not show because Matilda got the message instead. So, she thought it best we tell him of the mix-up so he did not think himself deserted,' Daniel said with a shrug.

'At 11 at night? You thought some poor man had asked a woman to meet him in the gardens at 11 at night? A man who is sneaking a message into bridal flowers?' Thomas exclaimed.

'Does sound terribly shifty,' Elijah added, himself now frowning that his siblings would put themselves in that danger.

'I did point that out to Matilda,' Daniel said, 'but as she was determined to go...'

'And so we went.' Matilda said.

'What happened?' Alice asked eagerly.

'Well,' Matilda said, keen to tell the story but with a sidelong glance at Thomas who she expected an angry reaction from once her story came out. 'We hid behind the trees and saw a very respectable man about our age waiting for someone. He was anxious and looking around, wasn't he?'

'He was. He did not look at all threatening or sinister,' Daniel said, which earned him a frown from Thomas.

'We decided we best tell him, or rather I decided I should tell him that I got his message by mistake. But Daniel wouldn't let me.'

'Thank God for that,' Thomas exclaimed, 'at last, a sensible thought!'

Daniel smirked at him. 'I said *I* would tell him.'

'I withdraw my comment,' Thomas said, and rolled his eyes, earning him some smirks and chuckles from the audience around the table.

Matilda continued: 'But he took off in an enormous hurry when Daniel approached, so I ran out as well as I realised he might have been having a dangerous liaison and thought Daniel was a husband or beau. I called after him, trying to explain that I had a letter in my bouquet by mistake, but he simply ran off.'

'We saw him running up one of the city streets a little later but then lost sight of him,' Daniel added.

'What city street?' Thomas asked quickly, his thoughts going to the recently roughed-up Alaric Osbourne and his suspicious behaviour.

Matilda looked to Daniel for clarification. 'What street was it, Dan?'

'It was a little lane that runs off Albert Street, there are a few there,' Daniel said.

Thomas's jaw locked.

'You know something,' Matilda said, studying him. 'I can tell. Something about our man?'

'I know lots of things and I am not telling you.'

'Is he a criminal?'

'I'm not saying,' Thomas said, and reached for his glass of wine.

'But I have told you everything,' she declared.

'As you should, and I have nothing to tell.'

'You do so, Thomas Ashdown, and if you don't tell, I shall pursue this mystery myself,' she declared, 'and my friends might help me.' She looked at Alice and Georgina, her expression one of hopeful expectation.

All three men spoke at once.

'—Over my dead body, Matilda,' Thomas said.

'—I don't believe that is a good idea at all,' Elijah said.

'—Don't even think about it,' Daniel snapped, and Matilda smiled along with her friends.

'Best you tell me then,' she said to Thomas.

'You are wasted, Matilda, our interrogation unit could use you,' he said, unhappily.

'Really? Do you think there's an opening there?' she asked, which made Thomas groan and Elijah and the ladies laugh some more.

'What did he look like?' Thomas asked.

Daniel answered. 'Tall, thin, brown wavy hair that needed trimming, well dressed.'

'Hmm,' Thomas said.

'What does that mean?' Matilda asked.

'It means that's interesting, but could describe half of the men in our town,' Thomas said.

'Do you know him?' Matilda asked.

'No.' Thomas said, and resumed eating his evening meal.

'Do you think it could be connected to Mrs Greenwood's murder?' Matilda asked.

'I can't say.'

'Except,' Georgina stepped in and added, 'the bouquet with the note in it came from the store in Bridal Lane, and we found out today that Mrs Greenwood supplied lace to that store and that she was brutally disposed of nearby. So, there is a connection.'

Thomas grimaced.

'Anything else, Thom?' Elijah teased.

'No, that's about all I know as well,' he muttered. 'Promise me you will stay away from that laneway now?' he asked of Matilda.

'I have no business to return as the bouquets will be delivered on our wedding day,' she said.

'Good,' he said, and smiled, pleased and somewhat appeased.

'So exciting,' Alice said. 'Your wedding day...'

'Who would have thought you two would end up attached?' Daniel mused.

'All of us, I suspect,' Elijah answered, and Matilda gave Thomas her most engaging smile.

All was temporarily forgiven.

Chapter 14

Detective Thomas Ashdown had a connection; it was all he could think about. Tea Lane, *Blooming Blossoms* in Bridal Lane, the death of Mrs Greenwood and the beating of Mr Alaric Osbourne were all linked somehow. He felt it, he knew it, and his partner could not arrive early enough that morning for his liking. He wrote what he could upon the board in his office, linking them, and checked the statement by Alaric Osbourne to get his address. He wondered if it would be a legitimate address when they arrived.

Thomas heard the familiar footsteps of his partner approaching his office.

'Ah, you are here!' he proclaimed on Harry's arrival in the doorway. 'Earlier than usual too.'

'You sound pleased to see me,' Harry said with a grin, removing his hat. 'It's Therese's church meeting morning, where I am sent out onto the streets with no breakfast and feeling sorry for myself. What's happened?'

'I believe they are all linked – the murder and the beating crime, the florist and the laneway. Unfortunately, the link came from Matilda,' he said, with a wry expression, and Harry laughed.

'She's missed her calling that young lady. She'd be after your job if she could get it.'

'Don't I know it. I haven't breakfasted either. Let's do so and I'll tell you what I know,' Thomas said.

Harry needed no persuasion and accompanied Thomas as they made their way to the dining room on the ground floor of the Roma Street police headquarters. No sooner had they joined the line to help themselves to a hearty breakfast than Thomas's old training partner and friend, Burton and his partner Lou, arrived. Like Thomas, Burton was the younger of the partnership; his partner, Lou, was closer to his sixth decade than his fifth.

'We don't find you here often, Golden Boy, nothing to work on?' Burton ribbed Thomas. 'Aren't you investigating the lacemaker's death? Got it stitched up already?'

Thomas chuckled. 'We are working it as we speak. Know anything?'

'Of course he does, Burton knows heaps about making lace,' Lou joked. 'Dainty work is his speciality.'

Burton chuckled. 'You'll keep, Lou.'

The men took their trays to a table for four and sat down, wasting no time in the consumption of their hot breakfasts and mugs of tea. Thomas held off on his briefing in the extended company.

'If you don't know anything about lace or the victim, what do you know about Tea Lane and Bridal Lane?' Harry asked, always keen to have insights, especially as one of Lou's tips on an earlier case made a difference.

'Yeah, nasty part of town that,' Burton agreed. 'That soothsayer in Bridal Lane needs to be given the hurry along.'

'We met her,' Thomas said, pushing the fried egg onto his toast. 'She saw the deceased on the day and the delivery boy chasing her, even though he denies it, but that was about as good as she got.'

'Couldn't ask the spirit world who murdered your lady then?' Lou asked.

'Apparently not,' Thomas said. 'I assumed the same but was told she's a card reader, not a clairvoyant.'

'She's a shrewd old girl, is what she is,' Burton said. 'I almost had her once on charges of bribery. Remember, Lou? But she's slippery.'

Lou nodded. 'She watches the comings and goings in that lane like a hawk, and told a few she'd keep her mouth shut about their activities for the right price.'

'That's interesting,' Harry said, with a glance at Thomas. 'I wonder how much she's not telling us then.'

'There's more going on at that florist shop than we first thought,' Thomas said. 'I'll get you up to speed later, Harry, on what I heard last night.'

'Where were you last night?' Burton asked, curiously.

'Dinner with my fiancée and her family, but Matilda was in Bridal Lane ordering her flowers around the same date as the crime took place and had a few insights. It's not far from Tea Lane where we found the lacemaker.'

'She's cluey your girl,' Lou said. 'You'll have to keep on your toes with her. Let her know if she ever tires of getting quotes from you two for that newspaper she writes for, she can talk with Burton and me.'

'Yeah, she'll be thrilled, thanks,' Thomas said drily, and the men chuckled. 'How's your case going? Have you got one?'

'Have we got one?' Burton said, and laughed, 'probably the most important case at the moment.'

'Yeah?' Harry asked amused.

'The handbag snatcher?' Thomas guessed.

'That's it,' Lou agreed, and they all laughed. 'No, we're working on the industrial murder at the railway.'

'Ah yeah, a messy one,' Thomas said, a little surprised he and Harry hadn't been assigned it given their success rate. Burton said what they were all thinking.

'Probably because you're going off and getting married in a few weeks, and Harry's taken leave at the same time, they gave it to us. It's not going to be solved any time soon, in my opinion.' He changed the subject. 'So, are you ready for matrimonial bliss? Don't know what that beautiful fiancée of yours sees in you.' Burton grinned as he stirred his friend.

'She's had a lot of time to notice me,' Thomas joked. 'I've been in her line of vision since I was seven. I started planting the seed early.'

'That's where you're going wrong, Burton,' Lou said. 'You just claim them for a night and they forget you by the time you get back to them.'

'Longevity, hey? Well, you'll be pleased to know we've got our suits pressed and ready for the day,' Burton said, finishing his breakfast.

'Never know your luck,' Thomas said to him. 'One of the wedding guests might be right up your alley. Speaking of which, we've got two alleys to visit and the home of the deceased.' He threw his napkin onto the table, declaring breakfast over.

'We're off then. Take care out there, boys,' Harry said.

'Mind that tarot reader,' Burton warned again, 'she's not all she seems.'

*****

At breakfast, Matilda hurriedly flicked through the pages of the newspaper to the letters' page. Mrs Lawson's letter had been printed several days earlier in response to Mr Allen's column, but the debate continued.

'Wonderful!' she said.

'What's that, dear?' Mr Hayward asked her, sitting at the head of the table as they partook in breakfast. Often it was just the two of them sharing breakfast and the newspaper, and Matilda had been most concerned about how her father would bear it when she married and moved from home. But now with Betty very much on the scene, perhaps the next lady of the manor—Mrs Hayward—may take up residence before too long if all continued to go well.

Matilda pointed to the paraphrased version of Mrs Lawson's letter. 'The responses to Mr Allen's column continue.'

'Ah yes, Betty told me. Goodness me, what doom and peril and nonsense he spoke.'

'Thank you, Pa,' Matilda said, and squeezed her father's hand. 'I am so glad you are my father and not Mr Allen!'

She scanned the letters to the editor and found quite a few supporting both arguments, and then glanced up to see the headline on her father's section of the newspaper.

'Oh Pa, a mugging in Tea Lane, that's near Bridal Lane where I got my flowers.'

Mr Hayward turned the paper around to re-read the headline.

'A brutal attack too, by the sounds of it. A gentleman by the name of Alaric Osbourne. Best you not go there alone, Matilda,' he said in a no-nonsense way. 'I am at your disposal.'

'Thank you, Pa. I have no need to return unless it is work related, but I won't go alone, I assure you. Georgina accompanied me last time, and I would only go at a respectable hour of the day. I wonder why *Blooming Blossoms* continue to operate from there.'

'Is this connected to Thomas's case, the lace-making lady who died?' Mr Hayward asked.

'Yes, I expect it is. And I bet he knew about that nearby mugging last night and would not tell me. He was hiding something,' she said, narrowing her eyes.

Mr Hayward chuckled. 'I suspect he'll be doing a lot of that in the years to come, Tillie. He needs to be discreet in his job.'

'Then we shall be discreet together,' she said with a firm nod.

'I am well familiar with that look on your face, young lady. You are not intending to go to the scene of the crime, are you?' Mr Hayward asked, concerned.

'No, I assure you, Pa, I am not. But I am a little involved as I'm writing a profile on Mrs Greenwood, and this morning, Georgina and I are going to call at her home in the hope the next of kin may provide some insights on the deceased lady.'

'Nasty business that.'

'I wonder if Mrs Greenwood was in the wrong place at the wrong time,' Matilda mused, 'or if she was exactly where she was meant to be.'

Chapter 15

The front door of Mrs Louise Greenwood's home was open. Mourners had placed floral tributes around the doorstep and wreaths hung upon the door.

'Well, someone's in residence today,' Thomas said, relieved and energised after a large breakfast.

The men walked up the small garden path and removing their hats, headed up the stairs of the respectable timber home with the attractive fretwork around the veranda. The sound of voices drifted out to them, but no one was in sight from the entranceway. Harry tapped gently on the door and moments later, a woman who resembled the deceased but was several decades younger walked towards them down the hallway. Dressed in black, and with a kindly face, she greeted them.

'You are acquainted with my mother?' she asked. 'I am Mrs Hester Rees, daughter of Louise.' Her voice hitched, and she held a handkerchief to her mouth.

'Mrs Rees, we are so sorry to intrude at your time of sorrow,' Harry said.

'No, not at all. I am pleased to see so many people calling to pay their respects. Please do come in.'

'I am Detective Harry Dart and my partner, Detective Thomas Ashdown.'

'Oh, you are here on police business,' Hester said, gathering herself. 'Thank you for anything you can do to find my mother's killer, I am very grateful.'

'Be assured of our full attention to the case, Mrs Rees,' Thomas asserted.

'Thank you. Please enter, take some refreshments,' she said, and the gentlemen followed her down the hallway. Thomas took the opportunity to study the deceased lady's house along the way, searching for anything out of order or curious. Nothing appeared to be. The bouquet they hoped to find—which might indicate Mrs Greenwood returned home before the attack—was now as impossible to find as a needle in a haystack with the overflowing gifts of flowers in every room.

They passed a room where an elderly couple sat drinking tea and continued to the back of the house, finding several larger rooms where small groups of people gathered.

'I am so pleased you have the family to support you at this terrible time, Mrs Rees,' Harry said.

'Everyone has been overwhelmingly kind,' she said, dabbing her eyes again. 'It was such a shock.'

'I can imagine,' Thomas said, as he followed Harry and Mrs Hester Rees into one of the larger rooms with the dark curtains drawn. It took Thomas a moment to realise what he had walked into as her words reached him.

'We are grateful the coroner released my mother's body to us for burial,' she said softly.

Thomas's eyes adjusted to the room they had entered. The clocks were stopped at Mrs Greenwood's estimated time of death, and a wall hanging—most likely a looking glass— was draped with black crepe for superstitious family members who feared that Mrs Greenwood's spirit would be trapped in the looking glass if it were not covered. The family photos were turned face down and Thomas saw behind Harry bountiful bouquets on a table. There, against the back wall, Thomas saw the deceased, Mrs Greenwood, laid out for viewing.

He gasped and stumbled backward, Harry turning quickly to see what was the matter, but Thomas looked stricken.

'Excuse me,' Thomas muttered and turned, departing the room hurriedly, heading for the front door as fast as he could without running.

*****

Harry cleared his throat and drew Mrs Hester Rees's attention back to him.

'I beg your pardon, Mrs Rees,' Harry said and tried to offer some kind of explanation. 'Thomas has faced considerable trauma of late and...' he struggled.

'Do no concern yourself, Detective,' Mrs Rees said, kindly. 'We all deal with grief differently and some rituals are more upsetting than others. I take comfort in having my mother here,' she said, glancing towards the coffin and her mother in the corner. 'But my younger sister cannot come into this room, it is too much for her.'

Harry nodded. 'Thank you for your understanding. I hoped to ask you some questions to assist us with the case, but if now is not the best time…'

'Please ask me. I am keen to ensure the perpetrator is punished and am at your disposal, Detective. Would you feel more comfortable if we moved outside and joined your partner?'

'If you have no objections, that would be preferable,' Harry said, and with a small nod to Mrs Greenwood against the back wall, he followed Hester Rees out to the front garden where Thomas stood, looking uncomfortable and embarrassed on seeing Harry.

To Harry's surprise, the ladies from the *Women's Journal* were with him – Miss Matilda Hayward and Miss Georgina Urry. Harry did the introductions.

'We are sorry to come while you are receiving callers, Mrs Rees,' Matilda said, and explained the purpose of their visit.

'You are most welcome and I am touched that you wish to remember my mother with a tribute piece, thank you,' Mrs Rees said and dabbed her eyes again. 'Shall we sit?' She indicated some garden furniture under a tree and the ladies sat, while Thomas and Harry remained standing.

'If the detectives would like to speak with you first, as I am sure they are very pressed,' Matilda said, 'we can rest here.'

'No need to move away, ladies, if Mrs Rees does not

'insist,' Harry said, 'our questions are routine but not for publication.'

Matilda looked pleased. Thomas did not.

'Of course, Detective,' Matilda said, 'we understand and perhaps our questions, if Mrs Rees permits, may be of interest to yourself and Detective Ashdown.'

Mrs Rees agreed and Harry glanced at Thomas and took over the questions. His partner was not well, his skin was an unhealthy colour, and he looked mortified at his actions. Harry could see Matilda was also studying her fiancé with concern. He began his questioning.

'Do you know why your mother would have been in Tea Lane?' Harry asked.

'No, Detective. I confess I had very little to do with my mother's business dealings. I am married with three children and have my own duties. My mother would regularly join us for tea, especially since my father passed away, but both my sister and I had little to do with her work. It was well established before we reached adulthood.'

'Would you like to have been more involved?' Matilda asked, out of the blue.

'Oh yes, but my husband was not keen on me working. Maybe when the children have left home and I have more time on my hands,' she said.

'What does your husband do, Mrs Rees?' Harry asked, keen to eliminate him.

'He is a baker. Up early, to bed early. He and my mother got on rather well; it was my mother who introduced us. My husband is the son of one of Mum's sewing friends.'

'Can you think of anyone who would do your mother harm?' Harry asked.

'I can't imagine why,' Hester Rees said, dabbing her eyes again and looking up at Harry. 'She was very good at what she did, most conscientious and always delivered as promised.'

Georgina spoke up. 'I heard from one of the ladies at the *Women's Journal* who was an acquaintance in your mother's circle that your mother was very community-minded and of good faith. It is difficult sometimes to be the voice of Christian values or so my mother tells me regularly.'

Harry and Thomas both looked surprised but pleased. That was exactly where Harry was going but was not sure how to get there diplomatically without implying Mrs Greenwood might have interfered where it was not wanted.

Mrs Rees nodded. 'That is kind of your work friends to say so, and yes, that is very true, Miss… I have forgotten your name, forgive me.'

'Not at all. It is a stressful time and so many introductions at once. Georgina,' she responded, 'Georgina Urry.'

Mrs Rees smiled her thanks. 'Miss Urry, you are very correct. My mother had a firm moral compass and was not deterred from it. She believed in giving back, faithful relations, industriousness and personal responsibility. She was quite vocal on the subject, which did not always put her in good stead with those who strayed from the path.'

Harry gave Georgina a small nod of thanks.

'Did she make any enemies from trying to live her faith, Mrs Rees,' Harry continued.

Mrs Rees hesitated. 'My mother was accused of being unswerving in her convictions on occasion.' She dabbed her eyes and no one spoke, hoping Mrs Hester Rees might contribute more. 'When we last spoke, Mum told me that she was not going to continue to supply lace to *Blooming Blossoms* and intended to tell them.'

'Forgive me, but do you know why a florist shop required lace, Mrs Rees? Would not ribbon be more useful for the tying and decorating of flowers?' Matilda asked, surprised.

'It does seem odd, Miss Hayward, but the owner, Mrs Dalton, has a small dressmaking business on the side with her daughter. I can't recall the name of it, but it runs from another venue. They are able to share contacts and business and I believe my mother made lace for the dresses and, if required, a sample to match the bouquet. That is my understanding. Perhaps it was a favour as my mother and Mrs Dalton have been friends for decades. I must say, my mother's decision did come as a surprise.'

'Did she say why?' Thomas asked, finding his voice and strength again.

'My mother said they no longer shared the same values but did not elaborate. I am very familiar with my mother's values, so I did not ask anything more, I confess,' Mrs Rees said. 'She would have told me in more detail in due course, she usually did share her matters of conscience...' she stopped, realising this would never happen again.

'Of course,' Thomas said.

Harry noted Thomas's gaze lingered on Matilda and wondered if his reticence to be in the same room as the deceased had some relevance to their shared history. Returning his thoughts to the case, Harry was pleased that at least now they had a little more insight into the woman of whom everyone was singing praises. He suspected Mrs Greenwood's vocal stand might be just what put her in the path of danger, and again it linked back to the laneways and *Blooming Blossoms.*

Chapter 16

Harry and Thomas thanked Mrs Greenwood's daughter and, bidding the young ladies good-day, departed the residence of the deceased. When they were some distance away, had hailed and were seated on the omnibus, Harry broached the subject.

'Thom, I will not sit in judgement. Do you not think it is time you told me what it is that concerns you about death? It is not the first time this has happened, and it is of no great concern, except to your health. But I might prevent your distress if I know,' he said.

Thomas swallowed and gave a small nod. 'It is a weakness I have – a fear of being closed in with the dead. I apologise as I know my actions today were unforgivable.'

'Nonsense. You did not offend and there is nothing to forgive,' Harry assured him. 'Remember when we had that murder at the cliffs and I could not go near them despite needing to see the victim and the evidence? So be it.'

Thomas nodded. 'I recall, but that was different. A lot of people fear elevation and falling from great heights.'

'A lot of people do not like to be around the dead,' Harry reminded him. 'But you are often by nature of our job. I know it is more than that. You attend crime scenes where we see bodies in all forms of death and do not even flinch. But what is it about a funeral home or a mourning room? Tell me, son,' he pressed.

Their stop came into sight and the two men alighted and walked up the street to the police station. Thomas took a deep breath and ran his hand over his mouth. He did not speak and Harry did not push him any further. When the building came in sight, he exhaled and explained.

'My mother died when I was six, my brother Sewell was 19 and had left home. I lived with my father who was older than Mum… nearing his fiftieth year, and he had no interest in raising a young son. It's fair to say, that he was very angry with her being taken at eight and thirty, and angry at being burdened with me.'

Harry listened attentively but did not interrupt.

'The day after Mum died, he found me playing with the boys in our street; we were playing cricket. He was ropeable that I wasn't mourning my mother properly.'

'You were six!' Harry said, surprised. 'Most children wouldn't really understand.'

'I missed her, but she was not a doting mother. My father punished me.'

Thomas glanced at Harry and away before continuing. 'For two nights, he locked me in the room with my mother's deceased body in her coffin.'

Harry cursed under his breath. Thomas cleared his throat of emotion and continued.

'I was terrified. Kicked and screamed until it wore me out. I vomited in the corner of the room, which only made him angrier the next morning when he released me.'

'Thom, that is an unforgivable act by your father.'

Thomas continued as if the floodgates had been opened: 'I couldn't sleep lying in the dark with my dead mother. I kept imagining her rising, looking at me with her dead face and eyes wide open. I was terrified she'd call for me. At morning light my father unlocked the door, I crawled out and he told me to take breakfast. I was so glad when Mum was buried.' He stopped and looked at Harry. 'That is the gist of it. We are not a close family,' he said and smiled.

Harry shook his head as they walked up the stairs to the building. 'Ah, Thom, a cruel and awful thing to do to a young lad.'

'It's alright. But I confess, I don't like being in a closed or dark room with a dead body.'

'I understand.'

'I was lucky, though. I met Daniel not long after and pretty much grew up in his household – no one noticed I wasn't one of the Haywards given there were four boys there already,' he joked. 'My father was only too happy for me to stay over as much as I liked, and Mr Hayward always welcomed me, despite having a houseful of children; he wasn't worried about one more.'

Harry gave Thomas's back a pat as they headed down the hallway to their offices.

'Did Mr Hayward know of that incident, or did you ever confide in him?' Harry asked.

'He did. I had a lot of nightmares in the early days when I'd sleep over in Daniel's room. One night, when he and I were both awake largely due to me, he made us both hot milk and we sat in the kitchen and spoke of it. He told me it would never happen to me again.' Thomas exhaled. 'I was better after that, kind of like having someone on your side.'

'You've turned out pretty good for a lad with a rough start,' Harry said, and Thomas laughed, embarrassed.

'Hardly a rough start. I had a good roof over my head, an education, regular meals, I was clothed.'

'Maybe, but love and affection never go astray in childhood. Look at you now... a good head on your shoulders, a great job, a lovely lady soon to be your wife.'

'And my partner's alright too,' Thomas joked.

'Yeah, you're a lucky man,' Harry said and laughed at Thomas's expression. 'Thanks for telling me, it makes perfect sense now.'

Thomas nodded, keen to change the subject as they removed their hats and jackets.

'Let's review what we know. We've got some interviewing to do,' Thomas said, relieved to have the incident put to rest.

*****

Left alone with the body of Mrs Greenwood in what was now the mourning room of the Greenwood home, Georgina finished the illustration having consulted both an old wedding portrait and the lady herself lying nearby.

Matilda studied the deceased with curiosity. She lowered

her voice, and with a glance around to ensure there was no one nearby in the hallway or doorway, said: 'I have just spoken with several people asking them for their remembrances of Mrs Greenwood for my piece, and they are not all generous in their recollections.'

'Goodness! Even today when they are here to mourn her?' Georgina asked, surprised. 'One would think they would wait until the deceased was buried before they spoke ill of her.'

Matilda smiled. 'Yes, and not still in residence.' She glanced at the deceased.

'Shall we go?' Georgina asked.

'Yes, happily. But would you object if we were to go to *Blooming Blossoms* on our way back to the office?'

'Have you not ordered your flowers yet?' Georgina asked, surprised as they moved down the hallway. 'At this rate, I'll be helping you pick them on the morning of the wedding. I'm good at the cutting, but I suspect Alice will be the best at arranging.'

Matilda laughed. 'Rest assured, that won't be necessary. I have ordered them. But I thought it would be useful to have a tribute to Mrs Greenwood from the store that she supplied her lacework to for many years. Especially if the owner, Mrs Dalton, and Mrs Greenwood were old friends.'

'Hmm,' Georgina smiled, 'I know what you are up to.'

Matilda laughed. 'Do tell?'

'You hope to wheedle out of Mrs Dalton about their fallout and Mrs Greenwood's decision to not supply lace to her anymore?'

'Yes, precisely, assuming Mrs Greenwood had told her of the decision before she died,' Matilda said.

'And if you do find out anything, you can tell the detectives,' Georgina said, with a smile.

'That would be satisfying indeed,' Matilda agreed with a small laugh, before sobering as they left the room and entered into another room with the mourners.

The two ladies sought Mrs Greenwood's daughter to thank her and promised to secure a copy of the article and illustration for her when published. They departed on foot to the nearest omnibus stop.

'Thomas will be most annoyed with you for returning to Bridal Lane,' Georgina said. 'If we don't find out anything, it might be best if you do not mention your visit.'

Matilda wrinkled her nose. 'But I am accompanied and it is daytime, so that dutifully meets his requirements.'

'If Mrs Dalton does not know or admit to knowing of her friend's decision, it will be interesting to watch her reaction when asked to speak on behalf of Mrs Greenwood.'

Matilda smiled. 'Yes, that's exactly what I want to see, too. Please don't feel compelled to accompany me, however, if you are uneasy about returning there. I can go with Daniel later.'

They arrived at the stop and saw the omnibus coming toward them.

'Absolutely not. I wouldn't miss it for the world,' Georgina assured her. 'I suspect I won't be much help to you though – I am better at reading the mood of cattle than people.'

'Truly?' Matilda asked, as they stepped aboard and took their seats. 'Are they moody?'

'Not really, but a cow's tail is a dead giveaway. When it is hanging down straight, the cow is very relaxed; if they tucked it between their legs, then they are not happy. When they are playful, it is often kinked.' Georgina laughed at Matilda's expression. 'I bet that information will be very useful to you if you are stuck in a social situation with a farmer.'

'Without a doubt,' Matilda nudged her friend good-humouredly. 'It is not dissimilar to people,' she observed. 'Look at that man over there, he is slumped with his head down. He looks most despondent.'

'True. And that lady's head is high, and she's glancing around. I suspect she is happy and curious,' Georgina added. 'Oh!'

'What is it?' Matilda looked around as the omnibus came close to their stop.

'That is the young lady, Rose, from *Blooming Blossoms,* isn't it? Over there talking with that man and boy on the corner. She does not look happy... in fact, it looks rather secretive.'

Matilda gasped, and alighting, she pulled Georgina against a building wall behind the light pole, to try and stay out of sight.

'That is the man that was in the park that night with Daniel and me!'

'And that is *Blooming Blossoms'* delivery boy,' Georgina added. 'I saw him coming and going when we were in the shop.'

'What are they up to?'

'Perhaps it is a friendly liaison?' Georgina said. 'But it looks somewhat tense.'

'I agree.'

They watched as Rose handed a bouquet to the delivery boy and the man rolled up a piece of paper and put it inside the bouquet.

'That's what happened to me! I found the note, his note,' Matilda exclaimed. 'I have a good mind to confront them and ask why he ran and what is going on.'

'Except if it is something sinister, that might not be wise,' Georgina said.

'I guess so. Let us go speak with the owner and see what happens when Rose returns. I wonder if Mrs Dalton knows what is going on.'

'There is something afoot, for sure! But I have another suggestion,' Georgina said, holding her friend's arm before Matilda took off down Bridal Lane.

'Do tell?' Matilda encouraged her.

'Why don't we follow the boy with the flowers and see where he delivers them? That might be telling.'

Matilda's eyes widened with enthusiasm. 'Why yes! Have you comfortable shoes on?'

'Always,' Georgina said.

Matilda squeezed her hand. 'Let's then, that's a brilliant idea.'

They continued to watch the three people engaged in a lively discussion on the street corner for a few minutes more and then the lad departed with the flowers, Rose gave a small bow and headed back down Bridal Lane, and the gentleman departed the opposite way.

'Thank goodness it is a busy area,' Matilda said, as they blended into the crowds upon the footpath, always keeping the young man in sight. 'I do wish he would slow down, though.'

'It's unfortunate he's young and male,' Georgina agreed, lifting her skirt a little more to allow for a longer stride. 'We would have no problem keeping up with the shop owner, Mrs Dalton.'

Several people moved aside to allow the hurrying young ladies to get ahead and they smiled their thanks, trying to look as natural as possible. The young delivery boy stopped abruptly and the ladies did the same, pressing themselves against a shop window so they could pretend to browse and look inconspicuous, should the occasion require. Then, he was off again and the ladies picked up the pace.

'I imagine to anyone watching from afar we look rather desperate,' Matilda said, between breaths. 'Chasing a flower deliverer down the road as if we know the bunch is for us.'

Georgina laughed and then both ladies could not stop giggling at their antics.

'I never thought I'd stoop to this for a bunch of flowers,' Georgina added between gasps and laughs, making Matilda laugh harder.

The ladies followed the delivery boy around a corner, down the busy town shopping strip and into a quieter street with a mixture of small businesses and little timber houses. They remained behind, and as he slowed his pace, they too wandered casually, as if they were heading home. The young lad crossed the street, took one more left turn, and not seeing the ladies peeking around a hedge on the corner, the boy selected a small white home with a garden full of flowers.

'He's stopping,' Georgina said, 'thank goodness for that.'

They watched as he took the stairs, knocked on the front door and waited. There was no answer, so the delivery boy put the flowers on the top step where they could not be missed and departed, coming back the same way. They looked around desperately for somewhere to hide in case he recognised them from the store. Georgina opened her copy of the newspaper, put it in front of both of their faces and exclaimed as he came nearer: 'There are new hats at Edwards and Chapman's in the city.'

'Oh my, and millinery,' Matilda added, peeking over the top to see the boy showed no interest in them, especially as they were speaking of ladies' shopping items.

They waited a moment longer before lowering the paper and making their way around the corner.

'No one is home, so what if I should just drop in and see what that message reads,' Matilda said, with a glance around.

'It is very risky, but we have come this far. There are other people in residence nearby should we find ourselves in trouble and need to seek help,' Georgina said, observing an elderly gentleman watering his roses further up the street and a mother coming down the opposite way with a pram.

'Let's do so quickly then,' Matilda said, and the ladies hurried across the road, and up the front path of the small home.

'I shall pretend to knock while you subtly check out the flowers,' Georgina said.

'Excellent idea. We'll look as if we have a delivery or are

visiting,' Matilda said, and arriving at the stair, moved the petals delicately until she secured the note.

Georgina knocked on the front door as the young delivery boy did, and waited, one eye upon Matilda, and then the door swung open.

Georgina gasped, and Matilda straightened beside her.

'Good morning, I am sorry I was off with the fairies and you startled me,' Georgina said, and smiled at the lady whom she guessed to be her mother's age, but was a little less worn from life in the city, not on the land.

The lady smiled kindly. 'I've been accused of the same myself. How may I help you?'

'We are from the *Women's Journal* magazine and undertaking research to find out what our readers might like to see more or less of in our issue.'

'I'm sorry it is not me that subscribes, but my daughter, Petronella. But she is not home at the moment.'

'Oh, that is a shame, but we are grateful for her subscription,' Georgina said, relieved that having a subscriber in residence added credibility to their visit and they did not appear to be randomly door-knocking around the neighbourhood. 'Well, I am sorry to have bothered you then,' Georgina apologised.

'You appear to have a flower delivery,' Matilda said, picking up the flowers and noting the card read "Miss Petronella Pettyfore".

'I thought I heard a knock before, but I was out the back in the garden,' the lady said. 'The second time, I was sure.' She took the flowers with thanks and inhaled their scent.

Seeing the note, she smiled. 'Ah, for my daughter, she has a very dedicated suitor. Shall I let her know you called?'

'No, please do not concern her,' Matilda said. 'It is just a random survey, so we shall continue with some of the ladies on our list. Thank you for your time and trouble.'

'Not at all,' the lady said, smiled at them and watched them walk down the stairs, before closing the front door once the ladies reached the footpath.

'Oh my,' Matilda said, exhaling sharply and trying to keep her expression neutral until they were well away from the area. They turned the corner and then she breathed out. 'What quick thinking on your behalf, Georgina! You are very good on your feet.'

'It was not too far from the truth, as we are seeking interviews, if not a survey,' Georgina said, her voice betraying her relief to be away from the house and delivery. 'I nearly toppled off the step when she opened the door. Did you get to read the note?'

'Yes!' Matilda said and grinned. 'Whoever Miss Pettyfore is, she has a note reading "*Burgess, Pad H, PAID. Next? BG8*" in her flowers. I must jot it down immediately before I forget,' Matilda said, and Georgina presented her pencil and the back of her illustrating pad.

'What do you think it means?' Georgina asked, studying the note.

'I am only guessing but it is something to do with a Mr, Mrs or Miss Burgess... Pad H... I don't know what that means, but I suspect they are meeting in the Botanical Gardens this evening at 8pm, and there is that paid reference again,'

Matilda said, reading her handwriting back. 'Well, that's a guess based on the last note I read, although I am surprised they would meet there again.' She re-read the note. 'They are meeting considerably earlier, perhaps that's part of his strategy to avoid trouble.'

'Promise me you won't go there,' Georgina said, as they walked more leisurely and rejoined the throngs of shoppers in the main town street.

'I promise, unless Thomas or Daniel is with me,' Matilda said, already thinking of her next move.

'If you are right, they will most likely meet somewhere different from where you last saw him. It is an awfully large area to watch,' Georgina mused. 'Perhaps we should all go and observe… we can cover all four corners.'

'That does make sense, even if Thomas puts up a fight,' Matilda said.

'I wonder what Miss Petronella Pettyfore has got herself caught up in,' Georgina pondered.

'I think it is something much more complex than a dedicated suitor,' Matilda said, and both ladies exchanged a look – a story was brewing.

Chapter 17

Thomas could not hide the displeasure or frustration from his face as Matilda, the Hayward brothers—Daniel and Elijah—and their lady friends, Alice and Georgina, gathered at the Hayward household to discuss the plan for this evening.

'I think this is completely unnecessary, potentially dangerous, and—'

'We know,' Daniel cut him off and gave his best friend, Thomas, a smirk. 'You don't want us there and you think we should leave it to the police.'

'Thom does have a point,' Mr Hayward agreed, as the group sat around the drawing-room, drinks in hand.

'But Pa, it might be just a lovers' letter and how silly would it be for the detectives and constabulary to be on hand?' Matilda pointed out. 'It was delivered in a bouquet, after all.'

'That's a reasonable thought too,' Betty said, and Mr Hayward nodded his agreement, although it is likely he would have agreed with anything Betty said in his current state of amour.

'There is no harm surely for us all to be enjoying a late dusk walk in the park and it will be the last light around that time of the evening,' Elijah said, supporting Georgina's desire to be there. He reached for her hand. 'There's bound to be many couples heading home through the gardens.'

'Yes, we can be on our way home from working at the madhouse,' Georgina joked with Elijah, 'and you from your asylum work, too.'

The group laughed at her cleverness.

'It does seem like a mad house at the *Women's Journal* on deadline day,' Betty agreed in good humour.

'As long as you just observe,' Thomas said. 'No one is to approach or be blatant in your study of what is going on. Remember, it could be—and is likely to be—a criminal incident. Can we agree on that?'

'Agreed,' Daniel said, and Thomas accepted the same from all parties present.

'Matilda?' Thomas pushed her.

'Yes, I agree,' she said and gave him a firm nod. 'So, we shall spread out and observe, and then meet again, let's say at 8.30pm, unless you have the man in your line of sight and are delayed.'

'What exactly are we expecting to see?' Alice asked.

'It's hard to say,' Matilda informed her. 'All we know is that the man in question has now had two bouquets delivered with notes in them and he ran when Daniel and I approached him to tell of the mix-up. The second note was delivered to a Miss Petronella Pettyfore—'

Thomas gasped and Matilda stopped. 'Are you quite alright, Thomas?'

He coughed and cleared his throat, the mention of a former paramour's name taking him by surprise. 'Quite alright, thank you. Sorry, do go on.'

'Well, the note was asking for someone—I'm guessing Miss Pettyfore since it was delivered to her—to meet him at 8pm. It may be romantic, or it may be a plot.'

'It does sound very much like a couple's liaison in secret,' Betty said.

'It does,' Thomas agreed, 'except that it may be more sinister and everyone needs to go in fully aware of the danger if you insist on doing this… since I have no power to stop you,' he said, with a less than happy look at Matilda.

'If you have suspicions, can you tell us if we promise to keep it to ourselves?' Georgina asked and tapped her nose. 'I believe that is the universal symbol for staying hushed.'

Elijah smiled at her with affection.

Thomas cleared his throat and shared: 'In strict confidence… we believe something illegitimate could be going on at *Blooming Blossoms* in connection with the death of Mrs Louise Greenwood.'

Matilda did not interrupt with questions even though she had many, hoping Thomas would continue. Fortunately, he did.

'Mrs Greenwood bought a bouquet, and we did not find it near her body or in her home. The tarot reader saw the delivery boy racing out of the shop straight after Mrs Greenwood departed, as if she had the wrong bouquet. Given the obscure note found in Matilda's bouquet and the outcome of Daniel and Matilda's observations in the park, maybe all is not legitimate, and underground messages are being passed.' The room was silent as Thomas painted the picture. 'Mrs Greenwood was also withdrawing her business from the shop owner, Mrs Dalton, despite their long friendship. Given she is known for taking the moral high ground, there may be a link between what she found out, her reasons for the withdrawal and her death.'

Alice shuddered.

'Perhaps it is too dangerous,' Mr Hayward said, looking more concerned. This time, Betty agreed with him.

Matilda had no intention of not attending. 'Or it could just be that this man is meeting Miss Pettyfore in secret and ran thinking we had caught him out.'

'That might be the case,' Thomas said with a shrug. 'I do not yet know this man or know if he is connected in any way to our investigation. There was a gentleman attacked in the same laneway in the days following Mrs Greenwood's death, but I am not aware of an association yet.' Thomas did not mention the gentleman's name or that he seemed to be hiding something on his person.

'Then we should be cautious and discreet,' Elijah said, 'assuming the ladies still wish to attend.'

'Absolutely,' Georgina said. 'Fortunately, we are in the company of a doctor if needed.'

'Very true,' Elijah said, with a grin.

'I still wish to go too,' Alice added. 'We will be careful.'

'That's agreed then,' Matilda said firmly.

'We should head off soon and each secure a different corner of the park while it is still light so we don't appear to all arrive suspiciously at once and take position,' Elijah said, getting into the cloak and dagger dramatics of the evening.

'It would be wonderful if one of us should overhear the discussion of the man and whomever he is meeting,' Matilda said.

'That might require some acting,' Daniel said. 'If we are that close, then we must look distracted.' He looked to his belle, Alice, seated next to him. 'I might have to kiss you in the name of research.'

Her small, pale, English face flushed with pleasure. 'Of course, if it is to benefit an investigation, then you must.'

'Does that apply to all of us?' Thomas asked, wryly, 'in the name of research, of course.' Daniel's eyes narrowed as he looked from his best friend to his sister.

Mr Hayward and Betty laughed, as Matilda smiled with delight.

'Shall we come along?' Betty asked, worried that Mr Hayward might want to go but be holding back out of concern for her safety.

'I thought we might dine alone, while we have a chance,' Mr Hayward said, with a smile at his young charges.

'Please stay,' Thomas said. 'The fewer people in danger the better, and no offence intended, but neither of you is as quick as you perhaps once were.'

Mr Hayward chuckled at Thomas's attempt to be diplomatic.

'That's a much better idea,' Betty agreed. She turned to Matilda. 'You can tell us what happened on your return. How exciting.'

*****

Matilda nestled up against Thomas, her arm linked through his as they wandered amid the beautiful grounds of the Botanic Gardens at dusk that evening. Thomas was prepared to admit the impromptu investigation did have some benefits, as he felt her small hand on his arm. The last of the day was upon them and a clear sky ensured they would have the benefit of moonlight. A light breeze provided heat relief after a warm day. The skirt of Matilda's blue dress swished against his suit leg and her intoxicating scent—a mixture of talcum and vanilla—teased his senses. He had to confess it was most distracting and not a problem he was usually faced with on the job.

'This is fun, isn't it?' she whispered, looking up at him with a grin.

Thomas raised an eyebrow and gave her a small smile. 'Important police business is not meant to be fun.'

She playfully hit his arm. 'Stop being Mr Very-Important-Detective and admit it is fun.'

'I am a very important detective,' he said with a grin and made her laugh. 'But we have to remember we are in the midst of a potential crime, even if it is nice to be doing this together,' he conceded.

'Yes, Detective,' she answered dutifully, and he smiled and shook his head at her. They stopped momentarily behind a tree, determining if the location would be of benefit. Thomas kissed her forehead as she looked up at him, and with a glance over her shoulder, he returned his attention to the park, keeping an eye on the other two couples as well as looking out for the man in question, although he had no doubt Matilda would manage that on her own.

'We are nearby where Daniel and I saw him last time,' she said.

'Would he recognise you?' Thomas asked.

'I think it is unlikely. He barely glanced back and was more intent on running away.' Thomas watched her studying the area. 'He was waiting by that tree there and we were almost where we are now. It is a good spot as we are a little obscured by the shrubbery.'

'There is a bench over there. Shall we sit and pretend we are having our own private liaison?'

'But what if he does not come to this spot again? We might not see him if we are sitting.'

'As you wish,' Thomas said, although he'd prefer to sit and have her out of trouble. 'We'll continue to walk slowly, doing a promenade around the courtyard. But don't forget to look at me now and then; otherwise, no one will believe we are not spying.'

Matilda glanced at him and then saw his mischievous expression and laughed.

'What if I look at you like this?' she said, making eyes at him. 'Like I am smitten and cannot live without you. Like you are the best thing to ever happen to me and my wedding day cannot come quickly enough.'

'I think that is working,' he said seriously, and then smiled at her. 'Wish that it were true.'

'Oh, but it is, Thomas, it is,' she assured him, squeezing his arm and making Thomas completely forget what they were in the park to do.

*****

Alice and Daniel peeked around a tree, saw the coast was clear and moved to sit on a bench in front of the lake where they could see right across the gardens.

Daniel wiped down the bench with his handkerchief and invited Alice to sit, enjoying the reward of her thanks and grateful smile.

'Isn't this lovely? I am sure none of us stops to smell the roses quite enough,' she said and sighed.

'So true.' Daniel agreed, relaxing and enjoying the last of the day. His thoughts were only half on the crime to play out. 'Since I have started court illustrating, I find I don't illustrate for pleasure anymore and you are right... I don't take in the beauty around me as much. Except for you, of course,' he hastily added, and she laughed at the late inclusion. He fully intended to propose to Miss Alice Doran, his English beauty, and ensure she stayed in Australia by his side for the rest of their days together. But he did not want to do so until after Thomas and Matilda's wedding to ensure he did not steal their moment in the sun. Besides, that was only a matter of weeks away, and both he and Alice were in the bridal party together.

'I am surprised Thomas allowed Matilda to talk him into this,' Alice said, as they sat watching the ducks on the water.

'She has been training him for years and years to go along with her crazy ideas,' Daniel joked. 'I swear she could talk him into anything.'

Alice smiled. 'That's so sweet.'

'Plus, he's no doubt a bit distracted with the wedding so close and happy just to keep the peace.'

Alice gave Daniel a look.

'What did that look mean?' he asked, intrigued.

'Men,' she said and sighed. 'You talk as if you have a lot of responsibility before the wedding. Has Thomas done anything except try on a suit and be forced to look at some flowers?'

Daniel smiled. 'Well, when you put it like that.' He straightened suddenly.

'Is he here?' Alice whispered, wide-eyed and looked around alert.

'No.' Daniel squinted as he looked across the park in the distance. 'I just saw Thomas kiss Matilda, out here in the open.'

'Do relax, big brother,' she teased him. 'He is honourable and they are engaged. Perhaps he is leading by example,' Alice said.

Daniel snapped to look at her. 'My word, you are right,' he said, and lowering his head to offer a kiss to Alice, she instead moved back slightly and gave a subtle wave to someone. Daniel frowned and turned to see Georgina and Elijah backing away from there and heading to patrol a different area.

'Nothing changes,' he muttered, watching Elijah who was very similar in colouring to him. 'The twins were always crashing my plans growing up and even now, one of them manages to interrupt my intent.'

When he turned back around, he found Alice leaning up and her lips right near his. He did not waste a second taking advantage of the moment.

*****

Georgina and Elijah moved hurriedly away, trying to pretend they did not know the handsome couple seated near the ducks and avoiding exchanging glances with Thomas and Matilda strolling on the other side of the park.

'Goodness, this cloak and dagger spy business can be quite tricky, can't it?' Georgina said, and Elijah chuckled.

'Especially to we novices,' he said, folding her hand through his arm and strolling on. 'Although I have become quite adept at avoiding the matron at work and the more persistent patients who insist they are maligned when there is nothing wrong with them.'

'Oh, I know what you mean,' Georgina said. 'Mrs Tuppence, a lady from my town, has a good heart, but should you ask after her health, you will hear about it in great detail. Should we visit, I shall point her out to you in advance. Once she knows you are a doctor, Mrs Tuppence will never let you rest.'

Elijah laughed. 'We shall visit regularly, shall we not? Perhaps one day we might consider taking up residence there. I could find work as a local doctor and you could assist me or your parents as you see fit, or perhaps care for our family.'

Georgina did not look directly at him; her emotions were a whirl.

'Would you not like that?' he asked, a little confused.

'More than I can say,' she answered, looking ahead. 'More than I care to dream about.'

He squeezed her hand slightly and cleared his throat.

'Please don't underestimate my feelings for you, Georgina.

I just hope in return your affections are as strong.'

She now turned to face him, her breathing increased, her eyes filled with devotion.

'Oh Elijah, please be assured they are and forgive me.'

'What for?' he asked, a little alarmed, fearing she was going to share some terrible secret that would drive them apart.

'I am inexperienced at expressing emotions. My family is very stoic and I have no siblings to have showered with love and affection,' she said sincerely. 'I would hate for you to feel I am indifferent to you because I cannot express it. I assure you, my feelings are as constant as the sun rising every day and the moon making way for her at dawn.'

Elijah took her hand and kissed it before returning his gaze to her.

'For someone so inexperienced at speaking your feelings, they are the most beautiful words I have ever heard, and the only person in the world I want to hear them from. Besides, you spoke to me of your affection in the portrait you did for me when we first met.'

She smiled. 'Ah, yes, the portrait I so boldly sent home with your sister.'

'I was so handsome in your drawing that I realised you were looking at me with rose-coloured glasses and must hold me in some regard,' he teased.

'I thought it remarkably lifelike,' she assured him, and then Georgina gasped. 'That is him!'

Elijah turned to see where she was looking. A young, tall man had just appeared in front of the iron fountain, the parliament building looming dark and large in the distant background.

'That is the man we are here to spy on,' she said again, and they both moved a little out of sight and watched.

Chapter 18

Matilda grabbed Thomas and kissed him right on the lips. He gave a small yelp of surprise before that became a soft moan of pleasure, placing his hands around her small waist and pulling her closer. Then, Thomas realised what was going on and he pulled back slightly and subtly looked around. Just on the other side of the bush where they were standing stood the man whose arrival they were waiting on. He held a bouquet and appeared to be impatiently glancing around. Thomas picked up Matilda in a show of passion and whirled her around. To anyone watching, including Daniel, it would appear as if two lovers were being playful, but Thomas was now facing the man and Matilda had her back to him. She gave him a frown but moved slightly to see the man in her peripheral vision. Then she saw the surprised expression on Thomas's face.

'What is it?' she asked, and confirmed: 'That is the man that Daniel and I saw that evening, who ran away as we approached.'

'Alaric Osbourne,' he muttered.

'You know him?' she stared in amazement, looking in Thomas's eyes and touching his face as if whispering sweet nothings. 'He's come back to the same spot, almost.'

'He is the man who was attacked in Tea Lane. Most likely after you saw him,' Thomas added. 'Now he is connected to the lane and bridal shop. So, what is he up to and whom is he waiting for?'

Thomas saw the man look around and quickly engaged Matilda in more amorous displays of affection, only pulling apart when they appeared to be no longer in Osbourne's searching gaze.

'I must say, this is an excellent assignment,' Matilda said, quite flushed and excited.

Thomas grinned. 'Indeed. I assure you my stakeout work with Harry has never been as rewarding.'

'I should hope not,' she teased, and then sobered. 'Look Thomas, someone is approaching him, a woman in a red dress with dark hair. Could this be Miss Pettyfore?'

Thomas did not turn around but waited until the woman had arrived in his line of vision. 'Have you seen her before?' he asked.

'Maybe, I do not know, she has a familiar look. Have you?'

He ignored the question, studying the pair.

'Did he kiss her on the hand or lips?' Matilda asked.

'Neither. But he handed her the flowers.'

'Then they are not lovers; this must be a business meeting of sorts. Let us get closer and listen.'

The pair moved towards a park bench below the

shrubbery line and sat close, holding hands in case they needed to engage in more amorous activity for their cover. Thomas strained to hear, only picking up the occasional word as the couple spoke in low tones.

'Sunday… deserves it… take this, Petty… you know what to do…'

Thomas squinted through the shrubbery as he tried to see what was going on, but could only see small glimpses. Then, the couple parted ways, each going in the opposite direction. Thomas grabbed for Matilda again as Alaric Osbourne passed nearby. Thomas was, however, more concerned that Miss Petronella Pettyfore would recognise and greet him. He knew her rather well, more so than he wanted to admit.

*****

'From where Alice and I were sitting, it looked like he slipped the lady a roll of notes,' Daniel said. 'Why would he be giving her money?'

'And what role has she to play in his subterfuge?' Alice asked, as the six young people reunited and started their walk home.

'What did you hear, Thom?' Elijah asked.

'Just random words,' he answered. 'But something is happening on Sunday and I suspect it is linked to the name and initials in the original note.'

Matilda thought aloud: 'The note said "*Burgess, Pad H, PAID. Next? BG8*" so we were right about the BG 8 being here and now, but could Burgess be a name and Pad H, could that be an address?'

'Possibly, but now it remains with Harry and me,' Thomas said to the group. 'No further personal investigations.'

'I agree,' Daniel said, 'we have done our civic duty, so solve it and let us know, Thom.'

Matilda did not look as convinced; Thomas could see her brow was furrowed, her lips pursed, and she was still thinking through the connections. He sighed and rolled his eyes, to the amusement of the others. As Matilda spoke with Alice, Daniel turned his attention to Thomas.

'You took quite a few liberties tonight in the guise of an investigation,' Daniel said, his tone slightly chilly.

Thomas looked at his best friend with surprise and did not speak for a moment.

'I saw you and Matilda,' Daniel added.

'I have no doubt you did. We agreed we would do what was necessary to appear of little consequence to the man we were studying, including protecting the ladies.'

'Well, you took that to the full extent,' Daniel said and scoffed.

Thomas stopped in his tracks, and Elijah and Georgina almost ran into the back of him.

'Is everything alright?' Elijah asked, sizing the two men up and feeling the tension in the air.

'Yes,' they answered in unison, staring at each other. The group stilled.

'Now you are the paragon of virtue and feel you need to protect your sister from me?' Thomas asked incredulously.

Matilda stepped in. 'It was I who threw myself at Thomas when I saw the man and feared how close he was to us. He might have recognised me or moved away because of our proximity to him,' she said. 'By kissing Thomas, I knew he would look away, as a gentleman should.'

Alice looped her arm through Daniel's and tugged him to keep walking.

'Best you look after my honour,' she said, in her lovely British accent. 'I am sure Thomas is most capable of protecting his fiancée.'

Elijah placed his hand on Daniel's shoulder and moved him in the direction Alice was suggesting as Georgina stepped in to break the tension.

'In my mind, I was sure I would make a very good spy, but in reality, I fear I am too tall,' she said. 'I was like a giraffe poking my head about the bushes.'

The group laughed. Even Thomas could not hide a smile.

'You have an advantage over me,' Alice said. 'I couldn't see or hear anything. Nevertheless, it was quite fun.'

'Except that now, Thomas, you have a serious job ahead,' Matilda said. 'I wonder what a lady as pretty as Miss Pettyfore, who seems to have a most sensible mother and resides in a very nice area, has got herself involved in and why.'

Chapter 19

Harry looked impressed. 'It is a clever ruse, is it not, to include a note in a bouquet? Who would think anything sinister was going on?'

'I agree, except I am sure the tarot reader knows more, and Alaric Osbourne was not mugged because he was in the wrong place at the wrong time, as he claimed, and somehow Mrs Greenwood's murder is linked to it all.' Thomas paced around his office.

'Well, your team of sleuths did a good job last night,' Harry joked, sitting on the side of the desk.

'I would have preferred none of them got involved, but Matilda had no intention of that. There is safety in numbers at least, even if Daniel felt the need to protect Matilda's honour after we were kissing to remain inconspicuous.'

Harry smiled. 'Did he now? Well, that's interesting.'

'How so?' Thomas asked, sitting on the edge of his own desk and giving Harry his attention.

'Well, the Hayward boys have but one sister whom I imagine was always one of the boys until the men became old enough to realise her honour needed protecting. They have never really needed to do so since you were her first and only beau, but perhaps Daniel is feeling like he is losing her to you. They are the closest pair, are they not?' Harry asked.

Thomas thought for a few moments. 'They are the best of friends and the closest, but you are right and I never thought of it. Her attentions have been transferred to me and even though he has Alice, perhaps he is feeling the loss of her affection.' He rubbed his chin as he thought. 'I shall mention this to Matilda and suggest she spend some time with him, like old times, without me present.'

'Good lad,' Harry said, pleased Thomas could empathise. 'So back to this other problem.'

'Yes.' Thomas straightened and cleared his throat. 'The lady who attended last evening to meet Mr Osbourne, I know her.'

'Do you?' Harry asked, surprised and interested. 'In what way?'

'In the way you are thinking,' Thomas said. 'Long before I started courting Matilda, of course, when I was younger and single.'

'How much younger?'

'Perhaps seven or eight years ago, when I was one-and-twenty. I met her at a club and, well, we enjoyed each other's company,' he said, with a grimace.

'I see. I suspect you didn't tell Matilda that?' Harry asked.

'Good grief, no. Who knows how she might take that. Women are strange creatures and hard to read,' Thomas said.

'That they are. From your memory or time with Miss—'

'Petronella Pettyfore,' Thomas answered.

'Miss Pettyfore, yes, was she involved in anything untoward?' Harry asked.

'Not that I knew of, but really, we only had a few liaisons. She was young and beautiful, confident and brash. Petronella attracted many successful and wealthy suitors, and a young police officer like me couldn't hope for her affections,' he said, truthfully.

'Any regrets then?'

'Absolutely not. I felt nothing when I saw her but curiosity. She was not wearing a ring, so perhaps she is still single, and I don't believe Alaric Osbourne is her suitor,' Thomas said. 'Speaking of which, I was keen to pay him a visit, but now I am not so sure. We might prevent happening what we want to catch in the act.'

'That makes sense,' Harry agreed. 'If our main players are Alaric Osbourne, Miss Pettyfore and this young delivery lad, let's find out more about them and the disagreement between *Blooming Blossoms'* owner Mrs Dalton and the deceased Mrs Greenwood.'

Thomas frowned as he stared at the board and their connections.

'What are you thinking?' Harry asked.

'*Blooming Blossoms* is a flower shop, but it is also a bridal shop with bridal bouquets and the side business of dressmaking,' Thomas said, working through his thoughts. 'So, is the *Burgess* at *Pad H* that was scrawled on the note a wedding client, perhaps? Has he paid for services but what does the "next" mean?'

'Or is this Burgess to receive the roll of money that Miss Pettyfore obtained and, if so, for what purpose?' Harry asked, putting up an alternative theory.

'I think we should be a little sneaky,' Thomas said. 'Are you up for it?'

'Of course, sneaky is my middle name,' Harry joked.

'I thought it was Francis,' Thomas shot back as he grabbed his hat and Harry did the same. 'I shall tell you on the way.' The two men departed the office.

They arrived on the street level and Thomas hailed a hansom. 'I suggest we go to *Blooming Blossoms* and wait until Mrs Dalton leaves for her lunch break or other business, and we catch young Rose alone. She does not look the type to be caught up in anything untoward and if there is a client by the name of Burgess, let's hope Rose will tell.'

*****

Matilda thanked Mrs Celia Dalton, the manageress of *Blooming Blossoms,* for her time, as they sat in a small tea shop in the main street, just around the corner from Bridal Lane. Matilda wore one of her better dresses gifted from Aunt Audrey, given Mrs Dalton was a successful businesswoman and always appeared perfectly groomed. Today was no exception with her lemon dress accessorised with pearls.

'It is my pleasure to assist,' Mrs Dalton said. 'It's nice to have a little break and besides, you are not only writing a piece on Mrs Greenwood, but you are also a customer.'

'The bouquet samples you gave me were beautiful,' Matilda said. 'I cannot wait to hold them on the day. Only a few weeks now.'

'Are you nervous?' Mrs Dalton asked.

'No, excited, yes,' Matilda said. 'Since becoming engaged, I feel like I have been waiting forever for this day, but then sometimes it is all happening too fast.'

Mrs Dalton laughed. 'I understand. When I married my dear husband, I was truly in love. My parents had another gentleman in mind for me, but I only ever loved Mr Dalton and as he was a good, hard-working man from a respectable family, they had no grounds to object. We are still happy to this day.'

They thanked the waitress, who put a small plate of delicate cakes between them, and Matilda topped up their teacups.

'That is what I want, a long and happy marriage, a meeting of minds and hearts,' Matilda said, and sighed. 'Given I have known Thomas almost all my life, I am sure it will be a good basis for a life together.'

They talked of pleasantries for a short while; Matilda hoping to engage Mrs Dalton's favour and trust, and succeeding when both ladies revealed they had lost their mothers in childhood and shared that in common.

'But best to business or I shall return to work without the quotes I need and I know you are busy,' Matilda said, after some time.

Mrs Dalton nodded. 'Can I be candid with you, not for your article?'

'Of course,' Matilda said. The result was as she hoped – Mrs Dalton opened up to her.

'Louise and I were parting ways, in business and friendship,' Mrs Dalton said, not knowing that Matilda was already armed with this information.

'Oh, I'm sorry to hear that. Was she retiring?' Matilda fished.

'No,' Mrs Dalton said and glanced around before continuing. 'Louise has always been so very firm in her faith and convictions, some admire that. I do not. I've never really understood that type of person who speaks of the good Lord's love but has no mercy. Surely God is the most merciful of all.'

'I am hoping so,' Matilda agreed, and Mrs Dalton chuckled.

'Perhaps this will offend you too, but my daughter, Katherine, and I have a side-business. I am a silent partner and run the flower shop, but I refer brides to her. Katherine has been assisting girls who must make a quick marriage by asking clients to donate their gowns if they so choose after their day or by making very affordable gowns that conceal the figure.'

'How very kind of her,' Matilda said, and Mrs Dalton looked relieved.

'I thought so too. She has always had a good heart, too good sometimes as she can be a soft touch.'

'And Mrs Greenwood did not like that?' Matilda asked.

'When she found out recently—and I don't know how she did—she was vehemently opposed. We had words about it on several occasions,' Mrs Dalton said and shook her head at the memory. 'I am sure Louise would see them all shunned from society.'

'So, she wanted to withdraw her business?' Matilda prodded, tasting one of the small cakes from the platter. 'Oh my, this is good.'

Mrs Dalton smiled. 'It is the citrus I believe, makes for a lovely taste. But yes, she intended to withdraw and I don't know what took her so long. I kept placing orders and she kept fulfilling them despite our frosty relations. And then, she visited to deliver an urgent lace order, bought some flowers which I admit was kind of her to support the business, and that was the last I saw of her. She was murdered that very night.'

'What sort of flowers did she buy?' Matilda asked, and Mrs Dalton looked surprised.

'I don't know… well, let me think.' She sipped her tea and thought for a moment. 'Oh, I remember now and I imagine her sense of charity was the reason she bought them… a wedding had been cancelled, the groom-to-be had taken ill. We had wedding flowers made and ready to go, which was sad for the family and unfortunate for us.'

'Would you not charge them anyway for the flowers?' Matilda asked.

'I could not bring myself to do so, it was unlikely the young man would live,' Mrs Dalton admitted. 'This all unfolded while Louise was in the store and she insisted on buying the bridal bouquet at full price. It was generous of her and mind you, the bouquet was breathtaking.'

'What became of it, the bouquet, do you know?' Matilda asked.

'I don't. Perhaps it is at her home. I never gave it a second thought,' Mrs Dalton said. 'But you know, Matilda, this discussion has been very good for me. It has made me soften my views of Louise just a little. I am ready to give you some lines for your story.'

Matilda was delighted with that outcome and reached for her pencil and pad. But she was more pleased with the information received. So, Mrs Greenwood took home bridal flowers. Did they have a note in them perchance?

Chapter 20

Daniel Hayward was out of sorts. Once he had cooled down, he knew he had been unreasonable with Thomas, and they rarely quarrelled, even as boys. He had taken the opportunity to kiss Alice when the moment presented itself, and he knew his sister was not the type to be compromised by his best friend. He owed Thomas an apology, but it rankled him to make it because after all, it was his sister who Thomas was kissing so out in the open for everyone to see. Well, he relented, anyone who was in the park at dusk.

He ran his fingers through his dark hair, contemplated that it needed cutting, and then his thoughts returned to the night in the gardens. Did Thomas recognise Petronella, Thomas's old flame, last evening? If he did, Thomas at least did the honourable thing and did not say so. That didn't excuse all the dishonourable kissing that went on right out in the open. He took a deep breath and scolded himself for being petty. But Daniel had a confession to make as well, and it involved Petronella. Given what had transpired, it might be relevant to Thomas's case.

With a two-hour mid-morning break between court cases, he decided to drop in to the Roma Street Police Headquarters and make peace with his friend and share his observation. It was a stone's throw from the court and he arrived there in good time.

'You've just missed him by about five minutes, sorry, sir,' John the desk sergeant advised Daniel. 'He's gone off with his partner.'

'Oh blast. I'm his future brother-in-law,' Daniel introduced himself.

'Ah, the lovely Miss Hayward's brother then?' the sergeant smiled. 'Mind, you look nothing like her.'

'No, but I'm just as lovely,' Daniel said, and gave him a wink, making the sergeant laugh.

'I overheard they were going to some florist shop. Perhaps it was a bridal stop on the way to duty,' he offered a small suggestion.

'Ah, I know just the place. Thank you, Sergeant,' Daniel said, with a nod.

'Good to meet you, Mr Hayward.'

Daniel headed off to Bridal Lane, knowing full well what Thomas and Harry were up to. Jumping on an omnibus, he arrived in time to see the two men walking towards the laneway; they must have headed there on foot.

'Thomas, Harry!' he called after them.

Thomas whirled around and Daniel saw Thomas's smile of recognition before his expression tightened as if expecting a confrontation. Daniel hurried to them.

'Do not look so concerned, Thom. I am over my

indignation from last night,' he said and slapped him on the back. 'Hello Harry, are you well?' he asked Thomas's partner.

'Very well, Daniel my lad, thank you. Shall I leave you boys to chat?' he asked.

'No, you're on police business, and that is why I am here too,' Daniel said, then looked a bit sheepish. 'I am sorry, I regret our falling out,' he directed his comment to Thomas.

'I understand,' Thomas said, surprising Daniel, who expected him to point out his hypocrisy and stupidity a couple of times at least.

'You do?'

Thomas nodded. 'It won't happen again… before we are married.'

'Then you will have Matilda mad at me,' he said and rolled his eyes. Thomas grinned and the boys left it at that. 'I have something to tell you and after last night, I thought it might be pertinent.'

'Excellent,' Harry said. 'Did John on the desk send you this way?'

'He mentioned you were off to a florist shop.'

'Are you not working at the courts today?' Thomas asked.

'Yes, but I have a few hours' break,' Daniel said, as the men stepped out of the way of a lady pushing a large pram up the footpath towards them. They moved toward the entry to Bridal Lane. Daniel saw Thomas scan the lane while Harry looked towards the *Blooming Blossoms* shop.

'What have you then, Dan?' Thomas asked, still studying the lane before returning his gaze to Daniel.

'Did you see Petronella last night?' Daniel asked, and seeing Thomas bristle, he held up his hand. 'I'm not asking you in relation to Matilda.'

'You're not? Well then yes, I saw her, but she did not see me as I was ensuring my cover held,' he said, with a twitch of a smile that Daniel did his best not to reciprocate.

'I saw her recently too,' Daniel said, 'somewhere else before last evening.'

'Where?' Thomas asked, and Harry gave Daniel his full attention.

'The evening that Matilda and I went to the Botanic Gardens to advise the gentleman we received his note and his lover was not coming, I saw her.'

'But I understood a woman did not arrive as she did not receive the note, and that the man, Alaric Osbourne, ran when you tried to talk with him?' Thomas asked.

'That is all correct. But when we departed, we saw Osbourne running through a city lane. As we passed the next corner, I saw Petronella standing as if to cross the road, while holding a bouquet. I didn't realise it was her initially because I just saw a woman holding an enormous bouquet and I looked at her face for but a moment.'

'But it was her? Are you sure?' Harry asked.

'Yes. When I saw her again in the gardens, I recognised her as the same lady immediately. I'm good with faces and detail, it's what I draw all day,' Daniel said.

'Of course,' Thomas agreed.

'I don't know why she was out at that time of night or where she was going with the flowers, it was but a momentary glance,' Daniel said. 'But it was her.'

Thomas nodded; his eyebrows drawn as he thought. 'That is very interesting, thank you, Dan.'

'What do you make of it?' Daniel asked.

'I do not know, yet, but it is something and the flowers are very relevant, I am sure of it.' Thomas glanced down the alley. 'Mrs Greenwood had a bouquet on her when she was murdered and when we arrived, they were nowhere to be seen.'

'Goodness, you don't think Petronella is capable of murder, surely?' Daniel asked.

Thomas gave a small shrug. 'I've thought many a person wasn't over the years only to be surprised. Dan, will you do us a favour now that you are here?'

'Of course.'

'We need to speak with the young shop assistant at *Blooming Blossoms,* but we do not want the owner present. Could you enter on the basis of buying Alice some flowers or better still...' Thomas brightened, 'as you are the best man, check that Matilda ordered the buttonhole flowers for the men.'

'Excellent. While doing so, ask if the manageress is in the house?' Daniel asked.

'Yes, and if she is, just offer her your personal thanks for making your sister so happy or something similar,' Harry said.

'Will do. My second mission in two days. Goodness, I will soon be undercover for a living.'

Thomas chuckled. 'Actually...' he looked at Harry.

'Why not?' Harry agreed as the two men read each other's

thoughts, something they had become adept at during their years of working together.

'Uh oh, what are you two plotting?' Daniel frowned.

'Whether the manageress is there or not, we are trying to determine if the name of *Burgess Pad H* that was scribbled on the note in the bouquet is a customer known to the store,' Harry said.

'I see. So, is Burgess a customer and something untoward is going on, or if the name is not known to *Blooming Blossoms*, then their bouquets are being used for ill means, possibly without their awareness?' Daniel asked.

'We'll make a detective of you yet,' Harry said, patting him on the back.

Daniel straightened and nodded. 'Leave it with me. I am on my way.'

*****

Thomas and Harry watched as Daniel adjusted his suit jacket and confidently made his way to the *Blooming Blossoms* store. He held the door open for a young lady who gave him a winning smile and then entered the premises. He was the sole customer in-store and Thomas saw the young shop attendant, Rose, come to attend to him.

'Nice to see you and Daniel back on friendly ground,' Harry said.

'It was out of character of him, but I'll be more careful, for the next month anyway,' Thomas said, watching the shop intently. 'No sign of the manageress by the looks of it.'

'Rose is reaching for a book,' Harry said. They saw her open a large ledger on the counter and run her hand down it. She smiled and looked up at Daniel. They exchanged a few more words and he thanked her, purchasing a bunch of flowers. He departed, placing his hat back on his head and casually strolling towards the detectives who moved out of the laneway and further up the street, lest they should be seen.

'Keep walking,' Daniel said, as he caught up behind them. 'Matilda has just come around the corner with a woman.'

Thomas glanced back. 'She's not going down Bridal Lane, is she?' he said, stopping but saw her bidding the woman goodbye and taking her leave down Albert Street. 'It is alright, she is going the other way. That's the owner of *Blooming Blossoms*, Mrs Dalton,' Thomas told Daniel.

'Why would they be in each other's company?' Daniel frowned as he too stopped and watched Matilda retreating while ensuring he was out of sight. Thomas kept behind Daniel until Mrs Dalton turned into the lane.

'I believe Miss Hayward is writing an obituary on Mrs Greenwood, who was an old friend of Mrs Dalton, the *Blooming Blossoms*' proprietor,' Harry informed him.

'Ah, that is right. Somehow Matilda always finds herself in the middle of trouble with stories she's writing for that blasted magazine,' Daniel said and shook his head.

'Tell me about it,' Thomas said and caught Harry smiling.

'Well, she's your problem next month, brother-to-be,' Daniel said, thumping Thomas on the back. 'I've got to get back to the courts. Are you walking that way and I will tell you what I learnt?'

'We are,' Harry said, and the men took the less busy streets so they could walk three abreast. 'Let us reimburse you for the flowers since it was a work expense.' He reached inside his jacket.

'No need, but thank you,' Daniel said. 'I am overdue to give Alice some flowers. Speaking of which, the lovely Miss Rose is happy to report that our buttonhole roses are ordered,' he said, beginning with the least important piece of news, and laughed at Thomas's grimace. 'As for Burgess… I said I had heard about an old friend of mine who was to marry, but we had lost contact. I asked if they might be a client so I could send my best wishes and flowers.'

'Good thinking,' Harry said.

'She was charmed by me, of course,' Daniel joked, 'and she flipped open her orders book. But sadly gents, there was no one on their books by the name of Burgess. I said what a shame, as it would be so great to see him again,' Daniel joked.

'Damnation!' Thomas swore under his breath. 'I was sure that would be the connection.'

'Rose doesn't just have the names of the brides in that log by any chance?' Harry said.

'Good thinking,' Thomas said.

'No,' Daniel nipped that thought in the bud. 'Rose asked me was Burgess the bride-to-be or the groom's name. I said the groom and she had both names, yours and Matilda's included. I saw them listed.'

'Well, there goes that lead,' Thomas sighed.

'Sorry to be the bearer of no news, gents,' Daniel said, seeing Thomas's disappointment and frustration.

'You did well, thank you, Daniel,' Harry said. 'But we still have a note in a bouquet with *Burgess Pad H* on it.'

Thomas looked at Harry. 'Why did Alaric Osbourne and Petronella Pettyfore need that information? Let's think bigger. Here is a couple meeting clandestinely in the park to discuss something related to a *Burgess Pad H*, and I still believe it must have some connection with a wedding given the focus is *Blooming Blossoms,* and Mrs Greenwood and her bridal lace.'

'And let's agree that a flower shop façade is a wonderful place for subversion,' Daniel said.

'Exactly,' Harry agreed. 'So why would you be planning and meeting in such a manner unless you intended some criminal activity, and did Mrs Louise Greenwood find out about such activities when she received the wrong bouquet?'

'As Matilda did,' Thomas agreed.

The men slowed their pace as they neared the courts where Daniel worked, and Harry said, 'I think we need to go through the electoral rolls and see if there is a Burgess in there and work backward.'

'It will take forever, it is not an uncommon name,' Thomas said, and sighed, resigning himself to the necessity of the task.

'But if *Pad H* is Mr Burgess's occupation or a suburb, that will narrow down your search area and voting list,' Daniel added.

'For suburbs, well, there are not too many that I can think of... Petrie for one,' Harry mused, 'but what is the H for?'

'Paddington,' Thomas added and then smiled at Daniel.

'Or *Pad H* – Paddington Heights. Yes indeed, brilliant suggestion, thank you, Dan.'

'Pleasure gents, I shall see you both on Wednesday if not sooner,' he said, departing with a tip of his hat.

Thomas turned to Harry. 'Right then, to the electoral office to find this Burgess character. It might also be worth our while seeing if there are any patterns with crimes of late.'

'Some connection with weddings like wedding breakfasts being burgled?' Harry asked.

'Yes, overcharging for goods and services and not delivering, or bribery if a partner has strayed perhaps,' Thomas mused. 'Seems all a bit petty though, and why would that end in murder?'

'If the latter was the case, then the last people the crime would be reported to is the police, I imagine,' Harry said.

'Yes. I suspect there is something more sinister going on and if it were not for the death of Mrs Greenwood, I would think the letters could be unrelated to *Blooming Blossoms*, and the bouquets are just a convenient ruse.'

The two men entered the building and made their way to see the boys in crime, taking the stairs to the second floor to the rooms they rarely visited.

'Nothing like that, Detectives, for the last six months while I've been here, but if you want to go back further...' a brash young constable told them.

'No, that's probably a reasonable time frame for what we are seeking,' Thomas said.

'If you were chasing pickpockets, muggings, or jewellery thefts, I'd have a lot of worthy candidates for you.'

Harry chuckled. 'We'll leave those with you, but thank you, Constable.'

Ten minutes later, they were back on the street.

Chapter 21

Matilda rounded the street corner onto Albert Street and waited a few minutes. Cautiously, she peered around and on seeing Thomas, Detective Dart and her brother, Daniel, were far enough away not to see her, she ventured back to Bridal Lane. She smiled at their attempts to hide from her, as if she would run up and ask them what they had learnt. She could do that later with Thomas and was confident she could wheedle information out of him.

Matilda intended to walk Mrs Dalton back to her *Blooming Blossoms* florist shop but on seeing the men trying not to be seen, she distracted Mrs Dalton on the corner for a few moments longer, before she bid her good day and then marked time. Now with the coast clear, she returned to Bridal Lane and, taking the opposite side of the laneway to *Blooming Blossoms,* Matilda slipped in to see the tarot reader.

It took her eyes a moment to adjust to the moodier surroundings lit only by a couple of candles placed on a table in the middle of the room, and to identify the musky scents burning.

'I've been expecting you,' the tarot reader, Madam Gerta, said, entering from a back room hidden by a curtain.

'Were you?' Matilda asked.

'Not for the reasons you believe. I didn't read in the cards that you would call in; everyone assumes I see everything in the spirit world, but I see more sitting here and watching the comings-and-goings in Bridal Lane,' Madam Gerta said, with a smile. 'I did, however, hear you were doing an obituary on Mrs Greenwood and I expected you to make your way here eventually.'

Matilda gave the tarot reader her name, took the indicated seat at the table, and the two ladies sat. Madam Gerta had several layers of loose fabric draped around her in shades of red and gold. A black hat was perched upon her head and both hands were adorned in bracelets and rings. Matilda expected to see a black cat, or any cat for that matter, but there was none to be seen. As she looked around, she stiffened, alert with surprise, on seeing two people outside *Blooming Blossoms* that looked very familiar.

'Goodness, that is the man and woman I saw in the park recently,' she said, hoping Madam Gerta might know who they were and enlighten her.

'They are often to be seen here. Miss Petronella Pettyfore works for Mrs Dalton's daughter who is a bridal dressmaker. They share ribbons and lace for the dresses and bouquets. And that gentleman is Mr Osbourne, his nephew is the delivery boy for the store. I believe Mr Osbourne is quite sweet on Miss Pettyfore.'

153

'Is that so?' Matilda asked. She turned around to find Madam Gerta studying her.

'You are a pretty little thing. I drew a card for you the other day.'

'Thank you. What does that mean?' Matilda asked curiously observing the pack of cards with the intricate drawings that sat on the table between them.

'It means that I thought about you and let the universe direct me to a card that would tell me your fate.'

'Ooh, that sounds intriguing. Can you tell me if my fate is pleasing?' Matilda asked, clasping her hands in her lap upon her notebook.

Madam Gerta wore a satisfied look. No one could resist asking. She tapped a finger on the top card in the pile. 'Given you were in the florist shop and took home some samples, I suspect your pending betrothal will make for very happy days. However, what I did see was that your curiosity may lead you into trouble.'

Matilda sighed and then gave a small shrug. 'It is a fitting card. The detective did not ask you to tell me that, did he?' she asked, suspiciously.

Madam Gerta laughed. 'No. But if you would like a reading, I can tell you more.'

'Thank you, but I'd prefer to ask you to share your thoughts on Mrs Greenwood, and her death if you would?' Matilda asked. 'I don't have to publish all your comments if you would like to share some thoughts but not necessarily with the ladies of our town.'

'I see,' Madam Gerta said. 'You want to know if I saw who murdered her?'

Matilda sat straighter. 'Well, yes, I imagine everyone does.'

'I didn't see what happened,' Madam Gerta said.

'Oh, how disappointing for the detectives and I confess, for me too. Curiosity and all,' Matilda said, sitting back again in her chair.

'I can tell you one thing that might help, though,' Madam Gerta said.

'Yes, please.'

'She deserved it.'

*****

The bride-to-be bit her lip to restrain emotion, but tears ran down her face as she stood in front of the mirror, being fitted for her dress by Miss Katherine Dalton. The bride was not crying because it overwhelmed her with delight to see herself in her wedding gown. Her impending nuptials were not the day she had planned or dreamed of as a young girl. Nor was she a blushing bride. She did, however, have proud parents and a loving groom who remained oblivious to her plight and distress.

Katherine rose from pinning the hem of the bridal gown and making the final adjustment. She took Sophia's hand.

'Dear Miss Emery, do not make yourself unwell. I assure you; no one will know on the day or in the future. You will look every bit like the beautiful bride and the blessed child within you will be born a little earlier than nine months. I was born a little early; many babies come in their own good time.'

Sophia Emery nodded. 'Thank you, Miss Dalton. It is more than I deserve.'

'Nonsense. Why do you deserve anything less?'

'It is a kind thing that you do,' Sophia said. 'I am grateful to you and your mother.'

'Believe me, Miss Emery, when I say you are not the first and you will not be the last. I ask but one thing….'

'Anything,' Sophia assured her.

'Perhaps one day return a kindness to someone who also finds themselves on the edge of society,' Miss Dalton said and smiled.

'Oh, I assure you, I will,' Sophia said most earnestly. 'Is that why you began your business? Did someone do a kindness for you along the way?' She hastened to add, 'not that I am implying you got yourself in the same kind of trouble as I am in.'

Katherine smiled. 'My mother has had several kindnesses shown to her, of which I have benefited,' she said and did not elaborate. She looked up as a woman gently pulled the curtain aside.

'Petronella, come in!' Katherine said, inviting her in. 'You remember Miss Emery.'

The ladies exchanged greetings, and Petronella admired Katherine's work.

'Oh Katherine, you have excelled yet again. You look most lovely, Miss Emery,' Petronella smiled.

'Miss Emery is naturally concerned…' Katherine said, and let the comment hang in the air.

'There is no need to be,' Petronella assured her, most

confidently. 'You cannot tell and believe me, being in the wedding business, Katherine and I have assisted many brides who went on to have very happy family lives.'

'It is true. Many young ladies,' Katherine said, with emphasis so that Sophie did not feel so isolated in her pain.

Petronella lowered her voice even though no one else was present, but to share a bit of wickedness. 'As well, we have helped some girls on the larger side who may appear to be in the family way and are, in fact not.'

Katherine gave a small giggle. 'True, and they were beautiful brides on their day.'

'Whereas, Miss Emery, you look most petite,' Petronella assured her.

Sophie Emery gave a small cry of relief and touched her hand to her heart.

'Thank you, thank you both. I feel ever so much better,' she said and gave a shaky smile. 'I just need to make it to this Sunday and after that, all will be well.'

Katherine helped Sophie out of her dress and when she had departed, again with her sincere thanks, Petronella gave Katherine a curt nod.

'It is all organised. Alaric will ensure it is done promptly and then justice will be done and you, my dear, will be compensated.'

'Thank you, Petty. Every time there is a job of this nature, I am concerned that it will be our last. What happens if Alaric is caught?'

'He won't be. Besides, a gentleman concerned about his own reputation will not press charges,' Petronella said.

'Alaric said the best thing to do if ever questioned is deny everything.' She studied the pretty and demure dressmaker. 'You know, I think Alaric is sweet on you.'

Katherine reddened. 'He is a lovely man but mother has not warmed to him. Besides, I believe you are mistaken – he only has eyes for you.'

Petronella sighed. 'He is not for me.' She helped Katherine to put away lace and the measurement tools from Miss Emery's final fitting. 'My mother despairs I am not yet married and is sure I am left on the shelf, but I can't bring myself to feel romantically about Alaric.'

'So you are not concerned about being unwed?'

'No, I rather like my shelf,' she said and laughed. 'But I did see a former beau just this day past. Constable Thomas Ashdown or I should say Detective Ashdown now. My, he has matured well and looked like a wonderful catch. He was young and inexperienced when I first met him.'

'He is to be wed,' Katherine said and paused. 'Oh, forgive me, I hope that has not pained you.'

Petronella sighed. 'No, I didn't see a ring on his finger, but thought he may have been betrothed regardless. What is the future Mrs Ashdown like? A sweet little thing who does what she is told and will keep his house?'

'I am not sure about that. I met them both fleetingly at Mrs Greenwood's mourning room when I was accompanying my mother to pay our respects. She is fair to your dark features and looks very bright. I believe she writes for the *Women's Journal*.'

'Does she now?' Petronella said, and smiled.

'Oh no, what are you thinking?' Katherine asked, narrowing her eyes at her friend.

'Nothing, I assure you. But it might be nice to make her acquaintance.'

'Petronella! You are wicked sometimes. You cannot tell her that you had relations with her soon-to-be husband.'

Miss Pettyfore laughed. 'I would not be so bold. But should he be there at the same time, now that would be fun.'

Chapter 22

Walter Burgess of Paddington Heights looked at the two detectives with a baffled expression on his face. He was groomed to within an inch of his life – his moustache, hair and even eyebrows cut neatly with precision. His pants, shirt and shoes appeared to be custom made but they did not hide his ruddiness. Beneath the gloss lay a rough exterior and hands that spoke of labour. He was not a tall man but was solid of girth and chest.

'I can't imagine why my name would be in a note inside a bouquet, detectives,' he said loftily, chasing away a member of his staff who appeared at the door to assist him with assurances that he would handle this.

'It is a mystery to us as well, Mr Burgess,' Thomas said.

The detectives had found the details for Mr Burgess of Paddington Heights in the electoral rolls and were pleased to find him in residence in his palatial home. He did not invite them in.

'And this is what our town's best are working on? Following up a note wrongfully placed in a bouquet?' he chuckled. 'I assure you I do not send notes or flowers to anyone but my wife, and the act of flower-sending is few and far between these days.' He smirked.

Thomas opened his mouth to snap back a reply, and Harry stepped in.

'We are not concerned with anyone's private life or flower deliveries, for that matter, Mr Burgess. However, the note, the bouquet, and the delivery service are connected with a murder and a mugging and your name and suburb amongst it all.'

Thomas saw they now had his attention.

'Murder! Good Lord,' he exclaimed. 'Am I in danger?' He looked around as if expecting to see dark and dangerous figures about to break through the shrubbery and storm the house.

'We hope not, sir,' Harry said, 'but if you know anything about a flower delivery, a note, or have recently had any dealings with *Blooming Blossoms* floristry—'

'I can unequivocally assure you I have engaged in none of which you just outlined,' Mr Burgess said, cutting Harry off.

'Well then, allow this to stand as a warning to ensure your personal safety at all times, as you or your property might be marked,' Thomas said.

'What are you to do about that then?' he insisted. 'Should you not provide security to me?'

Thomas reined in his frustration. 'As you previously pointed out, Mr Burgess, the residents of our town would not want their best police resources spending time on security duty just because there was a misplaced note in a bouquet. Good day to you, sir, and do let us know if you notice anything suspicious.'

Thomas turned to depart, Harry tipped his hat and followed his partner, concealing a smile until they were outside the gates.

'Arrogant twit,' Thomas muttered, and Harry laughed.

'I can see him involved in a bit of thuggery,' Harry said, 'and as a consequence, being the recipient of it as well.'

'You got that right, I almost hit him myself,' Thomas said, making Harry laugh again. 'What the hell is his connection?'

'Unless it is nothing to do with him,' Harry said, and Thomas threw up his hands in frustration.

'Let us see if Mrs Greenwood's daughter, Hester, knows Mr Burgess or if he was acquainted with her mother,' Thomas said.

'We should also speak with Alaric Osbourne and ask if he is familiar with the Burgess name. We need to speak to your lady friend too, Miss Pettyfore.'

Thomas grunted, displeased.

'I'm sure she'll be delighted to see you again,' Harry teased him and laughed at the wry look Thomas gave him.

*****

That evening at dusk, as Thomas and Matilda took a turn through the gardens, her arm looped through his, she smiled up at him. He slowed his steps to allow for her restrictive skirt and the length of her stride, which was half of his own.

'You never fell behind when we were younger,' he teased her.

'It is this infernal dress and...' she stopped herself.

'And?' he asked.

'The restrictive unmentionables which I shall not mention,' she joked, but still reddened at the word and implications.

Thomas was too gentlemanly to voice his thoughts – that in less than a month, he would be removing those very garments from Matilda's body. An uncomfortable silence where nothing was mentioned fell between them until Matilda cleared her throat and spoke.

'I have news that might help your case,' she said.

Thomas could not help but smile seeing her infectious enthusiasm.

'As do I,' he teased, adjusting his hat back off his brow so he could see more of his surroundings.

'Oh good, shall we trade?'

'No.'

Matilda's shoulders slumped. 'But my information might be very useful; I was talking with Mrs Dalton from *Blooming Blossoms* about the last encounter she had with Mrs Greenwood.'

'I probably have that information,' he said with a small shrug. He wasn't confident he did know what Matilda was referring to, but he did not want to trade, as Matilda called it.

'Oh well, if you say so,' she said, playing his game which niggled at him now. *What might she know?*

They walked for a while and Matilda hid a smile as Thomas cleared his throat to speak. It took him a little longer than she expected.

'Perhaps you best tell me then,' he said.

'Only if we trade,' she held resolutely.

'Matilda,' he said firmly, 'you cannot expect when we are married that every evening I will talk to you about my cases or trade information.'

'Why ever not?' she asked, looking up at him with genuine surprise on her face.

'Because it is police business and needs to remain as such.'

'But I will be your wife and you know very well that I have assisted you on several cases with my observations and clues, and I can maintain your confidence. When have I ever not?' she asked.

'I'm sure there have been occasions, and if you told your writing friends, I've no doubt you swore them to secrecy,' he said, eyeing her suspiciously. 'But none come to mind,' he conceded.

'Exactly. So, I shall tell you mine, but only if you swear to share your news.'

'Just one for one,' he bargained.

Matilda thought about that for a while. 'I guess that is fair.'

She offered her hand to shake, but he took it and kissed her palm instead, making her smile.

'I hope you don't enter all your agreements like that,' she teased.

'Only with Harry,' Thomas promised her and earned a laugh. 'I shall go first then just to keep you happy.'

'Really?' she said, surprised. 'Excellent, proceed.'

He smiled and took a breath before proceeding. 'We spoke to Rose from *Blooming Blossoms* today as Harry and I thought she was unlikely to be involved in anything untoward, but if she knew of something, she might tell. Well, rather, your brother spoke to her on our behalf.'

'Ah, I wondered who you were talking with in Bridal Lane.'

His brow furrowed. 'So, you saw us?'

'Yes. You, Harry and Daniel. It left a lot to be desired if that was your best attempt at subterfuge,' she told him.

Thomas made a frustrated humph sound. 'Do you want to know the outcome, or can you guess?'

'No, please tell me,' she said, inviting him to continue.

'Rose advised that there is no client by the name of Burgess, male or female, and observing her from afar, and from Daniel's report, she did not seem to be concerned about the name. I don't think she knows what is going on, but we did find the Mr Burgess in question.'

He finished and left the rest of the story hanging.

'Is that it? What happened when you found Mr Burgess?' Matilda asked.

'Well, that would be a second piece of information, would it not? I can't tell you unless your information is worth trading for it.'

She pursed her lips and kept walking. 'Well, the information I was going to share can wait as I have something more relevant to your Rose update.'

'Do tell,' Thomas invited her to speak. He did not take her insights lightly, as she had been of considerable assistance and in possession of relevant information on several of his past cases. He would be reluctant to admit that out loud however unless absolutely pressed to do so.

'Georgina and I saw Rose talking on the street corner only last week with the man that Daniel and I saw in the park, and the *Blooming Blossoms* delivery boy was with them.'

Thomas stopped suddenly. 'No!'

'Yes, I am afraid so,' Matilda said. 'Perhaps she is not as innocent as you think. It appeared to be quite an animated discussion and then the delivery boy ran off with a bouquet, to deliver it I am guessing. Rose and the man—'

'Alaric Osbourne,' Thomas interrupted.

'Yes, Rose and Mr Osbourne spoke only for a moment more before going opposite ways.'

Thomas swore under his breath and then apologised. 'I beg your pardon, Tillie, but that is not good news at all. Why did you not tell me this?'

She looked surprised. 'I did not know the relevance, as you so rarely share your cases with me,' she said smartly.

'What other piece of news do you have to share?' he asked, frustrated.

'It is your turn, I just told you about Rose, Mr Osbourne and the delivery boy. Shall we sit and watch the ducks for a moment?' she asked when they arrived at the lake.

'If you wish,' he said, feeling too frustrated to sit. He was sure now that Rose knew more and had played Daniel. She was bound to know about the letters in the bouquet and of the name Burgess as well. He waited for Matilda to sit, before taking the seat next to her and enjoying how her dress bunched against his leg as she sat as close as decency allowed. He took her hand and looked at his large diamond ring on her finger.

'It suits me, does it not?' she teased, and he laughed.

'Yes, you and you only,' he said and could tell she was pleased with his words.

'Your turn,' she prompted him.

'So, the Burgess Pad H that we found, is a Mr Burgess of Paddington Heights, but he did not know anything about a note, a flower delivery or even of *Blooming Blossoms*. I don't know if I believe him as he seemed quite affronted by the line of questioning.'

'Hmm, defensive?' Matilda mused, narrowing her eyes in thought as she watched the ducks gliding past.

'Maybe.'

'What is his connection then?'

'I do not know, but that is my job to find out, not yours. You are writing about Mrs Greenwood, remember?' he asked.

'Yes, Detective,' she answered curtly. 'Although there are quite a few who do not speak kindly of her, which brings me to my second piece of information...'

'I can hardly wait,' Thomas said and nudged her. She grinned.

'Just before her death, Mrs Greenwood delivered an urgent lace order to Mrs Dalton at *Blooming Blossoms*.'

'Yes, we know that,' Thomas said as if that were basic policing work.

'Don't be so impatient, Thomas,' she chided him. 'While there, a wedding was cancelled but the flowers were already completed, bunched and ready for delivery. The groom was very ill, and it left Mrs Dalton with the expensive wedding flowers, but she was not of a mind to charge.'

'That's generous,' Thomas noted.

'Indeed,' Matilda said. 'So, Mrs Greenwood insisted on buying the bridal bouquet, the most expensive of all the flowers. It was very kind of her and a great help to Mrs Dalton.'

'Very good of her,' Thomas said, not yet making the connection.

'That was the bouquet she left with… a large wedding bouquet of cream and white flowers.'

Thomas sat upright. 'Of course. But we found no flowers beside her.' He clicked his fingers, 'and Daniel said he saw Petronella with a large bouquet that same night you were in the park.'

'Petronella?' Matilda asked, and then Thomas realised he had put himself in the situation of having to address why he referred to Miss Petronella Pettyfore with such familiarity. He corrected that immediately.

'Ah yes, Miss Pettyfore. An old acquaintance of your brother and mine. He recognised her, but not at first.'

'On the same night that we met the man in the park?' Matilda said, putting it together in her head. 'Do you think she was supposed to meet him but got the wrong flowers and

I got her bouquet instead? Or...' she continued thinking fast, 'do you think this Miss Pettyfore was somehow involved in the murder of Mrs Greenwood and picked up the bouquet at the scene of the crime?'

Thomas didn't answer as he ran a hand over his mouth while thinking.

'What sort of acquaintance was she, Thomas, this Miss Pettyfore? The type who could be involved in something untoward?' Matilda asked.

Thomas frowned. 'I could not rule it out, but I would not have thought it likely.' He stood, keen to avoid any further questions of his knowledge of Miss Pettyfore. 'You have given me much to work through and think upon, Matilda,' he said, offering her his hand as she rose to her feet and they resumed their walk.

'Then perhaps when we are husband and wife, we should consult more often,' she said, giving him her sweetest smile and distracting Thomas from crime momentarily.

Chapter 23

Confident, beautiful and sassy Petronella Pettyfore opened the door of her home and gave a cry of delight.

'If it isn't former Constable Thomas Ashdown, now out of uniform and looking even more handsome,' she said, and laughed on seeing Thomas's uncomfortable expression.

'Petronella,' he said, removing his hat to address her. 'This is my partner, Detective Harry Dart.'

'How are you, Miss Pettyfore?' Harry asked with a warm smile, enjoying the scene as it played out.

'Very well, thank you, Detective. My, such handsome detectives on the police force these days.'

'It was a requirement when I joined, but it had been removed by the time Thom signed up,' Harry joked, and Petronella laughed.

Thomas gave his partner a well-earned grimace. Clearing his throat, Thomas returned his attention to Petronella.

'We were hoping you might give us a moment of your time to discuss a crime in Bridal Lane.'

'Bridal Lane,' she said, a little confused. 'Well, gentlemen, do come in.' She opened the door to the small timber house wider and both men followed her in, Thomas closing it behind him. Petronella led the way to an attractive sitting room featuring bay windows that overlooked a small back garden and allowed natural light to stream in. The room was tastefully furnished and modest. She indicated seats, offered refreshments, and when the men declined, sat, thus allowing them to do so after she was seated.

'I can't imagine what might bring the heavy hand of the law to my door,' she said, in a manner that was nothing short of amorous while holding Thomas's gaze as she spoke. 'And I hear you are to marry?'

Thomas shuffled uncomfortably, conscious that Petronella had the effect of making him feel like an inexperienced young man around her.

'Yes,' he answered. 'And you have not?'

'No. My mother and I share this home, but I may consider accepting a suitor's hand in the near future.' Again, she spoke as if Thomas might be the lucky man if he played his cards right and was prepared to break his current engagement.

'We are here about the death of Mrs Louise Greenwood,' Thomas said, getting to business.

'Oh yes, poor dear, Louise,' Petronella said. 'I knew her because I work occasionally with Mrs Dalton's daughter, Katherine, in her bridal dressmaking business.'

'What do you do if I may ask?' Harry said.

She gave a small smile. 'Of course. I bring in business by promoting Katherine's dress-making services, attending fairs and buying lace and fabric for her.'

'Does she not have a store front from which she operates?' Thomas asked.

'No. Katherine has established a sewing and display room in a separate wing of her home.' Petronella cleared her throat delicately. 'Katherine caters for the unconventional bride...'

'How so?' Harry asked, curiously.

'Let us say, a bride of limited means or a larger bride, be that from...'

'I understand,' Harry said, allowing her to show some discretion.

'So, your promotion of her services as such, would take you into some unconventional situations as well?' Thomas tapped in.

'On some occasions, yes,' Petronella agreed but did not elaborate. Thomas suspected she regretted opening that line of enquiry. He continued. 'Do you know of any reason that Mrs Greenwood might have come to harm?'

She smiled. 'Forgive me, Thomas, but it is so strange to see you all serious when you were always quite mischievous.'

Thomas felt Harry look at him with a raised eyebrow and a small smile.

'Well, I was a young man, and now I am not so young,' Thomas said.

'Goodness, you would not yet be in your third decade, and so serious.'

'It's a sobering job,' Thomas retorted. 'To Mrs Greenwood...'

'Ah yes, Louise.' Petronella sighed. 'She was lovely, and

she was not. She was a good person if you were a good person, but if you were not doing your Christian duty, then you were quickly shunned. I found her to be very nosy and very inflexible.'

'I know many people like that but they don't end up murdered,' Thomas said.

She nodded. 'I cannot think of anyone in my acquaintance or circle who might do her harm, Detectives, and I don't know why you think I might.' She sat back and placed her hands on her lap, doing her best to look demure, a contrast to her over-confidence but moments before.

Thomas exposed his hand. 'You were seen in the city holding a large bouquet not long after Mrs Greenwood was murdered. Flowers similar to the bouquet she bought that very afternoon from *Blooming Blossoms*, and that were not found beside her body or in her home.' The latter he could not be sure of given all the mourning flowers present in Mrs Greenwood's home, but Thomas was prepared to embellish the truth to study Petronella's reaction.

'Gracious!' Petronella said, her hand going to her throat in what Thomas believed was mock theatrics. She fluttered her eyelashes at him. Long and dark, and enhancing her dark chocolate eyes, Petronella was ensuring Thomas was well reminded of her charms.

'Where did you get your bouquet from, Miss Pettyfore?' Harry asked.

'You both think that I might have killed Louise and stolen the flowers after doing such a dastardly deed?'

'Or perhaps you found them, and that might assist us

in knowing which way the murderer left if they discarded the flowers as he or she departed. So, where did the flowers come from?' Thomas asked.

'I purchased them from *Blooming Blossoms,* of course. I often drop in ribbons from Katherine's dressmaking studio to her mother's florist shop. Especially if we wish to match the flowers to the bride and bridesmaids' dresses. At the close of business each day, Mrs Dalton discounts older flowers that have not sold, or sometimes she gifts them to her staff and colleagues. I was given a bargain price on a beautiful bouquet which I took home with me,' she said, coolly and calmly, as if challenging the detectives to say otherwise.

'But you must not have gone straight home as you were seen with the flowers late that evening,' Thomas said, pushing her.

'I don't know what evening it was, Thomas, but I may have gone to a show, or dinner with friends or out with a gentleman caller and not gone home prior.' She shook her head. 'Goodness me, you sound rather desperate to find the killer if you believe I am the very same and the only clue you have is a bunch of flowers.'

Thomas had to admit to himself it did sound rather weak.

'No need for alarm, Miss Pettyfore,' Harry spoke up. 'We are just investigating every avenue and if you did not find the flowers or see or hear of anything untoward, then that does not assist us in tracking the killer's movements. We shall be off then.' Harry rose and Thomas grabbed his hat from the chair and did the same.

'We should catch up, for old time's sake, Thomas,' she said, touching his arm.

He gave a small nod of acknowledgement and politely declined. 'Unfortunately, with my work and the impending wedding, I barely have time to see my nephew, Teddy, who is my ward these days,' he said, by way of an apology.

'Ah yes, the wedding. Well, I do hope to have the chance to meet the new Mrs Thomas Ashdown,' she said, with a glance that belied what she was saying.

The men bid her farewell and once out of hearing range, Harry said, 'I am glad you are not the type of man who would take a mistress or have one last fling, as I believe Miss Pettyfore extended the invitation.'

'She's an exciting lady, but not the type you wed,' Thomas said, with a glance back. 'And certainly not the type who would make you feel like the one and only.' Not like his Matilda, he thought and felt most content at the prospect until frustration and concern about just where and what she might be doing in his investigation seeped into his consciousness.

Chapter 24

Sunday lunch seemed to come around too fast for Thomas, he could swear it was twice weekly despite the impossibility of that sentiment. It was not that he didn't enjoy the large family gathering of the Haywards, presided over by Aunt Audrey and Mr Hayward, it was just that it came with the inevitable questions of when he might be attending church with the family before the lunch, and how soon after they wed did he and Matilda intend to start a family. The latter subject had fallen on him since Amos and Minnie had their first child. On the bright side, he no longer had to contend with questions about his intentions towards Matilda.

Mr Hayward's project—the conservatory renovation—was finished and ready for family gatherings, but the family agreed to use it for the first time for the wedding breakfast, now only weeks away. So instead, they crammed around a large table – Aunt Audrey at one end with Amos and Minnie on one side of her and Alice and Daniel on the other. Beside Alice sat Elijah and Georgina, with Mr Hayward and Betty at the head of the table and Thomas, Matilda and Gideon to his right. Gideon threatened to bring his new romance, the mortician Miss Phoebe Astin, but thought it best to wait until the family had migrated to the conservatory for Sunday lunches.

'You are very quiet today, Thomas,' Aunt Audrey said, and Thomas saw his best friend, Daniel's amused look in anticipation of the usual run of questions.

Thomas decided to beat Aunt Audrey at her own game. 'You are right, Aunt Audrey, I beg your pardon,' he said. 'I was thinking of a current case I am involved in, but I must learn to leave that at the door when I enter.'

'Indeed you must young man, for soon you will have a wife and children who will require your full attention once you are home,' she said, with a smile that implied she was teasing him but nevertheless there was truth in her words.

'Oh, and we will want your full attention,' Matilda said, squeezing his arm and giving a laugh. She dropped her hand to his leg under the table which did get his full attention. Matilda continued. 'Thomas Junior will need his father's guidance.'

Secretly thrilled at the thought, and somewhat surprised by his own reaction, Thomas still managed to smirk at Matilda, knowing she was teasing him.

'I'm sure we can come up with something better than Thomas Junior,' he said.

'Surely you will be naming your first born and all subsequent sons after their uncles,' Gideon joked. 'Gideon is a fine name, Elijah, Amos and Daniel can follow.'

Betty laughed. 'So that is four sons you must have, Matilda. I suspect you will have to give up your work at the *Women's Journal* if you are blessed with that many children.'

'I suspect I will need a stay in Elijah's asylum if they are anything like my brothers,' Matilda said.

'That can be arranged,' Elijah assured her.

'Lord help us,' Mr Hayward said, with a shake of his head. 'Perhaps we should let the young couple wed first and focus instead on Amos and Minnie's blessing, my first grandchild.'

Thomas gave his soon-to-be father-in-law a grateful smile for the diversion.

'And when might you start accompanying us to church, Thomas?' Aunt Audrey asked, and the brothers hid their smiles as Thomas slumped slightly, thinking he had a reprieve.

'As soon as crime stops happening on a Sunday, Aunt Audrey, I shall be there, relieved and worshipping.'

Aunt Audrey made a disbelieving sound and, to Thomas's delight, she turned her attention to the Hayward men.

'With all the lovely ladies around the table, it is time that you brother, and Daniel, Gideon and Elijah followed the fine example set by Thomas and Amos, and secure the hands of these lovely ladies,' Aunt Audrey proclaimed.

The ladies flushed with embarrassment except for Georgina, who was not the blushing type. She instead laughed at Aunt Audrey's forward comment. An uncomfortable silence stretched until Mr Hayward stepped up to honour the ladies.

'I could not agree with you more, sister,' he said, and

Audrey smiled with satisfaction. 'I for one am delighted and amazed that Betty sees fit to spend time in my company, and nothing would make me happier than to see my sons married to these fine ladies.' He threw the comment back at his sons with a raised eyebrow and a challenge.

Elijah cleared his throat and spoke: 'Nothing would give me more pleasure, but of course we must allow Thomas and Matilda their moment in the sun.'

Daniel and Gideon looked at him as if he were a genius.

'Absolutely,' Daniel said. 'Our focus is definitely on the soon-to-betrothed pair.' He offered Thomas a beaming smile, which Thomas did not return, nor did he appreciate the re-focusing of attention on himself.

'You need not think you are so smart, Daniel,' Aunt Audrey berated him. 'I know exactly what you are up to and I expect to go to all your weddings soon. I am not getting any younger.'

'But we do have a mortician in the family, Aunt Audrey, or may soon if Gideon declares his intentions,' Elijah said, and the family laughed.

'Thank you, Elijah,' Aunt Audrey said, 'but I won't be needing those services any time soon, hopefully.'

'Perish the thought, Aunt Audrey,' Elijah agreed with great seriousness.

'Georgina, what of you, dear?' Aunt Audrey enquired, getting her nephew Elijah back for his impertinence. 'Will you be taking our beloved Elijah back to the country with you?'

Matilda's expression relayed her surprise at Aunt Audrey's bold question, but Georgina spoke up confidently.

'I hope that I am securing his heart, Mrs Bloomfield, little by little. My father always says if we faithfully plant seeds, we will reap a harvest. So time will tell what we shall reap and where we shall reap it,' she said with a smile and looked to Elijah.

'Well said, young lady,' Mr Hayward raised a glass in Georgina's direction. 'May you all grow from the time you spend learning about each other and may Audrey and I be around to see you reap that harvest.'

'To harvests,' Elijah said, with a grin at Georgina, and the glasses clinked as the toast was made.

As Audrey began her inquisition on Minnie and her baby, Daniel leant across the table and asked Thomas: 'Did you look into why Petronella was wandering around the city late at night with a bouquet?'

'Oh, yes, Thomas mentioned she was an acquaintance of both of you,' Matilda said, turning to Daniel.

'How do you know her?' Alice asked, looking up at her beau with curiosity given his familiarity in calling Miss Petronella Pettyfore by her Christian name.

Thomas gave Daniel a look that would have frozen his custard and Daniel offered a pained expression as an apology.

'She frequented a club we used to visit when we were young and wild,' Daniel answered. 'Forgive me, it is not suitable talk for the table.'

'So, you admit you both got up to unsuitable activities then?' Matilda said, teasing both men.

'Well, not for our age and we were never taken to the

watch-house,' Thomas said, with a glance to Gideon whom he had rescued from there not that long ago.

'Ah yes, that,' Gideon said. 'Most uncomfortable those watch-houses. I don't know how one is supposed to sleep anything off on such a hard bench.'

Elijah laughed at his twin as Thomas apologised for the inconvenience.

'I wish I had been involved in more unsuitable activities,' Georgina added and enjoyed a round of laughs from the table guests.

'I am sure you have done many things of which we can only imagine,' Betty said, with fondness. 'Have you birthed any animals?'

'Oh many,' Georgina said as if everyone did that regularly. 'Sheep, calves, but they always seem to come at the most inconvenient time.'

'Yes, the young are like that,' Mr Hayward said drily, with a look to his children around the table. 'Amos was most considerate and came just after 11 o'clock in the morning.'

Aunt Audrey patted Amos's hand. 'And considerate every day thereafter,' she said.

Minnie glanced at the nearby crib and smiled. 'I hope our child is the same.'

'Have you seen a snake?' Alice asked Georgina, her expression of terror conveying her dread at the thought.

'Oh, quite a few. I am not fond of them,' Georgina agreed. 'But still, an unsuitable activity might have been fun,' she mused on her previous thought.

'I think, whether you like it or not, Matilda has led you

into several memorable activities for the right and wrong reasons,' Elijah said, with a glance at his sister.

'Well, I wasn't to know that a woman was embalmed in the cupboard where we were having lunch, or that Thomas would go get himself experimented upon in an asylum now, was I?' she said, in her defence.

'I wouldn't have missed out for the world,' Georgina assured her.

'So what have you got for us next?' Alice asked, most enthusiastically.

'Nothing, hopefully,' Thomas answered, giving his fiancée a look.

'Well, that is just boring, Thomas,' she retorted. 'We have a note in the bouquet mystery plus a beating, and a murder. I shall update you ladies later.'

Thomas groaned as Matilda announced his case to the table and, as expected, Aunt Audrey piped in again.

'Goodness me,' she said. 'I can't bear to think about it. Although theft does seem to be rife in the town at the moment, Thomas. What is the constabulary doing about it?'

'I do not know for sure, Aunt Audrey, as they are a different department, but the crime lads did say during the week that theft was on the rise. Do you know of someone personally who has been affected?' He asked out of duty more so than interest and anticipated she would ask for him to flag her acquaintances for special attention.

'Well, I was at my church parish meeting just yesterday and Mrs Burgess said their premises had been broken into recently and a large sum of cash and jewellery had been stolen,' Aunt Audrey said.

Thomas straightened. 'Burgess?'

He saw in his peripheral vision that Daniel and Matilda had caught the importance of the name given it was that very name that was on the note in the bouquet Matilda brought home.

'Yes, they live at Paddington Heights,' Aunt Audrey said. 'It's an expensive suburb so I imagine it invites some attention from those with bad intentions on their mind.'

'Does Mrs Burgess's husband go by the name of Walter, by any chance?' Thomas asked.

'That is him. Quite a proud man. So proud in fact, that Mrs Burgess said he would not report the theft, and he did not want police traipsing through his house.'

'Is that so?' Thomas said. 'Most interesting,' he mused under his breath.

As the conversation moved on, Matilda leaned closer to Thomas and said under her breath: 'You think there is a reason Mr Burgess would not report the crime, Thomas? Perhaps something he is involved in?'

'That's exactly what I am thinking,' he said, and surprised her, as he rarely shared his thoughts without much provocation.

Matilda persisted: 'And that Mr Osborne and the lady he was meeting that night with the note in the flowers are somehow involved in that crime?'

'So it would appear now, as that cannot be a coincidence,' he confirmed. 'But you will leave that with me, of course.'

'Of course,' she said and smiled at him. Thomas was less than convinced at seeing the thoughtful expression on her face. 'Oh, did I mention that the tarot reader thought Mrs Greenwood deserved all that came her way, even death?'

'No. You did not and when did you speak with her?' Thomas asked in a low and very annoyed voice.

Matilda waved her hand around. 'Recently, when I was in Bridal Lane with Mrs Dalton for the story.' While not quite true, it was not far from the truth as she was in the lane and had been with Mrs Dalton.

Thomas sighed. 'Tell me then.'

'I don't think I will, Thomas, given you are so ungrateful.'

He leaned in closer to whisper in her ear. 'How can I be grateful when my fiancée places herself in grave danger to get information that is not worth getting should she be harmed?'

'Well, the tarot reader was hardly going to harm me.'

'You do not know that. She may have killed Mrs Greenwood.'

'What are you two speaking of in whispers?' Aunt Audrey asked.

'Bridal Lane, Aunt Audrey,' Matilda answered truthfully. 'I have ordered my flowers from *Blooming Blossoms*, but it is a most unsavoury lane.'

'I hear it is dreadful these days,' Aunt Audrey said. 'It wasn't always. Mrs Greenwood—God rest her soul—was just saying to me a few weeks ago that she no longer wished to do business in that lane.'

'Mrs Louise Greenwood? You knew her then, Aunt Audrey?' Thomas asked, again amazed that the matriarch of the family was such a source of information at today's lunch.

'Only from the church committee. She was a hard-working lady and I hate to speak ill of the dead, but her charity work only extended to those who she deemed suitable for charity. It does not always work like that.'

'It certainly doesn't,' Amos agreed. 'From the cases we take on at the law firm that need affordable legal assistance, many are good people who find themselves in unfortunate situations.'

'Exactly,' Aunt Audrey agreed. 'Mrs Greenwood was all fired up about exposing a business that she claimed was aiding and abetting unwed mothers into hasty marriages. I am not sure what is wrong with that given they certainly need to be married, but Mrs Greenwood was trying to close the stable door after the horse had bolted.'

'Most interesting,' Thomas said again. 'You are the source of some helpful insights today, Aunt Audrey.'

'Aren't I always, young man?' she asked, and before he could stumble out an answer, she laughed and Thomas breathed a sigh of relief.

He glanced at Matilda. 'We shall talk later about the tarot reader.'

'Maybe,' she teased, 'if I have forgiven you for being so bossy.'

He rolled his eyes.

'I shall work out an appropriate penance,' she said.

'Oh good,' he retorted, and couldn't help but smile in anticipation.

Chapter 25

T homas pounced on Harry the moment he arrived at work on Monday morning.

'We have some new information,' he said before his partner had barely stepped into the office, 'and I think it might help us crack this case.'

'Good morning, Thom, well thank you, and you?' Harry asked with a grin.

Thomas smiled. 'Very well, too.'

'Did you enjoy the Hayward luncheon?' Harry asked, teasing Thomas.

'It was pleasant as always,' Thomas said, keeping his answers short and sharp as Harry placed his hat on the desk and sat on the edge. He looked at Thomas and smiled.

'Tell me then, before you combust.'

Thomas smiled. 'We need to go to *Blooming Blossoms*. Mr Burgess was robbed recently but did not report it, and Aunt Audrey said Mrs Greenwood was trying to stop an unwed mothers' marriage scheme, and we know the note in the bouquet had Mr Burgess's name on it,' he said, trying to tell Harry everything at once.

'Son, none of that makes much sense, so let us go and you can start from the beginning on the way,' Harry said, grabbing his hat and placing it back on his head. He led the way with Thomas in pursuit.

*****

Mrs Dalton looked surprised as she sat opposite the two detectives in the back room of *Blooming Blossoms*.

'Well, that is most surprising,' she said, and reclined in her chair, webbing her fingers under her chin. 'So let me understand this. You believe we are running a side business to get pregnant brides wed fast and accepting cash payments to do so? Are we taking the money from the bride's family or the irresponsible father-to-be, or both?'

Thomas realised it did sound rather fanciful and ill-thought-out once said out loud and given the surprise reaction of Mrs Dalton, he was not sure that if it was happening under her nose, that she was aware of the scheme.

'That remains to be seen,' he answered, truthfully. 'But from recent activities, I believe the money is being taken from the male perpetrator.'

'So he pays one way or the other,' Mrs Dalton said and gave a wry smile. She was, after all, a woman of some worldly experience. 'I can't say I object to the idea. In fact, it has merit.'

'How so?' Harry asked.

'Well, if a young lady is compromised and the man in question is not willing to stand by her but willing to provide her with a dowry, for want of a better word, then she can be matched to someone who needs funds and will be a provider and father. Is not the problem solved?'

Thomas explained: 'Unless the man in question is not willing to provide for the woman he compromised and instead, a party robs him to do so. He, of course, will not report it to the police for fear his indiscretion may come out if he was already married. This is a criminal act.'

'Oh, I see, theft is involved,' Mrs Dalton said, with an understanding nod. She was extremely calm under pressure and gave the impression of knowing nothing about the ruse. 'Justifiable,' she murmured, almost too low to hear.

'And,' Harry continued, 'if Mrs Greenwood found about it, and given how strict her beliefs were, she may have been killed to prevent her exposing the practice, the victims, the men in question and the thefts.'

Mrs Dalton nodded. 'Yes, I can see that, although it seems extreme to murder her for that. She would have to prove it was going on after all.'

'If she came to us with her suspicions, we would have to investigate it,' Thomas said. He cleared his throat. 'We have experienced it first-hand. My fiancée received a note in her bouquet which was not meant for her.'

'A note in the bouquet from my store, from *Blooming Blossoms*?' Mrs Dalton's voice rose as she finished her sentence.

'The very one,' Thomas said.

Her shocked expression revealed her genuine ignorance of the situation and Thomas felt deflated. 'What sort of note?'

'Inviting her to a liaison,' Thomas said, not wanting to go into detail and feeling as if the conversation was being derailed.

Mrs Dalton's eyes widened. 'I don't wish to cast aspersions on your lovely fiancée, Detective, but are you sure she was not meeting anyone?'

'Absolutely not,' Thomas said, his lips thinned with anger. 'She did attend the scene with her brother and witnessed a matter which she reported to the police. Hence, why we are here.'

'It is all very confusing,' she said, with a look to Harry as if he would shed light on the matter.

Harry frowned. 'Pray tell, what reason did Mrs Greenwood give you for not continuing her business relationship with you, if she did not accuse you of this practice?'

Mrs Dalton pursed her lips before continuing. 'I need to be assured of your discretion if I tell you Louise's reasoning.'

'We give you our word,' Harry said, 'unless you are involved in the crime, of course.'

She nodded, satisfied with that response.

'My darling daughter, Katherine, who is a dressmaker, is one of the few generous souls who accept brides-to-be in the family way and on their way to the altar. She is a charitable and kind girl, and the dresses Katherine makes allow the girls to have a dignified wedding without being disparaged.'

'Mrs Greenwood found out about this and confronted you?' Thomas asked.

'Yes. Katherine used Louise's lace on several of the dresses and Louise heard of a bride being rushed to the altar in one of those dresses. She was outraged,' Mrs Dalton said and rolled her eyes. 'For pity's sake, have you ever?' she asked, frustrated, and Thomas and Harry restrained their smiles. 'As if someone would point to the lace on the dress and declare Louise complicit with the poor state the bride was in.'

'It does seem extreme,' Thomas agreed.

'It certainly was. So, Louise and I had a parting of the ways, but she did not stop delivering. I kept expecting her to do so.'

Thomas nodded. 'So, you are saying you know nothing about men being held to account, having to provide for their sins, or being robbed?'

'I assure you, Detectives, I know nothing of those practices, but I can't in all honesty, say I object to them.'

Harry gave her a firm nod, that would appear to be somewhat complicit with her thoughts, and Thomas sighed and said, 'Then I think we best talk with your daughter, Katherine. Perhaps she knows more about the brides or the dowries or the sending of these notes.'

'I doubt that very much, Detective, but if you must.' Mrs Dalton scribbled down the address of her daughter's home and workroom.

'Do you know Mr Alaric Osbourne?' Thomas asked.

'Indeed, I do. His nephew is gainfully employed by me as our delivery boy. It was Mr Osbourne who applied on his nephew's behalf,' she said. 'Why? Is he in some trouble?'

'No, nothing like that,' Harry said, nipping her query in

the bud. 'Mr Osbourne was recently attacked, but he may not have told you. Men have their pride.'

'Goodness me,' she said. 'It is getting more and more dangerous in our town.'

'Sadly, that appears to be the case,' Harry said.

'And Miss Petronella Pettyfore? You know of her?' Thomas persisted.

'Yes, I know Miss Pettyfore as well. She is a friend of my daughter's, although I find her a bit spirited for my liking. She delivers ribbons and fabric colour swatches sometimes between my daughter and me, so we can match our bridal bouquets to the bridesmaids' colours. And what of her then?'

'Do you recall her buying some flowers from you when a wedding was cancelled recently?' Thomas asked. 'I believe you gave them to her at a good price.'

Mrs Dalton snorted with laughter. 'Not Petronella. She scrimps and saves to meet the rent and put food on the table. Buying flowers would be an outrageous decadence. I have on occasion given her flowers, of course, when they are not suitable to be sold, but that has not happened for months. Our sales have been very good.'

Thomas stored this information, remembering Daniel had seen Petronella with a huge bouquet that she claimed to have bought at a discount price. That was clearly an untruth.

He gave Harry a nod and the two detectives rose to depart, thanking Mrs Dalton for her time and frankness. Once out of Bridal Lane, Thomas added Miss Petronella Pettyfore to the growing list of people he intended to visit today.

Chapter 26

The din in the office surrounds of the *Women's Journal* was always louder than usual at the start of a deadline week. Betty and her team were furiously racing through the last-minute copy to ensure its accuracy and to provide headlines and fact checks; the illustrators—two in total, of which Georgina was one—hurried with last-minute drawings, mostly for advertising clients who had been tardy; writers including Matilda had either finished and were quietly working on their stories for next issue, or hurriedly trying to finish off their copy and send it to Betty for the current issue.

In her peripheral vision, Matilda saw her editor, Mrs Lawson, rise and come to the door of her office. Mrs Lawson beckoned and Matilda hurried in with her notepad and pencil.

'How are you, my dear?' Mrs Lawson asked, her face kindly but her body a display of tidiness and rigidity.

'Very well, thank you, Mrs Lawson. Is everything alright?'

'Perfectly,' she said, and put Matilda's mind at rest, inviting her to sit. 'I have read your obituary for Mrs Louise Greenwood.'

'I fear it is perfunctory, but aside from her exceptional lace work, her life was… well strait-laced,' Matilda said, and sighed, making Mrs Lawson laugh at Matilda's pun.

'That's not a bad thing, dear, and would make for a great title for your article but it might be a little derogatory. I think you did a good job, especially capturing how her life was cut short and the bereaved family left behind. However, I know enough of you and your writing style to read between the lines.'

'Oh, dear.'

'Oh yes. Don't worry, I am sure no one else will detect the underlying current unless they are personally acquainted with Mrs Greenwood, or perhaps familiar with the principle of double effect.' Mrs Lawson raised an eyebrow and gave Matilda an enquiring look. 'There is a bigger story than what you have written?'

Once again, Matilda was in awe of her editor's powers of perception and gave a small nod.

'Yes, Mrs Lawson. Everyone gave me the standard and expected replies about Mrs Greenwood, her talent, and her Christian views, and every one of those comments was laced with some dislike for her inflexibility of those very views.'

'We are always most diplomatic when it comes to speaking of the dead,' Mrs Lawson agreed, 'but I suspect those readers who were not a great supporter of Mrs Greenwood will appreciate the nod to her exacting views and how your piece is not pure flattery.'

'I hope so.' Matilda thought before she continued. 'When I was a child and my father had his law practice, he used to speak with me about the principle of double effect if his case won when it shouldn't have. Well, it wouldn't have I imagine if Mrs Greenwood was the judge and jury.'

'I suspect you are right. Do go on,' she encouraged.

'Mrs Greenwood was most unforgiving of those who fell by the wayside, who sinned or were involved in something she felt was immoral. She was withdrawing her lacework from Mrs Dalton's store because Mrs Dalton's daughter helped unfortunate brides-to-be. Mrs Greenwood could not see, or refused to accept, that it may be morally permissible to care for these young women, even if the result might be not to her liking or society's standards... a wedding of necessity, a man paid the dowry to step in and be a husband and father. It is hardly evil but rather a less desirable outcome so that some good may come of a bad situation. Am I being too moralistic now?'

'Well, I for one wholeheartedly agree with you,' Mrs Lawson said, to Matilda's great relief. 'Your last paragraph—a quote from your detective that Mrs Greenwood may have been in the wrong place at the wrong time, but then adding her daughter's thoughts that her values may have contributed to her death—will hopefully provide some correspondence to the journal from our readers.'

'Do you wish me to amend it and finish with our condolences?' Matilda asked.

'On the contrary. I expect the crusaders like Mrs Greenwood will hold their ground, but I do hope we get some dissenters. Off the record, you have your own theory on her death?'

'Yes. Thomas is working on the case—the murder of Mrs Greenwood—and I think in her self-righteousness, she discovered something and was about to expose it or someone. Time will tell.'

'Then I hope the case will be solved before your wedding day and you can write the story for us before departing on your honeymoon. Perhaps you should begin it now, writing what you know of the whole sorry story and add the conclusion when it reveals itself. As always, a quote or two from the detectives would not go astray.'

'I will make it my mission,' Matilda said with a smile, and thanking her editor, departed to pursue the story.

*****

Miss Petronella Pettyfore saw the detectives outside *Blooming Blossoms* and hid from sight. She was on an errand, dropping off some ribbon and lace to Mrs Dalton from her daughter, in order to match a bridal trim with a bouquet. It was hard for Petronella to remain inconspicuous as she was a strikingly handsome woman, but she did her best to window shop on the main street and not return the looks of gentlemen who passed and glanced her way.

She subtly studied the detectives as they stood in the doorway of *Blooming Blossoms*, about to depart the store. Petronella was struck by just how dashing Detective Thomas Ashdown was, and now very successful as well. She turned her face as they departed and headed towards her, but not before she noticed Thomas's confident gait.

He was not as sure of himself when she knew him. He was kind, considerate, and very inexperienced, as was his young friend, Daniel. Look at him now. What a good catch he would make, and might he have rekindled his interest in her if that fiancée was not on the scene?

When they were out of sight, she entered the laneway but did not get to the bridal store; the tarot reader beckoned. Petronella delayed her visit to Mrs Dalton to enter the premises of Madam Gerta's dark shop.

'Petronella, I have some information,' Madam Gerta said, not bothering to waste time with greetings and formalities.

'I have not the funds to pay you for anything further,' Petronella said.

'But you will have soon. I ask just a coin or two my way – a shilling, which is cheap by anyone's standards.'

Petronella nodded. 'Not by mine, but I can meet your fee if the information is worth it.' She accepted the offer to sit, her back to the lane in a chair opposite Madam Gerta, whose hands automatically cut and opened the card deck before her.

'I know why Louise was withdrawing her lace business from the mother and daughter,' Madam Gerta said, with a nod to the flower shop across the lane from her store.

'That hardly surprises me. There is very little you do not know about, but that is news not worth my coin,' Petronella said.

Madam Gerta chuckled, pleased. 'You are right, and that is not the news I have to impart or expect to be compensated for revealing. It is about the woman writer.'

Petronella raised an eyebrow. 'Do tell. Is this the dainty one who was visiting Mrs Dalton for quotes for an obituary on Mrs Greenwood?'

'The very one. She will bring about your downfall.' Madam Gerta overturned a card as she made the prediction, revealing an image of a tower with fiery flames in all its windows – the card representing destruction.

Petronella laughed. 'I know you are prone to dramatics, Gerta, but that is a wonderful piece of theatre.'

'Ignore me at your peril, Petronella,' Madam Gerta said, and sniffed with disdain, gathering the cards and reshuffling the pack. She placed the pack in the middle of the table and pulled her red robe tighter around her, as if protecting her secrets.

'Alright then,' Petronella sobered, 'I shall play the game. How is this woman intending to bring me to my knees?'

Madam Gerta raised her chin, not one to be disrespected or dismissed. 'My price for information has gone up. It will cost you two shillings before I say anything more.'

Petronella sighed, not convinced she was not being conned by a master confidence artist, but gave a brief nod of consent. 'Make it worth my while,' she said unhappily.

Madam Gerta gave a small smile of victory. 'That dainty lady, as you call her—Miss Hayward—is a very sound investigative writer. If you read the *Women's Journal*, you will know that she was party to solving several crimes and first on hand to report them.'

'I do read the journal, but I did not make the connection. Regardless, what has this to do with me?'

'She was recently in here when your friend, that awkward man, visited *Blooming Blossoms* and walked you out.'

'Awkward friend… oh, you mean Mr Alaric Osbourne?'

'She said she recognised him and yourself as the lovers from the park. I disputed the fact, saying I did not know you to be lovers. But she said Mr Osbourne presented you with flowers.'

'Flowers? Why was she there?' Petronella realised she had said too much. Her expression changed as she considered that someone—the woman writer for one—had seen them in the gardens using the flowers as a ruse.

'Then, Miss Hayward followed the young delivery boy when he took the bouquet to your home. She was watching the lad talking with Rose and Mr Osbourne on the corner for some time, and then when the boy ran off with a bouquet, Miss Hayward and another young lady followed him.'

Petronella laughed. 'How would you know this? Do you have extended vision now?'

'I did not know at first. After I saw him run off and Rose return to the store, I saw Miss Hayward and her very tall friend in pursuit in the direction the lad went. When he returned, he dropped in here when summonsed and I asked him where he delivered that bouquet. I was curious.'

'Of course you were.'

'He said to your home.'

'When was this?'

Madam Gerta thought. 'Last week or so. The lady writer questioned why you would receive two bouquets from a man who was not your lover or whose intentions you did not accept.'

Petronella frowned as she thought. 'Mother said two ladies from the *Women's Journal* had dropped in. They were undertaking a survey.'

'Interesting... and clever. Ask your mother for a description, it will match,' Madam Gerta said, cockily. 'After the murder of Louise, Miss Hayward has been most diligent in her questions. She not only asked me for some words about Louise, but about Louise's character, what I might have seen, and what I believe Louise had gotten herself into.'

'Hmm, I don't like it, but I can't see how she would connect me with the death of Mrs Greenwood just because I have two bouquets given to me.'

'Can you not? Perhaps you are right, although she most likely has access to more information about the crime as it unfolds. She is, after all, the fiancée of that handsome young detective.'

Petronella looked as if she had been slapped. 'That is Detective Ashdown's fiancée?'

'The very same – Miss Matilda Hayward soon to be Mrs Thomas Ashdown.' Madam Gerta smiled, satisfied she had earned her keep and delivered a sound final blow.

'That is all I have,' she added with a satisfied look.

'On this occasion, you have earned your keep,' Petronella said. 'Thank you, Gerta. I will deliver the shillings as soon as I receive them.'

Petronella rose and hurried out, keen to deliver the lace and ribbon to Mrs Dalton at *Blooming Blossoms* and to get home. She had to find a way to speak with Miss Hayward, and more importantly, to put any story to rest. It was then that she had another idea, how she might achieve several ends at once. She just needed a bouquet and a favour from Jacob, the delivery boy.

Chapter 27

Thomas and Harry made their way to the home of Miss Petronella Pettyfore, deciding to prioritise a visit to Petronella before that of the dressmaker, Miss Katherine Dalton.

'If we tell her we know the truth, that she did not buy nor was she gifted the flowers, and we believe she was the last person to see Mrs Greenwood alive, we may just break down her bravado,' Thomas said.

'She is worldly, but it is worth a try. Failing that, we'll see if the gentler Miss Dalton reveals anything under pressure.' Harry sighed. 'I feel we are so close, Thom, but yet the answer is out of reach.'

'Frustrating indeed,' Thomas agreed, his frown matching his feelings. 'Petronella is no fool and well used to handling the opinions of men. But the threat of imprisonment, especially wrongful imprisonment, may encourage her to expose her hand.'

The hansom pulled up outside the Pettyfore's modest home and Harry asked the driver to wait a few moments, lest no one be home. Petronella's mother opened the door moments later and the men removed their hats.

'I'm sorry detectives, she is not at home. I believe she is at work with Miss Dalton today,' she responded to Harry's question.

'We have that address, thank you, and we are sorry to disturb you, Mrs Pettyfore,' Harry said.

'Not at all. She is not in any trouble, is she?'

'No, nothing like that,' Thomas assured her. 'We are speaking to a number of people who knew Mrs Greenwood.'

'Yes, of course. Poor Mrs Greenwood. I saw her at church every Sunday but was not in her circle of acquaintance.'

The two men thanked her again and re-entered the hansom cab, giving the driver Miss Katherine Dalton's address.

'Well, we shall hopefully catch the two ladies together,' Harry said.

'If need be, we will speak with Miss Dalton separately. I suspect Petronella will take the lead and dominate the conversation,' Thomas said.

'You do not seem to be that fond of Miss Pettyfore. Did it not end well?' Harry asked.

'It never started,' Thomas said truthfully. 'She was my first love, but I was mistaken in thinking she felt the same or that I was her only love. Very mistaken.'

Harry nodded. 'Can you be objective?'

Thomas snapped to look at him and laughed. 'Of course. It was a decade ago and I was a naïve young man. It wasn't Petronella's fault; it was mine for being presumptuous.'

He gave a small shrug. 'As lovers go, she was an excellent teacher.'

'Good to know that Miss Hayward has something to look forward to then,' Harry ribbed his protégé and got another rare laugh from Thomas.

*****

'More flowers,' the receptionist at the *Women's Journal* announced as she walked down the middle of the room, pretending to veer towards different ladies and enjoying the laughs that followed. Finally, she stopped and gave them to Matilda.

'Oh, for me?' Matilda asked, surprised. Thomas usually presented flowers to her in person and they were smaller than any past arrangements she had received.

'They are lovely but not from Thomas?' Alice asked, joining her and sharing the same thought.

'No,' Matilda said, and looked around the bouquet for a card but could find none.

'They are lovely, nevertheless,' Alice said and hurried off with a small wave as the deadline beckoned.

Matilda studied the flowers but could find no indication of the sender, and then she saw the slip of paper inside the bouquet and with a glance around to make sure she wasn't being watched, retrieved it and put the flowers down.

Unfolding it, she read: *'Miss Hayward, let's talk. Today, 3pm. Petronella Pettyfore.'* An address was scribbled underneath but Matilda recognised it was not the address where Petronella and her mother resided, as discovered when she and Georgina chased the flower deliverer. Matilda felt a rush of excitement; an audience with Petronella Pettyfore. The very same woman the tarot reader identified, the woman she had seen in the park when undercover with Thomas and her friends and family, and the woman she had seen again at *Blooming Blossoms*. Not to mention that despite his discretion, Miss Pettyfore was possibly Thomas's former lover. What could Miss Pettyfore possibly know and want to share? Matilda wondered.

A clue at last, something that might be useful for her story and for Thomas' case. She knew the address and it was a respectable area. Matilda had less than forty minutes to get there.

She tidied her desk, advised Betty she was following a lead and with a quick wave to Georgina and Alice, raced out the door to meet the lady she believed was somehow caught up in the whole mystery.

Fortunately, an omnibus was nearby and moments later she stepped on board, taking a seat and running through the situation in her head, trying to arrive in a state of preparedness. Perhaps that was Miss Pettyfore's intention – to have Matilda a little rattled and on the back foot. Or maybe she was an ally who wanted to help or needed help.

Matilda alighted at the nearest cross street, checked the address on the slip of paper she had folded into her notepad and proceeded up the street. It was a lovely little area, and the house in question was but four from the corner. Her concern about coming alone to an unknown address was erased when she saw the sign on the gate reading '*Bridal wear. Dressmaker: Miss Katherine Dalton. Please enquire within.*' Looking up from reading the sign, Matilda saw the curtain move slightly and she made her way up the pathway lined with rose beds on both sides.

*****

'She's here. I shall speak with her in the back room if you have no objections?' Petronella asked, with a glance to Katherine working in the corner, pinning up the hem of a beautiful white satin gown.

'If you think that is best,' the docile Miss Katherine Dalton responded, and bit her lower lip with worry.

'I do. Let me handle this.'

'I most certainly will,' Katherine said, alarmed. 'I am not sure what you are doing or why you called her here. But I am not comfortable with it.'

'I know, trust me, all will be well,' she said, and smiled at the worried dressmaker.

Petronella moved to the door and opened it as Matilda went to knock.

'Miss Hayward, thank you for coming. We have not formally met.'

'Miss Pettyfore?'

'Yes. Please do come in.'

Matilda glanced behind, and feeling quite safe in her surroundings, entered the cottage.

'Have you met Miss Katherine Dalton?' Petronella asked.

'I believe we were both at Mrs Greenwood's mourning room, but we have not been formally introduced,' Matilda said, and Katherine rose to greet her.

'We shall leave Katherine to her work, as I have a matter to discuss with you if you please,' Petronella said. 'Will you kindly follow me?'

Matilda nodded, and the ladies walked down the small hallway to a room at the back of the house. Petronella entered, closing the door behind Matilda, and revealing on the window seat Alaric Osbourne and a young girl of no more than six or seven years.

Petronella read the look of surprise, fear and hesitation in Matilda's eyes and her glance at the door. But the wheels were now in motion and Petronella wanted answers.

Chapter 28

Alaric Osbourne stood as manners dictated, and the little girl studied Matilda and smiled at her.

'Hello. You're pretty,' she said, pulling at her own fair plaits.

'Thank you, and so are you,' Matilda said with a small smile of relief. Surely, with a child present, the discussion would not escalate into any kind of violence.

'Miss Hayward, this is Mr Osbourne, won't you be seated?' Petronella said, and with a nod to Osbourne, Matilda selected the closest chair to the door and Osbourne resumed his seat. Petronella sat beside the little girl and continued without introducing the child. 'We understand that you have a fine mind for a mystery... I subscribe to the *Women's Journal* and have read your work, although, at the time, I confess I didn't make the connection that you were the paper's crime writer and the very same writer who was gathering tributes for Mrs Greenwood.'

'I would hardly call me the crime writer. I just happened to be there at the right time.'

Petronella smiled. 'I imagine your fiancé has assisted greatly with being in the right place at the right time. Has he told you who I am?'

'Yes,' she responded, deciding not to give the confident lady who was holding the floor the satisfaction of Matilda looking uncomfortable. After all, Thomas had informed her that he and Daniel knew Petronella when he was a younger man and had said no more, so she assumed there was no more. Matilda could see her response did not satisfy Petronella.

'We were very close for a while,' Petronella said for a reaction and glanced at the child.

Matilda's eyes widened. 'Are you telling me...'

Alaric Osbourne spoke up. 'Miss Hayward, whatever you might think is going on between myself, Miss Pettyfore, Miss and Mrs Dalton and *Blooming Blossoms* requires clarification. We are working in the best interests of women with little prospects.'

Matilda interrupted him. 'Mr Osbourne, it is hardly my business.'

'But you appear to be making it so,' Petronella said. 'The tarot reader said you followed the delivery boy to my home, and that you identified me from the park. What were you doing in the park if not watching me? Was Thomas with you?'

Matilda thought for a moment before responding. 'It was innocent, I assure you. I collected my bridal flower samples and found a note within one of the bouquets. I was most worried that a suitor might be waiting for his beloved to arrive, and believe she did not come, when in fact she didn't get the note.'

'Ah, that was you accompanied by a man in the park that evening,' Alaric said, putting it together.

'It was, but you did not give us the chance to explain.'

'And?' Petronella demanded.

'What would like me to say?' Matilda asked.

'Why were you watching us the second time, why did you follow the delivery boy, to my house?'

Matilda sighed as if she believed the situation to be most obvious. 'I am writing the obituary from Mrs Greenwood and naturally, I would like to know what happened to her or help the police if I find out anything. Not wishing to speak ill of the dead, but from the comments shared with me, she is regarded with some...' she searched for the word.

'She was a hypocritical, bitter and conniving woman,' Osbourne spat out, surprising them both with his venom. 'You'd be best to write an article about how she deserved her death.'

'Then tell me the story. Let me write something that reflects her true life and that which might have led to her death,' Matilda requested, trying not to sound too keen, but she was terribly interested in hearing his version.

Osbourne glanced to Petronella and back to Matilda.

'I will, but you are not to mention us by name in the story.'

Matilda thought for a moment. 'I will have to seek my editor's thoughts on how to do that, it is not my call.'

'Then there is no story to share with you,' he said firmly.

'Alright then, I shall agree to your terms,' Matilda said. 'I shall find a way.' She opened her notebook and with her pen at the ready, encouraged him to begin.

'Let me begin by saying, I did not kill Mrs Greenwood, neither of us was party to that.'

Matilda nodded and he began his story, a tale that had its roots in his childhood. He neared the end of his tale and finished abruptly.

'I am sorry for your hardships, Mr Osbourne,' she said sincerely, recognising his misfortune and knowing she had a story her readers would appreciate. 'But I am afraid that you sound very much like a man with a reason to take the life of Mrs Greenwood.'

'But I tell you I did not,' he snapped angrily, 'and if you do not believe that, then the story cannot run.'

'It is a little late for that given you have imparted it,' Matilda said, with surprise. 'May I ask why you felt the need for the clandestine meetings? Could you not meet at *Blooming Blossoms*, or here at Miss Dalton's business, or call on Miss Pettyfore at her residence?'

'How many times might I do that without raising suspicion?' he asked. 'A man without intentions would eventually look dishonourable and I have to think of the ladies' reputation before my own.'

Matilda nodded, accepting this. They heard male voices outside, and Petronella and Osbourne exchanged quick looks.

'Who is that?' he demanded.

Matilda recognised Thomas's voice. 'It is the detectives,' she said, rising.

Osbourne leapt from his seat and pushed her back down into the chair, keeping a firm hand on her shoulder. 'I want your assurance—'

'—unhand me,' she interrupted him, shocked at his treatment.

'Stay where you are,' Petronella hissed. She moved to assure the little girl there was no need to be frightened. 'Do not worry, darling, everything is fine.'

'What is going on?' Matilda asked, realising she was in more trouble than she first believed. That perhaps they were not here to share their story or ask for fair representation, but to keep her silent.

'Thomas!' she yelled, and Osbourne slapped her hard across the face. The shock momentarily delayed her actions and a determined look swept her countenance. Matilda was no stranger to pushing past males – she had been part of many play scrums with her brothers when younger, and she applied the same technique. Head low, Matilda shoved Alaric Osbourne with all her might and grabbed for the door, only opening it but inches before a hand slammed it shut and threw her across the floor.

It was long enough to call out Thomas's name once more – clearer, louder and with all the might she could muster. She heard him racing down the hallway, and the sound of footsteps behind him indicated Detective Dart was in pursuit.

*****

211

Thomas could not believe his ears. His heart thundered with adrenaline, fear and anger as he glanced at Miss Dalton before racing towards the back rooms down the hallway, where he heard Matilda's voice. Harry followed closely behind.

He heard Miss Dalton crying out an apology of sorts and reaching a closed door, he pushed against it, only to be repelled. Hurriedly stepping back, Thomas rammed against it, sending Alaric Osbourne flying. Matilda was on the floor, lying on her side, her face a stinging red on one side where she had obviously been struck. Thomas hurried to her and Harry issued orders.

'Do not move, either of you,' Harry said, looking from Alaric Osbourne to Petronella Pettyfore. He glanced at the little girl hidden behind Miss Pettyfore's skirts.

'Hello there, why don't you go out and wait with Miss Dalton, little one,' he said kindly.

'Yes,' Petronella pushed her slightly forward, and with soothing words, sent the little girl down the hallway to Miss Dalton.

'Explain yourselves,' Thomas said, assisting Matilda to her feet and shielding her.

'It was just a friendly discussion, providing the writer with some facts,' Petronella said, with a derogatory glance to Matilda, as her jealousy flared at Thomas's possessiveness.

'Is that so, Miss Hayward?' Harry asked. 'Why then was the door locked and you look to have been struck to the ground?'

Matilda nodded. 'I was invited here and I assumed it was

to discuss Mrs Greenwood, but we did not finish before we heard your voice, and Mr Osbourne reacted most angrily.'

'You best start talking then,' Thomas said to him.

'We have done nothing that merits the time of the police force, nor do I have anything to say,' Alaric Osbourne said.

'You have come to our attention several times this month, Mr Osbourne,' Harry said, 'as an injured party and now you appear to be involved in something nefarious – including an attack on a young lady.'

'Hardly an attack!' he scoffed.

'Thomas, this is not warranted,' Petronella demanded.

'I'll determine that,' Thomas answered. 'We were coming to speak with you, Petronella, about being in possession of Mrs Greenwood's flowers... the very bouquet that was in her arms on the evening of her death.'

She began to defend herself and deny the allegation when Thomas held up his hand.

'Do not tell me you purchased or were gifted the bouquet, which we know from Mrs Dalton is not the truth,' he said, giving her a look that put an end to her tirade. 'You were there, somehow, you were involved, and from the looks of what we came upon here, I suspect you both were.'

'Petronella has nothing to do with it,' Osbourne said, standing taller and defending her, his admiration of her evident. 'It was my doing...'

'Be quiet, Alaric,' she angrily hushed him.

'Go on,' Harry encouraged him.

Osbourne cleared his throat and then thought better of saying anything further and refrained from speaking.

'If you have nothing to say, you can cool your heels at the station for the night and see how talkative you feel in the morning,' Harry suggested and pointed down the hallway for Osbourne to head out of the house.

'I shall return to speak with you and Miss Dalton in a moment, remain here,' Thomas ordered Petronella as he signalled to Matilda that she was to depart. 'I shall see you safely in a hansom and home.'

Thomas's words did not move Matilda as she looked at Petronella before returning her attention to Thomas.

'Is the little girl yours?' Matilda asked of him.

Thomas's jaw dropped with surprise. 'What? No!' He snapped to look at Petronella. 'Did you tell Miss Hayward we had a child together? Why would you do that?'

'I did not,' she said, smugly.

'You inferred it,' Matilda said.

'Surely, she has no rights in your past, Thomas?' Petronella asked.

'That may be true, but I do not need to play witness to his indiscretions,' Matilda said.

'She is my past and my future,' Thomas said, his face a mask of anger. 'You have gone too far, Petronella.' He turned to Matilda. 'The child is but seven or eight. Our very brief time together was a decade ago if it were a day.'

Matilda nodded her acceptance of this, and walking in front of him, exited the room and strode down the hallway farewelling Miss Dalton on the way; Thomas hurried to keep up with her.

*****

Matilda was no sooner on the street where Detective Dart was securing a hansom to return himself and Alaric Osbourne to the station, when she felt Thomas at her side, taking her arm and leading her away from the pair.

'Are you hurt?' he asked, scanning her face for pain or distress.

'I assure you I am not, but I am very pleased you came when you did,' she said, looking at him gratefully. 'I did get a very insightful story which you need to know about.'

Thomas shook his head and looked away.

'What is it?' she asked, surprised at his anger and feeling the tight grip he placed on her upper arm.

He returned his attention to Matilda, and took in a deep breath before speaking in a strained low voice: 'Are you truly out of your mind?'

She snatched her arm from his hand.

Harry called out as a hansom pulled up. 'Thom, I shall leave you to finish up here while I escort Mr Osbourne. Good day, Miss Hayward.'

Matilda bid him farewell and Thomas gave him a wave of acknowledgement, asking the driver to send back the next hansom they encounter. Matilda could see one just on the corner near the busier road. Thomas returned his attention to Matilda for the few minutes before her ride arrived.

'Do you have any idea of the danger you have put yourself in, not to mention that you might have impeded an investigation?' he asked, talking in a manner she had never heard him use with her before – low and calm, brimming with restrained anger.

'This is what I do, Thomas. Miss Pettyfore invited me here and I hoped for a story. Would you have me decline for fear I might not like what I hear? Do you approach the gentlemen journalists and ask the same question of them?'

'Of course not,' he scoffed. 'They can handle themselves and I care not what happens to them.'

'This is my business,' she said.

'No, it is my business.'

They stared at each other, as they did when competing as children; neither yielding an inch of ground to the other.

'You know this is what I do and yet you put yourself in danger and risk getting us both in trouble. Can you not choose stories like Alice writes? Pieces that can be safely researched and written from the confines of the *Women's Journal* office? Daniel does not have this aggravation, nor does Elijah,' he pointed out, keeping his voice low as he led her towards the approaching hansom cab. 'Do your readers desperately seek stories of crime and violence?'

Matilda refused to let him take her arm again.

'They seek newsworthy stories, Thomas. You have known me all my life, why should it come as a surprise to you that I would do the best job I can with the story I am presented with?' she stopped, demanding an answer from him.

Thomas exhaled in frustration. 'It is not the writing, it is… it is the deception,' he said. 'You could have told me you would be here.'

'Why? I do not call you every time my editor sends me to write or cover a story.'

'But this relates to an ongoing case,' he said, 'as you know.'

'And if I had told you, would you have stopped me or rushed over here to accompany me on what might have just been a personal piece about Mrs Greenwood?' She did not wait for his response. 'Before coming, I determined it was a very respectable neighbourhood and the shadows of the day are not long yet.'

His jaw locked as he looked away, conceding the point. He turned back to face her.

'Will this be what it is like when we are married? That you are underhanded for fear of me protecting you? That you will put yourself in situations most unsuitable? If we had not arrived this afternoon...'

She swallowed before answering.

'This is who I am, Thomas, and what I do. I am not asking you to change what you do for fear that I may one day get a knock on the door telling me you will never be home again.'

She shuddered and he removed his jacket to drape it around her shoulders.

'I do not need it, thank you.'

'You have had a shock, let me see you home. We will talk about this later.'

'No, Thomas, we will talk about it now.' She asked the driver to wait one moment. 'Are you to forbid me from doing what I wish to do, or wait until we are wed before you attempt to do so? Because it is best you know now that I have every intention of continuing this work,' she said, directly.

'I doubt forbidding you would make any difference,' he said curtly. 'Are you to continue to deceive me to achieve your end?'

'If that is the word you choose to use, even though you find it quite acceptable to never tell me the full story,' she said.

'That is hardly the same thing when I am working on a current criminal case.'

'No, of course it is not,' she said, her voice indicating she believed, in fact, it was the same thing. 'I cannot see how we can go on, Thomas.'

Matilda could tell Thomas felt her words as if he had been slapped, but he too had his pride, and he masked his feelings.

'If your work is more important to you than our impending marriage, then perhaps you are right,' he said, surprising Matilda. She expected him to capitulate, or at least say she was being hasty.

They stared at each other for what seemed like a very long time, waiting for the other party to back down, to concede they could find a middle ground, but both hot under the collar, neither did.

'I shall see you home,' he said again.

'You will not, thank you.'

Fuelled by anger, she slipped off her engagement ring and handed it to Thomas. His face spoke of his disbelief and anger, and he accepted it, pocketing it quickly.

Matilda turned and walked to the hansom cab. Thomas followed and gave the driver Matilda's address. He slipped the driver the fare.

'You need not do that,' she said, annoyed, and refusing his hand to enter the hansom.

He closed the door once she was seated and stood back as it drove away.

Chapter 29

Daniel pushed open the front door of the Hayward household and hurried in to find his father, Harriet, and his younger brothers, Elijah and Gideon, in a quiet and sober conversation in the drawing room.

'What has happened?' he asked, searching their faces and concerned about being summoned home. The family waited for Mr Hayward to tell his son the news.

'Matilda has called off her engagement to Thomas,' Mr Hayward said.

'Why? Where is she? Where is he?'

'Slow down,' Mr Hayward said, raising his hands in a calming manner. 'Tillie is upstairs. I don't know where Thom is, but it did not happen here. I believe they met at the scene of a crime.'

Daniel groaned.

'She won't say any more and has gone to her room, asking not to be disturbed,' Harriet said. 'I shall take her up a cup of tea soon. She has taken off the ring.'

Daniel groaned again.

'We were waiting for you before we head off to find Thomas,' Gideon said, 'to find out what this is all about.'

'And to check on him,' Elijah assured Daniel. 'I am sure it is nothing dishonourable, knowing Thomas, just a misunderstanding.'

'I will speak with her,' Daniel said, ignoring their calls behind him that Matilda insisted on not being disturbed. 'Don't leave without me; I need to find Thom,' he called back as he took the stairs two at a time, knocked on her bedroom door with gusto, and impatiently waited a moment, his hand on the doorknob.

'I am coming in with or without an invitation,' Daniel called, waited a few moments more in case his sister was not decent and then entered, closing the door behind him. Matilda was standing in a darkened room, her back to the door, looking out the window at the evening sky.

'Go away, please,' she said, not turning to face him, nor caring.

Daniel went to her side. 'Look at me, Tillie.'

They were the closest of the siblings, not by age, but by temperament and affection held for each other.

'Oh Daniel, I have lost him,' she said, her eyes glassy with tears and a look of distress that he had never seen from Matilda before. He pulled her to him and held her for a brief moment, before pushing his sister away, grasping her by the shoulders and looking down upon her.

'There is no one else for Thom but you, so this can be remedied. Do I need to go give him a good kick in the pants?' he asked, and Matilda smiled, shaking her head.

'No, I suspect it is my doing,' she said, with unladylike sniffing.

'I suspect it is too,' Daniel agreed, engaging another smile from her. 'Sit and we shall work it out.'

Matilda sat on the edge of her bed while Daniel took the chair by the window. He loosened his collar a little and with a deep breath, as though preparing to hear a confession, said: 'Tell me all that transpired and don't embellish to make you sound like the innocent party.'

Matilda was just about to deny she would do so, but Daniel's expression deterred her.

'I know you, and your wiles, out with it,' he said.

'Well, you can't interrupt with your own scolding or agreeing with Thomas,' she warned.

'Cross my heart. Begin then,' he said, and while Matilda told him the story, Daniel was prone to sigh and shake his head slightly in the retelling.

'What is to be done of it?' she asked, once finished. 'Perhaps it is best we have called off our engagement. I am sure Thomas could find a much more suitable wife.'

Daniel snorted in disbelief. 'I am sure there are many pretty, docile ladies keen to marry a detective and keep his house. But he would be bored in a heartbeat and never leave the office to return home at night. No, this requires compromise.'

'We tried that,' Matilda said.

'Not for five minutes while you are both hot under the collar and refusing to yield ground. Real negotiation and compromise long-term, to determine how you can both make it work so that you are not of major concern to him and in order to allow you some freedom to do your work.'

Matilda frowned at him. 'When did you become Mr Maturity?'

'When it doesn't relate to me,' he said and chuckled. 'One moment.'

He rose from his seat at the windowsill and went to the door, opening it and yelling out, 'Elijah, you are needed.'

He heard Elijah thumping up the stairs at a good pace and on his brother's entry said: 'You are the family peacemaker, Elijah. We need a negotiation strategy and a diplomatic solution, including what compromise both parties might need to make to get them to the altar.'

Elijah exhaled at the challenge before looking at Matilda sympathetically.

Daniel continued. 'Meanwhile, Gideon and I shall go seek Thom to ensure he has not done something stupid, like fallen prey to the bottle.' He turned to Matilda. 'Work with Elijah; I will do my best to bring Thomas back or to organise for you to meet to talk. Are you willing?'

She nodded.

'Then prepare what you will and won't accept, and if I cannot get Thomas here, I can at least present it to him and request the same in return.'

'Consider what you are not prepared to lose,' Elijah added. 'Thomas? Your career?'

'No,' Matilda fired up for the moment, the anger diminishing the flame of her pain. 'He cannot expect that of me.'

'He does not, from what I understand, as you have been

working this whole time,' Elijah said. 'But I cannot blame him for not wanting you to put yourself in danger.'

'I agree. You often rush in without thinking of the consequences,' Daniel said, siding with his best friend, Thomas. Seeing Matilda's expression, he added, 'but of course I understand you do not want to sit and paint or read poetry all day.'

'Daniel, be off with you,' Elijah said, turning to Matilda. 'Let us determine your conditions.'

Matilda nodded, calming a little. 'Thank you, Daniel, Elijah.'

And with that Daniel departed, taking the stairs just as quickly for fear his friend might be in a sorry state. He grabbed his coat and hat, and calling Gideon to his side, the two men departed swiftly.

*****

'Any idea where he might be?' Gideon asked, quickening his step to catch up with Daniel.

'Yes, several thoughts. We'll start at his home and if he is not there, Teddy might have some idea,' Daniel said, leaping on the omnibus as it arrived, Gideon following suit. 'We can drop in on Harry, too. He might know where his partner in crime could be. There's always the police department – he might be working late, or at our club, or there's a place Thom goes where the constabulary drink. Worth a look, too.'

'Tell me what Matilda said,' Gideon asked, and Daniel relayed the conversation.

Gideon exhaled after it was finished. 'I can't see how any husband would put up with that.'

'Hmm,' Daniel said 'that's why I asked Elijah to broker a peace deal.'

Gideon grinned, and the men rose to alight. A few minutes later, they were knocking on Thomas's front door. No one was home, not even his nephew, Teddy.

'Harry's home then?' Daniel asked.

'It's closest,' Gideon agreed. 'Don't stress, Thomas is a big boy and he's had his share of disappointments. He's not going to do anything stupid.'

Daniel wasn't as convinced. Thomas had changed since the engagement. Daniel couldn't remember seeing his best friend so content, ever. It was as if the security of his future provided him with some inner sense of worth.

Their search proved fruitless.

'Sorry lads,' Harry said, concerned, as he stepped out onto his verandah to address them. 'I haven't seen him since we parted ways this afternoon.'

'How was he?' Daniel asked.

'Well, now that you mention it,' Harry pondered, 'he was distracted and glum. I thought he might have been tired – he doesn't sleep well and works late. I suggested he visit Miss Hayward and enjoy some relaxation.'

Daniel nodded, grimacing at the advice.

'What has happened?' Harry asked, noticing and now concerned.

'Just a lover's tiff,' Gideon responded, playing it down.

'I will come with you to find him.'

'No, Harry, thank you, but that is not necessary,' Daniel said, placing his hand on Harry's arm before he retreated inside to get his hat and coat. 'We will head off now and are bound to find him. We have only just started our search.'

Harry nodded. 'You will let me know should anything be untoward.'

'Of course,' Daniel said, and they farewelled Harry.

'Next?' Gideon asked, as they walked with long strides down the path lit by lamps.

'The club he frequents with his colleagues,' Daniel answered. 'I don't believe he has gone to our club or he would have fetched me first.'

They walked a short distance before taking advantage of an omnibus coming their way and heading into the city. The club was a short walk from the police headquarters. Entering, Daniel scanned the faces and Thomas's was not amongst them.

'He was here,' the bartender told Gideon. 'Left about ten minutes ago, I'd say. Could still walk upright, so he'll be alright. Drink, lads?'

Daniel swore under his breath. 'Uh, no, thank you. Any chance he mentioned where he was going?'

'Not to me. Try his group,' he said, indicating a table where half a dozen well-inebriated men sat with several women in various stages of disrobing. The two young men ventured over, and Daniel recognised Burton, one of Thomas's colleagues and friends.

'Had his heartbroken,' Burton said. 'The ladies offered to take his mind off it, but he decided to go home and mope instead. Sorry lads, you just missed him.'

They thanked the group and departed the rowdy venue.

'Back to Thomas's house then,' Daniel sighed. Their walk to Thomas's abode took them along the riverfront and they had not progressed far before Gideon grabbed Daniel's arm.

'Is that not him?' he asked, looking at a figure standing on the rocks on the edge of the river.

Daniel did not wait for an answer but ran towards Thomas, calling his name. As they drew closer, Thomas came back onto land and walked away from them, gaining pace.

'Thom, wait,' Daniel said, and reaching him, saw he was not welcome.

'No Haywards, not tonight,' Thomas said, looking from Daniel to Gideon, and turning to go.

'Thom, you are as close to us as a brother,' Gideon said, following him, 'and therefore cannot elect to dispense with family. That is not how it works.'

'We have come from speaking with Matilda,' Daniel said, and Thomas faltered momentarily before continuing to walk towards his home.

'Do not say her name to me,' he said, his voice breaking.

'Stop,' Daniel insisted and Thomas did, running his hand across his eyes, not wanting to be seen as emotional.

'She is as miserable as you clearly are and this needs to be resolved,' Daniel continued.

'It cannot. Matilda made that perfectly clear.' He stopped and faced the men. 'She is no doubt right, we should step away now. To marry would be a mistake.'

'You don't mean that,' Daniel said.

'Leave me, Dan, Gids… go away.' He stumbled slightly and Daniel grabbed for him.

'I shall see Thomas home and stay the night,' he told his brother. 'Return home and advise there will be no discussion tonight as neither party is capable… well, one party in particular. Tell Elijah if he succeeded, I will need the conditions in the morning. He will understand.'

Gideon agreed and bidding them farewell, departed, leaving Daniel walking beside Thomas.

'You do not need to see me home,' Thomas mumbled.

'What were you doing by the river?'

'Not what you think. I was just resting a while.'

They walked in silence, broken only by two more attempts by Thomas to send Daniel home, before he stumbled up the front stairs, and the door opened. Teddy stood aside, a look of concern on his face.

'You are not looking well, uncle,' he said, with a nod to Daniel.

'It's been a rough day,' Daniel told him, and subtly pointed at his wedding finger and then touched his heart to indicate matters of the heart were at stake.

Teddy gave a nod. 'I'll make some tea then.'

'I'm going to bed,' Thomas called as he continued down the hallway to his bedroom. 'Goodnight Dan.'

Daniel followed him into the bedroom. 'I am not leaving you tonight, so give up on it.' He threw off his coat and hat and picked up Thomas's from the floor where he had just thrown them.

'Where is the ring?' Daniel asked, and patting down the pockets of Thomas's jacket, found it, and placed it in the top drawer beside Thomas's bed.

Thomas sat on the edge of his bed struggling with his boots. Daniel dropped beside him to help.

'I can do it!' he insisted. 'Go home.' He struggled for a few moments more, then swearing, dropped back onto his bed, boots and all.

Daniel pulled them off, along with Thomas's overgarments. Seeing him comfortable, he readied the couch in Thomas's large room to sleep on; it was not the first time he had spent the night there after many late nights together on the town.

'Elijah is brokering a peace deal. Will you listen to it?'

Thomas did not respond.

Daniel tried again. 'Do you want to discuss what happened?'

'No.'

With that, Thomas closed his eyes and said not another word.

*****

He did not expect to sleep and nor did he. Thomas spent hours staring at the ceiling, playing the scene over and over in his head, while Daniel slept nearby, the sound of his breathing low and constant providing some comfort. Thomas had feared this; feared that by losing Matilda—the only woman he had ever loved—he also lost the only family he had really known. The effect felt catastrophic.

She had always been his compass. Knowing where she lived, waiting for her to come of age to consider him a suitor, winning her hand. Now, it felt as if he had lost everything.

The room was dark, and he guessed it was close to three o'clock when he heard stirring and then a voice.

'Are you awake?' Daniel whispered.

'No.'

Daniel chuckled. 'Thom, I spoke with Matilda.'

There was silence. Daniel continued.

'She is as distraught as you are.'

'It is her doing.'

'You are both as stubborn as each other,' Daniel sighed with frustration.

'What would you have me do, Dan?' Thomas asked. 'I am a detective. I like my role and I am good at it.'

'You are,' Daniel agreed.

'I cannot give it up or change to ensure Matilda's safety, and she would not respect me if I did. I also need to provide for her comfort.'

'No one is expecting you to change your career, Thom, but you know how much Matilda's work means to her as well, whether we agree with it or not.'

Thomas said nothing for a time, the only sound being that of their breathing, before speaking again.

'Tell me, Dan, if Matilda was to be hurt or, Heaven Forbid, die, because of her investigation, how would you and the brothers, and Mr Hayward, regard me? Would you believe I failed her and the family? Would you all blame me for not being able to protect her or for not curbing Matilda's activities to ensure her safety?'

Daniel thought a moment before responding. 'Thom, I will discuss that with the family, as it is an understandable concern, but I know now what they will say. The same as I shall tell you – we know Matilda better than you, believe it or not.'

Thomas listened.

'We know what she needs and what she is like,' Daniel said. 'If you cannot be that for her, that person by her side despite her choices, she will find it in someone else. Could you bear that?'

'You know I could not,' he said in a low voice. 'But can I bear the other option?'

'Elijah was with Matilda when I left, working on a compromise. I suggest you spend tomorrow, or rather, today given it is morning, deciding what you could compromise and we meet this evening at home to discuss.'

'I appreciate what you are saying, but it is for us to resolve.'

'She is my sister and I will not have her abandoned. We will all resolve it,' Daniel said firmly. 'You would still have her?'

Thomas scoffed. 'She is my world,' he said again and cleared his throat of emotion.

'I know,' Daniel said. 'Seven o'clock – a meeting with Matilda and Elijah. We will fix this, Thom.'

'And if we can't?' he asked and rolled on his side away from Daniel. 'No.'

'No?'

'No. There will be no meeting. Matilda has declared her intent. So be it.'

Chapter 30

Matilda did not sleep. Earlier that evening when Daniel departed, she had spent an hour with Elijah talking in circles until he declared they could not fix the problem overnight and she should rest. Grateful to have her work to occupy her the next day, Matilda told not a soul—not even her two closest friends, Alice and Georgina—of the calling off of her engagement. She could not bear to say the words aloud and feared she would be inconsolable once she did. That brief respite was coming to an end as it was imperative to get Alaric Osbourne's confession to Thomas and Detective Dart, and she could not deliver it herself; she would have to write it and beg a favour of a friend or find a delivery boy, and that was bound to raise questions. She considered that Mr Osbourne may have recounted his story with the detectives after a night in the lock-up, but nevertheless, Matilda felt it was her duty to share the story before it was published. Thus, she finished up the first draft and went to speak with her editor, who welcomed her to take a seat and took the offered copy.

As Mrs Lawson read, Matilda sat silently waiting, her mind drifting, her eyes looking out across the room of working women but seeing nothing. She thought of the endless adventures with Thomas over the many years of their childhood, but her mind drifted to the moments of late. The stolen kisses, the way she felt seated so close to him at the Hayward table when she could sense his strength and know that soon they would be intimate. The thought made her shift in her seat and return her attention to Mrs Lawson, who was on the last page of Matilda's copy.

Shuffling the papers, Mrs Lawson declared: 'Excellent work, Matilda, and may I say what a turn up for the books,' she said, sitting back.

'Thank you, and yes indeed, Mrs Lawson,' Matilda said, with a smile. 'I shall keep the story close to my chest, and hopefully, should the murderer be revealed before we go to press, I will begin the story with that detail and fill it out.'

'If not, we shall write the piece about the petty bridal crimes and suggest Mrs Greenwood's demise was possibly a result of her being in the wrong place at the wrong time. Readers will infer what they might. Do you believe Mr Osbourne that he did not commit the murder?'

'I do, and only because I think he wanted to harm Mrs Greenwood himself,' Matilda said, and explained, realising that did not make a great deal of sense. 'As he was recounting his story to me, I had the strangest feeling that he was somewhat annoyed he did not get to perform the deed, it was most extraordinary.'

'I imagine then that her brutal demise is somewhat satisfying for him, even if he didn't have the stomach to do it himself,' Mrs Lawson mused. 'I believe we are all capable of violence if provoked or under duress, and that is a long-held grudge.'

'Yes, did it boil over or has it cooled somewhat?' Matilda mused. 'With your permission, Mrs Lawson, I would like to give a copy of my story now to Thomas and Detective Dart before we go to print... they arrived after Mr Osbourne's outburst and then Mr Osbourne refused to speak.'

'I think that is probably best,' she agreed.

Matilda thanked her, rising hurriedly and gathered the papers so as not to encourage any discussion about the detectives and to produce a copy for the two men. She could not deliver it herself, but should she, and take the opportunity to see and speak with Thomas? But why had he not called on her now that he too must be of a cooler head? Her heart told her it could not be over, but the ill feeling in her stomach suggested otherwise.

*****

Thomas had thrown himself into his work with a gusto that alarmed his partner, Harry. He was on edge from no sleep, barely touched any food that Harry tried to put in front of him and had a short fuse that even Alaric Osbourne looked somewhat concerned about.

'You can keep me in here all you like, Detectives, but it won't make me admit to a murder I did not commit,' he said again. 'All I am guilty of is trying to right wrongs. If more people did that, then your job might be easier.'

'If you did not waste our time, our job would be easier!' Thomas started forward, his hand flexed, and Harry stepped in.

'Mr Osbourne, if we are to believe your story—and we do not encourage the public to take the law into their own hands—who might you suggest killed Mrs Greenwood?'

'I cannot imagine.'

'I imagine you can,' Thomas hissed. 'And what of the flowers in Petronella's possession?'

'You are on a first-name basis with her, ask her yourself,' he snorted with derision and jealousy.

'Don't worry, I will,' Thomas assured him. The two men glared at each other. But Harry read Osbourne's reaction; he did not want Miss Petronella Pettyfore involved or accused of anything illicit.

Harry was right. Alaric Osbourne swallowed and said: 'I found the flowers and gave them to her, or rather, I asked my nephew to give them to her on my behalf.'

The two men studied him.

'Where did you find them?' Harry asked.

'On the ground near a bin in Bridal Lane.'

Thomas's eyes narrowed as he watched the man, reading his face for lies. His patience—and there had been precious little to begin with—wore out. 'Enough then,' Thomas snapped, 'let's go and bring Petronella in,' he said to Harry and went to stand. Osbourne held up his hands to halt him.

'Wait, wait,' he said, hurriedly. 'If I tell you the truth, you will think I killed that woman and I did not. I need your assurance you will hear me fairly.'

'You have our assurance of that, Mr Osbourne,' Harry said calmly. 'Proceed.'

Osbourne did not proceed until Thomas gave a small nod of agreement and sat again, webbing his fingers, placing his hands on the table and leaning forward, like a foreboding presence. Alaric Osbourne took a breath and began his story.

'I confess to having taken money from Walter Burgess, not stolen, but rightfully taken what he should have provided Miss Sophia Emery after getting her in the family way,' Osbourne said, his voice harsh. 'He has plenty, and he just discarded—'

'—yes, yes, we get it, move on,' Thomas said.

Alaric Osbourne reined in his anger. 'Burgess found out I was involved in the break-in at his premises. I was seen but fleetingly on the day, but enough to be recognised by one of his people… I have my suspicions it was his man who delivers his books to us—he is a client of Mr Dalton's accountancy practice—or the lad in the stable who I thrashed at poker or—'

'Mr Osbourne! We don't have all day,' Thomas growled, and Harry gave Thomas a frustrated look. They had all day when it came to a confession and solving a murder, and Harry did not want to miss out on any clues that might help their case.

'Proceed to the crime please, Mr Osbourne,' Harry suggested, giving Thomas a look that suggested he settle in. He would never berate the younger detective in front of another, but Thomas understood and appeared somewhat contrite by sitting back and settling down.

'Burgess came looking for me. I was on a break from my work and I had come downstairs to Bridal Lane. He wanted me to follow him and I did not want to go with him. I knew he would thrash me. He is strong and brutish, good with his fists.'

Thomas agreed with the summary from his meeting with Walter Burgess and motioned for Osbourne to continue.

'I didn't want him making a scene out the front of my workplace and *Blooming Blossoms*, so I moved away but he started on me before we had cleared the premises… angrily venting. When I turned, I saw Mrs Greenwood. She had left the shop after delivering lace and must have overheard some of what Burgess said. She had that self-righteous look on her face,' he said with a sneer.

'And then?' Harry asked.

'Burgess pushed me up the street and she's following behind, gobbing on and giving us both a sermon about morality.'

Thomas and Harry exchanged looks; Osbourne continued.

'He's getting stuck into me, she's hammering away at both of us and following us, people are looking. She was as good as dead the moment she opened her mouth in Bridal Lane. Burgess forces me into this service lane and she keeps following. By now, I'm fearing for my life, he's a big man,' Osbourne said, and stopped, taking a breath and licking his lower lip.

Neither man interrupted as Alaric Osbourne had arrived at the part of his story they most wanted to hear.

'Then, the old bag says she knows Burgess's wife and she was going to tell her that Burgess had sexual relations outside of his marriage. He nearly exploded, and he dropped his grip on me and turned and shook her. Next thing, he's grabbed this bit of lace she's holding, wrapped it round her neck and he's strangling her.' He stopped, breathing fast.

'And what did you do?' Thomas asked, expecting him to say he ran.

'I yelled at him to stop and then her feet went from under her and she fell. I couldn't get past them to run, and I admit I wanted to, but Burgess was like a man possessed. He didn't leave it at that, because Mrs Greenwood was still moving. So, he picked up a bottle that was lying near a bin and clubbed her with it, good and hard. I didn't like her but she didn't deserve that. I jumped over her and began to run but he caught up with me and said if I tell anyone it would be his word over mine and no one would believe me.' Alaric looked from one man to the next to gauge the reactions.

'So you did what he said, kept your mouth shut, left her there and ran?' Thomas asked.

Osbourne nodded. 'I couldn't save her; Burgess was too big for me to take on. He'd be no stranger to hitting women.' He said the latter with disgust.

'Perhaps some reflection on your own character might not go astray, given you just struck a young lady,' Harry suggested.

Osbourne lowered his eyes and had the good grace to look ashamed. 'I'll apologise to Miss Hayward.'

'Keep right away from her,' Thomas growled, and Alaric Osbourne nodded quickly, getting the message loud and clear. 'Continue. So, you left Mrs Greenwood and Burgess in the alley…'

Osbourne sighed and continued: 'I grabbed the big bouquet she'd been carrying because I didn't want anything in the lane that might lead the constabulary to *Blooming Blossoms* or finding out about our work, and I ran. When I got back to work, I told my boss that Mrs Greenwood gave me the flowers to give to my sweetheart. Later, I called to my nephew when I spotted him from my upstairs window, and told him to give the bouquet to Petronella. He's young,' he said with a shrug, 'mixed things up. He was supposed to put a note in it that I'd given him—I wanted to tell Petronella what had happened—but he had a few bunches on him for delivery and put the note in the wrong bouquet, or so he says.'

'That's why she didn't meet you that night and why Miss Hayward had the note in her bouquet?' Thomas said, accepting the pain that saying Matilda's name caused him.

Alaric Osbourne nodded. 'Honest truth,' he said. 'I don't know where Petronella was all night before she was seen with the bouquet, but that's how she got it.' He sat back, finished and spent.

'Then how did you get beaten up and left for us to find the day thereafter?' Harry asked.

'Burgess didn't leave it at that. He thought I needed another reminder, so his thugs tracked me down on my lunch break and with their fists, delivered the message to keep my mouth shut. That's it. I swear.'

'The first note said "PAID". What did that mean?' Thomas pushed on.

Alaric Osbourne swallowed, getting deeper and deeper into his admission of guilt. 'One of our subjects paid and we could provide the money to the jilted woman. That one was not Burgess, I would have to find his name—'

Harry cut him off, concluding the interview. 'Thank you, Mr Osbourne, that won't be necessary at this stage.'

'What part did the clairvoyant play in it all?' Thomas asked, not finished yet and surprising Osbourne, who shrugged.

'Nothing that I know of, or can recall.'

Thomas waited, staring at Alaric Osbourne until he relented and said: 'Burgess paid her and my nephew to say they'd never seen him and he'd never been in the lane.'

Thomas shook his head, swearing under his breath. He rose and Harry joined him; the two men turned to depart, hearing Osbourne calling out behind him.

'You cannot leave me locked up like this without telling me what you intend to charge me with?'

'We can,' Thomas assured him, and Harry calmed the young man.

'Sit tight, Mr Osbourne, I'll be back shortly.' He followed Thomas out and onto the street.

'Ease up, Thom. If no one has a charge to press against him and we have not caught him in the act of committing a crime, we have little on him. Why did you ask about the clairvoyant?'

Thomas ran a hand through his hair. 'I remember

Matilda saying something about the clairvoyant had a lot to say about the murder, but I never found out what that was. Maybe she saw what Osbourne just described, but regardless, both Madam Gerta and the boy have been lying to us, wasting our time.'

'Steady up.'

Thomas turned, frowning at Harry, who held up his hands in a conciliatory manner.

'I'm not saying they weren't in the wrong. I'm downright annoyed that they've made us chase our tails,' he said. 'But you've got to remember Burgess probably paid Madame Gerta and the delivery lad more than they'd earn in months. It's easy to have morals when your belly is full. When it's not, who knows what we might do in the same situation.'

Thomas looked at his partner and gave a nod. 'You're right.'

'Really?' Harry said with a smile. 'I like the sound of that,' and Thomas chuckled. Harry continued: 'So, do you believe Osbourne? I am convinced his story holds truth.'

Thomas sighed, put his hands in his pockets and looked skyward, closing his eyes as he felt the sunlight on his face. 'I think it was the truth – he was involved, but he didn't do the deed. She was not a small woman and it would have taken some strength to strangle her – he is not the strongest of men. Besides, there was no call for him to do so when he had little to lose. Burgess had a lot more.' He shrugged. 'I don't care, let him go if you see fit.'

'We could call on Miss Hayward and ask what Osbourne confessed to her and what the clairvoyant said. Did you not say she had information to share?'

Her very name caused him a sharp pain in his chest as if he could not breathe, and his eyes opened as he grimaced.

'Ah, Thom, what is going on?' Harry asked.

He looked away and mumbled: 'She returned her ring.'

Thomas heard Harry's gasp of surprise. 'No,' Harry groaned. 'You can fix this, Thom. You two are destined.'

'Please, Harry, let's not talk about it. Not here, I can't do that.'

Harry nodded. 'Alright, but I am here when you are ready or need to talk. Stay a moment while I see Mr Osbourne is released for now.'

Thomas nodded and leaned against a street lamp post as he waited for his partner. On his return, they walked around to their station's headquarters, neither saying a word and both uncomfortable in the revelation and silence. Their thoughts were interrupted the moment they set foot in the building.

'Detectives, I have a letter for you,' John the desk sergeant said, waving a small missile in their direction. 'It's addressed to both of you.' He handed it to Thomas, who was nearest.

Thomas pulled the papers from the envelope and recognised the writing immediately.

'Who dropped this in, Sergeant?' he asked.

'A young delivery man, just fifteen minutes or so passed.'

'Thank you,' Thomas said, disappointed. Had Matilda dropped it in herself, she may have come to see him, may have wanted to speak with him, but she did not.

'What is it?' Harry asked.

'It is Matilda's pending column and Alaric Osbourne's

confession to her. She has made a note that she will complete the story when we solve the case.' He handed it to Harry without reading it. 'We don't need to call on her now, it's all here.'

'Come then. Let us make a cup of tea and we shall read what Mr Osbourne had to say to Miss Hayward,' Harry said and led the way as Thomas struggled to regain his composure of indifference.

Chapter 31

Sunday lunch was a sober affair – a luncheon for the married or widowed women as it happened. Alice could not accompany Daniel due to a commitment with her guardian, Elijah was on his rostered shift and thus, Georgina had taken the opportunity to visit her parents for a number of days in the country, leaving Minnie, Betty, and Aunt Audrey to round the conversation with Mr Hayward, a restless Daniel and Gideon, and a very unhappy Matilda.

As soon as it was polite to leave, Matilda rose.

'Please excuse me, I am feeling very weary today,' she said.

Mr Hayward reached for her hand. 'Are you alright my dear? We can call for the doctor, or Elijah for that matter.'

'No, thank you, Pa, that won't be necessary,' she said. 'I am just very tired.' She departed the room, leaving her father to explain in more detail why Thomas wasn't present and the cause of her discontentment.

Matilda had only been settled for ten minutes when she heard a knock on the door. Aunt Audrey entered.

'May I?' her stately aunt enquired.

'Of course,' Matilda said and indicated the seat opposite to where she sat at the window.

Aunt Audrey sat, and Matilda felt her aunt studying her before she cleared her throat to speak. 'If your heart is so broken, child, why have you not put an end to this and spoken with Thomas?'

Matilda looked dismayed at her directness. 'I have no way to solve the problem, Aunt Audrey. It is our nature, what are we to do when neither of us can change who we are?'

Her aunt nodded. 'I am not so sure of that. The problem could be solved if you were prepared to accept a different course of action, a different role perhaps. Could not Betty help assign you to something you would enjoy that would also provide peace of mind to your husband-to-be?'

'Perhaps. She does not know of the termination of our engagement, although I suspect Pa has just told her.' Matilda blinked away tears and continued: 'You have been active in the community for many years, Aunt Audrey, as has Mrs Lawson, Betty, and many women. Is it about picking a partner who will accept that work or do I have to be a mother and wife and wait until, heaven forbid, I am widowed to do the work I want to do without censure?'

'I think every woman must make their own decision, Matilda dear, but for me, love always prevailed. I did not wish to reach old age and regret not having had true love or pursued true love. I can live without achieving all I was capable of, but the regret would be larger if I had not experienced the love I shared with Samuel.' She paused to gather herself and added, 'I would give up all my community work in a heartbeat for one more day with him.'

'Oh, Aunt Audrey,' Matilda's voice quavered and she turned her gaze out the window, taking in her aunt's words.

She replied in a whisper: 'I don't know how to be without him, but I don't know how we will go forward without these constant battles.'

'Then the question is, are you prepared to lose Thomas for your work? Does it mean that much to you? And I am guessing from the state I find you in, you know you cannot give him up or imagine either of you with other partners.'

The thought visibly affected Matilda, her hand going to her heart.

'Dear girl, fix this before it is too late.'

'He doesn't want to see me,' Matilda said. 'He refused to come home with Daniel when invited. Pa dropped in on him the other evening but he was not home and Teddy said he would let Thomas know. He has not repaid the visit.'

'Thomas, too, is in a lot of pain, I imagine. But I know that young man and the respect he holds for your father. He will come if James summons him; I shall see to it.'

With that, Aunt Audrey leant forward, placed an affectionate kiss on her niece's forehead and went to issue orders to her brother to summon Thomas now.

*****

Thomas felt as ill in the stomach as he had after a wild night of imbibing alcohol with Daniel, but this time, he was stone cold sober. Mr Hayward had summoned him to the house where, as a young man, he had spent a great deal of his childhood, to speak with the man who was more a father to him than his own, and the thought filled him with dread. Matilda would be there, in the house. Or what if she was not? That would be even worse. He couldn't bear to be in the house he spent most of his life in and not have the happy future he had foreseen. But he could not ignore the request to call on Mr Hayward; that would be the height of rudeness and disrespect. He had to go.

'It was bound to happen at some time, Uncle,' Teddy said, as they drank tea together on the verandah of Thomas's house late Sunday afternoon. The renovation work was almost complete to make it a suitable home for Thomas's new bride, and Teddy had found himself alternative accommodation with a fellow apprentice chef. Everything was planned, except now it did not matter. There would be no wedding and Thomas would be here alone.

'Sorry?' Thomas turned to Teddy, 'did you say something?'

'Yes, I've said lots of things this week that you've missed,' he jested, and Thomas gave him an apologetic smile. 'The visit… it had to happen at some time, you have to see the family… you and Daniel are best friends, it is inevitable. Best get on with it.'

'I know,' Thomas agreed.

They sat in silence for a long while, as men do, comfortable with not speaking, until Thomas said in a low voice: 'I am exhausted with the effort of trying not to think of her, but yet I don't want to not think of her.' He groaned, embarrassed by his honesty and pained by the separation. He felt Teddy's hand on his shoulder.

'I have never known you to be affected by anything as much as this, Uncle, and understandably so. I wish I had some way to help or some words that could be of use.'

Thomas nodded and recovered himself. 'I will be well soon enough, but thank you.'

They finished their tea and then Thomas rose to groom himself and change before dropping in on Mr Hayward and facing the pain head-on.

*****

The luncheon guests had long gone when Harriet hurriedly knocked on the open door of Mr Hayward's study.

'He's here?' Mr Hayward asked, rising, and she gave a quick nod.

'He's coming up the path now,' Harriet said and left the room. He heard the loyal housekeeper hastening up the stairs to see Matilda. They had agreed on a strategy… Harriet would distract Matilda on Thomas's arrival so that Mr Hayward could talk to the young man before hopefully summoning Matilda to his study as well. He did not want Matilda seeing Thomas and confronting him or worse still, skipping out of the house before James Hayward had a chance to work through the issue for both parties who seemed at an impasse.

Mr Hayward was unsure what to expect from Thomas. The young man had been absent now for a week, long enough to work through his emotions, and Mr Hayward had expected his visit well before now. Would Thomas be despairing, perhaps distant and cold, or belligerent?

He moved to the front door, took a deep breath and with a glance upstairs, he gave Harriet a nod. She knocked on Matilda's room and entered, making enough noise and fuss to distract from Thomas's entrance until Mr Hayward could get him safely ensconced in his study.

He opened the door before Thomas could knock and Thomas removed his hat, accepting the invitation to enter. Closing the door behind him, Mr Hayward hurried Thomas to his study, closing the door behind them. He saw Thomas's relief to be behind closed doors.

Mr Hayward was taken aback by the young man's appearance. Thomas was thinner, his eyes were dark with exhaustion and he had the look of a haunted man.

'Oh Thom, I am sorry. I should have insisted upon your visit earlier. I try and let my children—and that includes you—work out their problems before I interfere, it was remiss of me.'

Thomas shook his head. 'It is… that is… it can't be helped…' his voice trailed off, unsure of what to say. It was of consequence. His separation from Matilda was the pain that racked his body from dawn to dusk and all through the night, buried only by excessive drinking to aid in sleeping.

Mr Hayward approached the young man and placing his hands on Thomas's shoulders, pulled him in and embraced him. He felt Thomas's confusion, his rigid stance – Thomas was not a man accustomed to affection from a parent.

'Sit, please,' Mr Hayward said, pulling away. 'Would you like a tea or something stiffer?'

'Whatever you are having, thank you,' Thomas answered, and Mr Hayward poured them both a drink of whiskey, before settling on the couch opposite. Thomas fidgeted, cleared his throat and took a large gulp of his drink before placing it down on the table.

'If it is of any consolation, Matilda is as bereft as you appear to be, son,' Mr Hayward said and watched as Thomas drank in his words and seemed to take comfort from them.

'Do you still love her?'

'Of course. Forever,' he answered quickly.

Mr Hayward nodded. 'Do you still wish to marry her?'

'Yes. It is not I who declared it otherwise.'

Mr Hayward nodded. 'But yet you could not compromise to marry on her terms.'

Thomas's jaw clenched and he went to speak, but then stopped, letting the statement hang in the air. At this time, he would have agreed to anything, but that would not provide a resolution when they next fought and he knew that was inevitable.

Mr Hayward sat back. 'You know, Thom, I have never raised my hand to any of my children, you included.'

Thomas frowned. 'Are you to start now? I am a bit old for it.'

Mr Hayward chuckled. 'If I could get away with it, I might. I say this because there is a recollection I wish to share with you.'

Thomas nodded. 'Please.'

Mr Hayward continued. 'I was strapped as a young man, my father was very stern, a strict master.'

'As was mine and I too felt the strap from him often,' Thomas added.

'I know. When your father went away on business for a month and I suggested you remain with us rather than go to your great aunt, your father permitted me to punish you then or anytime I saw fit.'

'I bet he did,' Thomas said with a grimace. 'But you didn't.'

'No. From my own boyhood experience, I believe whipping and strapping a child does nothing but instil fear and humiliation. I hoped that respect, the sternness of my countenance and the threat of missing out on things that a child desires, does the trick. However, having said that, there was one occasion I came very, very close to administering the strap to you and Daniel. I was so angry.'

Thomas frowned. 'I don't recall ever coming that close to a strapping.'

'It was the time when you boys were about three-and-ten, Matilda was nine years or so, and we were enjoying the weekend at my brother's farm when he was alive, you were with us.'

'Uncle Lawrie,' Thomas said and smiled.

'That's him, dear Lawrence. Anyway, you and Daniel were forbidden to take the boat on the dam or go near it without an adult present, but regardless, boys will be boys,' Mr Hayward said, narrowing his eyes.

Thomas groaned, remembering what was to come.

'Matilda was with you, as she always was, and despite

your beliefs that nothing would happen, you capsized, and she could not swim as capably as both of you.'

Thomas nodded at the memory. As terrifying now as it was that day when he thought she might drown.

Thomas said, 'I remember once we did all get to shore, Daniel racing to get you and your anger. Uncle Lawrie looked after us and you raced off, carrying Matilda.'

'I couldn't look at either of you for a day or so. I was so angry,' Mr Hayward said.

'I know. That was worse than any strapping I got from my father.'

Mr Hayward smiled. 'Once I calmed down and got the full story, I learnt that of course Matilda had insisted on coming with you when you told her she was not to come.'

'That was very much how it always was,' Thomas said, relaxing a little and smiling.

'And I learnt that while Daniel could barely save himself, you pushed Matilda to shore, even at the risk of your own life. It was you, Thom, who saved my little girl.'

Thomas looked away with discomfort.

'And what if I can't save her? That day may come,' he said, in a voice almost inaudible.

'That is my point,' Mr Hayward said. 'Matilda has not changed. She is still following you around, meddling in your business. She will always be headstrong and do what she sets her mind to doing, and to some extent, I take the blame and credit for that.'

Thomas gave a knowing nod and a small smile.

Mr Hayward continued. 'You will always do your best to

protect her, Thom. Should you fail, then it is not for want of trying. But you have never cut her down, clipped her wings or tried to change the person she is before so that you may seek comfort in her safety.'

'I want to, I will not lie. I love her and her sense of adventure, but there is not one day that I am at work that I am not worried about what she is doing and where she might be,' he confessed and rubbed a hand over his face.

'I know, son. But would you like her if she was a bird in a cage?'

Thomas buried his face in his hands, emotional with exhaustion and loss. Mr Hayward leaned over and placed a hand on his shoulder.

'We have no expectations of you, son, except to love her and make her happy for all the days you have together.'

Thomas sat up straighter, wiped his face and nodded. 'Thank you, sir.'

'Soon you will have to get used to calling me Pa like everyone else,' he joked. 'Now, would you like to quietly leave, or do you need some time, or would you like to see Matilda?'

'Matilda, please,' Thomas said, rising as Mr Hayward did and wiping his face again on his coat sleeve.

Mr Hayward glanced once more at Thomas from the doorway to ensure he was under control. Thomas gave him a nod and James Hayward smiled, relieved to see the young man looked as if the world had fallen from his shoulders. Satisfied, he hoped his daughter would feel the same way. He turned and from the open doorway of the study, called her name.

Harriet ventured from Matilda's room. 'I shall fetch her, Mr Hayward,' she said, with a knowing smile.

Matilda appeared moments later in a soft lilac dress, her hair loose and long, her face pale and wan.

'Pa?' She looked over the railing down at her father. 'Is all well?'

'Yes, my dear. Could you join me in my study for a moment?' he asked, and watched as she came down the stairs towards him. He moved inside, out of the doorway, and she entered, halting and emitting a gasp.

'Thomas!'

'Matilda,' Thomas said her name shakily.

And then, in keeping with her unconventional upbringing and often disregard of the appropriate rules of conduct, she ran to him and wrapped her arms around him in an embrace that he had to step back to balance. Thomas lowered his head, hiding his face in her hair and holding her tightly as she wept.

Mr Hayward smiled and leaving his office door ajar, stepped away, trusting the two young people to reconcile appropriately.

Chapter 32

Women's Journal
Tuesday, 12 March 1889
Fortnightly edition Vol.1, No.37.
Price, 3d.

The mysterious notes in the bridal
bouquets

FEATURE STORY: A crime of passion, a
murder mystery, and the flower shop
at the very heart of the story. A
SPECIAL FEATURE by Matilda Hayward.
Illustrations by Georgina Urry.

--oOo--

This tale that ends with death began
with good intentions. A boy disowned

seeks, in his adulthood, to ensure women like his mother are never abandoned and left destitute. He aims to find justice for them, but events conspired against him, leading to the death of a well-known community member and worker, Mrs Louise Greenwood. We cannot name the boy, now a man, as to date no charges have been laid, but he has agreed to share his story with the Women's Journal in exchange for his anonymity. We shall call him Mr O.

The story began two decades ago. Mr O's mother, an innocent young woman with dreams of her own, worked in the household of Mr Gaston Greenwood – in a grand house with extensive gardens and where regular social events were held. Mr Greenwood was a dashing young man in his twenties and popular with his peers and the ladies. He had recently taken a wife and the joining of families further secured his wealth.

Unbeknown to his wife, the late Mrs Louise Greenwood, he continued to seek the company of women and took advantage of the young ladies in his employ. Mr O's mother was one of these ladies. To her dismay and distress, she found herself to be with child, but Mr Greenwood vehemently denied his involvement and dismissed her, penniless and with no reference.

The story we recount is what Mr O recalls of his childhood as an illegitimate child. His mother was disowned by her family and alone and pregnant in the world, but she would not give up her child, a child to which Mr O recounted she gave the best life that she could and loved with great affection. Mr O was but a boy when his father, Gaston Greenwood, died – a father who never claimed him and he never met. His mother made him swear he would not make himself known to the family despite her treatment, and that he would be his own man and make the best life for himself.

That he did, but Mr O was bitter. 'To make ends meet, my mother worked as a seamstress, washed and cleaned. She took any work she could get, so we had board and food on the table. She told people she was widowed as it was more respectable,' he said. 'But my mother told me Mrs Greenwood was as much to blame as her husband. She knew of her husband's philandering, that he had forced himself upon my mother, but regardless, Mrs Greenwood dismissed his mother and several other women in the family way with no compassion, nor assistance.

'She drove the young women away, laying shame upon them. If she could have made them wear a scarlet letter "A" for adulteress, I've no doubt she would have,' Mr O said, referring to Mr Nathaniel Hawthorne's 1850 novel of the same theme. Mr O later learnt of several women in the Greenwood's service who took their own lives when faced with nowhere to turn.

Moving forward to today, almost three decades later, Mr O is a successful young man with an honest trade. His beloved mother passed with fever and exhaustion not long after he came of age, gone now these ten years. His position affords him a comfortable life, but Mr O wanted more. He wanted to honour his mother and so partnering with a young lady—we shall call Miss P—discovered a way to help abandoned young women in the family way.

A house on the southside of our city

provides a temporary shelter for these young ladies who share in the duties to support each other. Mr O and his companion, Miss P, then seek to obtain a one-payment dowry from the gentleman in question, to assist the mothers-to-be. If the ladies choose not to wed, they have the funds to start again somewhere and raise their child. If they would like to be wed, Mr O and Miss P find a gentleman of good nature and kind heart, who will benefit from the dowry and accept and care for his new wife and child with genuine affection.

A young bridal dressmaker who helps brides-to-be in the family way also assists, providing modest and discreet bridal dresses for the hurried exchange of vows.

But how do these three charitable people meet and share information with the utmost discretion? They have set up a system of delivering small notes in bouquets from Blooming Blossoms to communicate when help was needed and identify their subject. Many a child and young woman have been saved by Mr O and his partners' efforts but not all men pay willingly, in the same manner as Mr Gaston Greenwood shirked his responsibilities decades earlier. Thus, some were removed of their funds unlawfully but were not in a position to report the theft to the police without uncovering their own involvement which may have caused a scandal.

Some of our readers will not support Mr O's work or moral stand, but Mrs Celia Dalton, proprietress of Blooming Blossoms flower shop recently learnt of the notes being sent in her bouquets and does not object. Mrs Dalton believes the community has a Christian duty to protect its most vulnerable members.

However, Mrs Louise Greenwood—a victim of her husband's infidelity—did not support the work and when she discovered what was afoot and that the letters were passed in bouquets from Blooming Blossoms, Mrs Greenwood advised Mrs Dalton that despite their lengthy friendship, she intended to withdraw her lace and ribbon supplies. It is unknown how Mrs Greenwood came about this information. Later, on overhearing a discussion between Mr O and another man she recognised as Mr Walter Burgess, Mrs Greenwood learnt

Mr Burgess was being asked to pay the bounty and she threatened to tell his wife.

In a fit of rage and ensuring his indiscretion remained a secret, Mr Burgess murdered Mrs Greenwood, strangling her with a piece of lace she had upon her, and ensuring her demise with a blow to the head. Mr O was present at the time and was also threatened. Ironically, Mrs Greenwood did not know that Mr O was the illegitimate son of her husband.

Brisbane's finest detectives, Thomas Ashdown and Harry Dart, have put to bed this case, charging Walter Burgess with the murder of Mrs Louise Greenwood, and dismissing Mr O with a warning on this occasion as no one has stepped forward to press charges. The tarot reader, Madam Gerta, was the last to see Mrs Louise Greenwood alive as the community worker and lacemaker followed Mr Burgess down Bridal Lane.

As for Mr O, he vows to continue his work in memory of his mother, and his partners have acknowledged their commitment. So be careful gentlemen, for your liaisons and dalliances have the power to ruin lives or in some cases, maybe your own.

Readers wishing to make donations to the southside unwed mothers' home or any ladies requiring assistance may contact the writer care of the Women's Journal.

Chapter 33

Thomas sighed and placed the *Women's Journal* down on his dining table. He looked over at the three men in his company – Daniel his best man, and the groomsmen, Harry his partner and nephew, Teddy.

'She had to put in that last line,' he said and shook his head.

Harry laughed. 'Never mind, Thom. Miss Hayward has promised you she will be accompanied on all her assignments out of the office from now on, a compromise of sorts.'

'I think if you held out another week, she might have given up the job,' Daniel said, and seeing Thomas' look of surprise, gave him a wink and laughed.

'I'd help you with that necktie, but I might accidentally strangle you,' Thomas retorted, making Daniel laugh again as he attempted to tie it correctly.

The men were dressing for the church and Thomas' anxiety was evident to all present.

'Relax and enjoy the day, Uncle Thom. It has arrived at

last, and soon you will be celebrating as husband and wife,' Teddy said, moving to assist Daniel.

Thomas drew a deep breath. 'I will relax when Matilda says "I do" and I know she hasn't changed her mind on the way to the church.'

Daniel cheered Thomas up by saying. 'She said the same, more or less, about you.'

Thomas smiled, relieved to hear this and moved out of the room away from the men momentarily, to the front verandah. Tonight, he would lay with Matilda. He was a strong and determined man, not one easily alarmed and somewhat hardened by his experiences, but Thomas involuntarily shivered at the anticipation of what was to come and how their evening would play out. He had loved Matilda since the first day he set eyes on her. It was as if the sun had turned its face to him and lit him with life and purpose.

Sure, on that day and the many others that followed, he was there to play with Daniel and his brothers, games full of warring and misadventure, but his eyes always sought Matilda out. That strangest of creatures – a girl, the Hayward brothers' only sister and today, his wife.

They had played at romance over the years and had their fights, God knows she is stubborn – was then, is now, he thought with a small smile. He had enjoyed his years as a young man sowing his seeds with Daniel when Matilda was too young to be of consequence or of age to be social, and once she came out in society, he waited. Tonight, he would say "my wife" when he introduced her. Who knows what was to follow but he would love to have a family soon, a daughter and a son, especially a daughter – a rarity in his family line. Seeing Petronella's daughter momentarily stopped his heart, but she was too young to be his child; another potential impediment to the altar, but one quickly removed.

Once he had a family, he could then be anxious about Matilda and the children, but it might keep Matilda out of the office and away from his investigations. A silver lining indeed.

'Come on then, Thom,' a voice said behind him and he turned to see Daniel, resplendent in his morning suit. 'Let Pa hand Matilda over to you for keeping.'

Thomas smiled. 'At last.'

*****

Matilda hugged Harriet who had started dabbing her eyes very early that morning.

'You shall have no tears left for the wedding,' Matilda scolded her, 'and you are the only one I can rely on to cry. Aunt Audrey is not likely to do so, and my brothers are only too happy to see me out of the house and off Pa's hands, I imagine.'

'I have been saving my tears so fear not, there are plenty to last the distance,' Harriet assured her with a smile. 'You look so beautiful.'

Her maid of honour and bridesmaids agreed. Matilda thanked Minnie, Alice and Georgina. She had hoped her two closest friends from her schooling years at the Girls' Grammar could attend but one was heavy with child and not able to travel from interstate where she now resided with her husband, and her other dear friend was abroad. Nevertheless, her firm friendships with the three ladies present, who were all likely to be sisters-in-law like Minnie in the near future, delighted her.

'What is your earliest memory of Thomas?' Georgina asked as she tamed a stray curl that had fallen from her coiffure style. She was not used to being so preened and fashionable, having hailed from the farm, but the effect was most pleasing.

Matilda had only to think for a moment before she broke out in a smile and embraced Harriet in her memory.

'The very first time Daniel brought Thomas home, they raced in, wet and dirty from the creek where they had met and decided to fish before falling in.'

Harriett laughed. 'I remember. I was always cleaning wet and muddy boot marks off the floor,' she said and sighed as if she missed the exercise.

'Do you remember, Harriett, that Daniel said, "this is Thom, he lives down the street?" He then said: "Thom, this is Harriett and my sister, Matilda," and then Thomas bowed to me,' Matilda said, her hand going to her heart at the memory. 'I was very touched and surprised and felt very important, being all of about five or six at the time. He was the first gentleman to bow to me except for Pa when he was play-acting.'

Harriett laughed again and said: 'If memory serves me,

Daniel then said, "you don't have to bow to her, she's just my sister".

The ladies laughed and Alice declared, 'How charming.'

'Thomas was always a charming child,' Harriett said. 'He was a good-looking, well-dressed young lad and I believe his father was very strict about good manners.'

'He was very strict about everything, from what I hear,' Matilda agreed, and allowed Harriett to preen over her a little more.

'Will he be here? Mr Ashdown senior?' Minnie asked.

'No,' Matilda said, somewhat relieved. 'He was not well enough to travel, but Sewell, Thomas's brother and Sewell's wife are coming, along with numerous friends from the police force and some of Thomas' school friends as well,' Matilda said, a little nervous at parading before them as she walked down the aisle.

'I declare you the most beautiful bride,' Harriett said, stepping back and stopping short of saying 'that she had ever seen' given Minnie was present.

Now Matilda felt weepy, and her bridesmaids stepped in to ensure she did not cry.

'I will feel much better once we are formally wed, and it is official. Then I shall relax and enjoy the celebration.'

'I can't imagine anything would keep Thomas from the altar today,' Georgina assured her. 'He loves you so completely and he does seem quite tolerant and open to adventure,' she teased.

'And well you know from the scrapes I've led you into,' Matilda said and shared a laugh with her eccentric friend.

She glanced once more at her reflection, and pleased with the outcome of the painstaking dressing, suggested: 'Let us join Pa downstairs for the church ride. I am ready to become Mrs Thomas Ashdown.'

*****

Daniel stood beside his best friend at the altar, fanned out next to him were Harry and Teddy. He was looking forward to seeing his belle, Alice, walk up the aisle in her bridesmaid apparel, but he could not help but be fascinated by his best friend. He had known Thomas was in love with Matilda, Thomas had been for years, but his usually stoic and conservative friend was heightened of emotion, a rare thing given how deliberated Thomas's usual actions were around Matilda. Truth be known, it made Daniel feel quite emotional as well. His sister, the Hayward family member he was and always had been closest to, was marrying his dearest friend. He placed a hand on Thomas' shoulder and Thomas turned to smile at him.

The church was almost full of guests now – a few late-comers rushed in to take a seat before the bride, her father, and bridal party made their appearance to walk down the aisle. The priest had joined the men at the altar, and Daniel smiled as Harry whispered to Thomas to stop fidgeting and Thomas grimaced. All was as it should be.

Aunt Audrey was seated in the front row and caught Daniel's eyes. On one side of her sat Betty with a space left for Mr Hayward to slip into the seat next to Betty once he had handed Matilda to Thomas's care. Aunt Audrey gave Daniel a small smile and nod of approval. After all, the muddy boys had grown to be responsible men and the bridal party did look most distinguished. Daniel was concerned if Matilda did not arrive shortly, Thomas might self-combust. And then the organ music started and Thomas drew in a deep breath and turned to face the back of the church, as did all eyes including those of his groomsmen.

Minnie arrived first, walking up the aisle looking beautiful, and sought out her husband to give him a special smile; Amos was seated on the other side of Aunt Audrey as expected – he was her favourite. Following was Georgina and then Alice, the ladies, wearing white embroidered muslin dresses, blue sashes, and white sailor hats. Their bouquets featured the blue forget-me-not flowers that so perfectly matched their sashes and hat trim.

Then Daniel saw his father appear with Matilda on his arm and, like Thomas beside him, he drew in a breath, stunned by his tomboy sister's beauty.

Chapter 34

When Matilda thought back upon that day, as she did often, it was as if it were a blur. The time went so quickly and she felt as if she were playing a part in a stage play destined for one performance only.

The images played in Matilda's mind: walking down the aisle of the church they attended every Sunday, but this time with their closest family and friends in attendance, her hand resting assuredly in her father's and her dear bridesmaid friends in front of her. Passing by the seat where Betty and Matilda's dear Aunt Audrey sat, steadfast in her loyalty and love. Beside Aunt Audrey, Amos and Elijah, whose partners were in the bridal party, and Gideon with his belle, Miss Phoebe Astin. There was Harriett and cook Mary and her husband. Scattered through the church were friends and acquaintances from the *Women's Journal*, her school days, and colleagues and friends of her soon-to-be husband including Thomas' brother, partners in crime Burton and Lou and their wives, and Mrs Teresa Dart, Harry's wife.

The look in Thomas' eyes when she reached him was one

of pure love and hope for their future, and when he said the words "I do" and she reciprocated, Matilda felt security she had never known, happiness she could not imagine, relief she could not express.

The well-wishers, the celebration afterwards and the speeches were heartfelt and enjoyable, a day of celebration for all and Harriet's gift to the newlyweds was delivered that day – cleaning ladies prepared Thomas' house for the bride and groom to spend the evening before they left for their honeymoon the next morning.

As expected, and pondered over by both Matilda and Thomas on numerous occasions before their wedding day, Thomas gallantly carried Matilda over the threshold of her new home and to the matrimonial bedroom for a night she would not forget.

*****

Thomas desperately wanted to unwrap Matilda from the pure white gown and be the first and only man to make love to her. He did not stop to lower her feet to the floor as they entered his abode, now their abode, but would have if she had asked. Instead, he enjoyed her arms wrapped around his neck, the inviting smile on her face as he carried her to the bedroom and lay her on the bed. She did not remove her hold of him and so encouraged, he lowered himself upon her, stopping long enough to kick off his shoes. He hesitated, which took an inordinate amount of self-control.

'Would you like time to… uh, do whatever ladies do?' he asked.

'What is that?' she asked, a glint of amusement in her eyes.

'I have no idea. To change maybe.'

'Will you not undress me? I thought that is what would happen next.'

'Of course, happily,' he answered, realising this was going to be a somewhat unorthodox first love-making session and wondering how much Matilda knew of the process, if anything. 'I am sure I can find you somewhere in there,' he teased, as the voluminous layers of skirt hid her and her fitted bodice appeared to be moulded to her.

'I best stand. All the buttons are down the back, and you will want to undress too,' she said practically, releasing her hold of him.

It was typical Matilda but not quite the romantic passion he had envisaged. Still, Thomas was not complaining and was a very willing participant in the undressing. He rose off the bed, offered his hand and gently pulled Matilda up but before she turned to be undone, she wrapped her arms around his waist, pressed her face to his chest and held him. It was surprisingly endearing and he felt overwhelmingly protective. Reciprocating her hold, she raised her face to him and he kissed her deeply, passionately, for longer than he had ever been able to before, until there was no denying the impatience of his need and her heavy breathing indicated the same.

He stepped up, as Harry had recommended in his advice—be confident, manly, enjoy learning together, and laugh at anything that does not go according to plan—and Thomas spun Matilda around which engaged a surprised laugh from her as he began to disrobe his bride of the many virginal white layers she wore. When he could see her creamy skin, she turned back around and his breath hitched.

'Oh Tillie, my God you are beautiful,' he murmured, his hand on her arm and the other gently touching her chin.

He saw the unshed tears in her eyes, and as she reached for his shirt, he assisted, undressing hurriedly and discarding his elegant groom's attire. He felt her eyes studying him, the shape of his arms and shoulders, feeling his skin as she touched parts of his slightly stubbled jaw, trailing her hand to his naked chest as he removed his own garments.

He gently lowered her to the bed. It had been many years since he had made love to a virgin, and he tempered his passion, and controlled his desire and pace. It was agony. Matilda responded to his touch, to his kisses, returning his action in kind and exploring him without trepidation.

She moaned with pleasure, arched and dug her nails into him, signs that pleased him that he was pleasuring her. She gasped as he touched the parts of her body that had never felt a man's touch before, and her eyes widened with surprise.

'Tillie?' He paused—despite the effort of doing so—to ensure all was well.

'I have felt nothing like that before,' she said, in a hushed voice that was almost reverent. 'It is so good.'

Thomas gave a small laugh. 'I am pleased to hear that on both counts.'

'Don't stop,' she directed him, with impatience in her voice.

'Then stop talking to me,' he retorted, kissing her to stop her from answering back as his hands continued to explore her, bringing her to the edge of passion until he tipped her over, her pleasure exciting him.

When she had breath to speak, she whispered, 'But there is more?'

'So much more,' he said, 'but we don't have to do it all on our first night together.'

'But you have not been inside me. I know that happens,' she insisted, her hand touching his face, the other caressing his chest.

'I intend to, be assured of that. I am just letting you catch your breath,' Thomas said.

'Do you need to catch your breath?' she asked.

He chuckled. 'No. Trust me, if you knew how much self-control I am displaying, you would not think me capable of it.' He ran his fingers over her skin as he spoke, and again her impatience kicked in.

'Do it, Thom, please, do it now,' she begged, wanting to lose herself to him.

He did not need any further encouragement. The strain of waiting and the effort of holding himself in check were mighty painful.

'I will do my best not to hurt you,' he whispered, positioning himself over her and pressing into her, ready to become man and wife in body.

She gasped, and he stopped.

'Will it hurt?' she asked, looking alarmed.

Thomas froze, his body still. 'Only a little, the first time, maybe, or so I am led to believe.' Then he saw the smile on her face and muttered, 'Tillie, you are teasing me and putting off my concentration.'

'I hope that is all I am putting off,' she said and gave him a teasing smile.

'You are impossible,' he puffed out the words, feeling less merciful now. Nevertheless, he entered her slowly, and trembled with the exercise of doing so when she was so perfect, tight, and welcoming of him. He heard her gasp and stopped.

'Don't stop,' she uttered, digging her nails into his back, and Thomas grimaced as he continued to move inside of her until they were complete as one and he felt he was about to burst.

'Is that alright?' he whispered, amazed by the feeling of her all around him and trying not to move to prolong the pleasure.

'Oh yes, it is more than alright. Is that it?' she asked, and he laughed again and moved slowly, rhythmically.

'Oh my,' she murmured, as their passion built and Thomas' body tightened, his muscles bunching. He tried to make the lovemaking last for as long as he could hold on, as Matilda moaned with pleasure beneath him. Then the release came, the release he had hoped for and dreamt about for so long. He heard Matilda gasp, and Thomas let go of his control. He too, gasped, closing his eyes and enjoying the sweet release until his body eventually stilled. Thomas too was sated.

After a few moments, he lifted his head to look at her and finding Matilda's lips, they kissed slowly and leisurely.

'It is an amazing feeling, I could not believe you would fit,' she said, practically.

He laughed softly. 'Thank goodness I did.' He looked at her in awe of the moment. 'I shall never love anyone else but you for the rest of our days together.'

'Nor I, I never have,' she assured him. 'A perfect day,' she said and sighed.

'With a perfect ending, Tillie.'

'Mrs Thomas Ashdown,' she corrected him, and for once, he was happy to let her win that point.

THE END

Author's notes and research for this story:

While this is a work of fiction, I try to be as accurate to the era as possible, in this case – 1889. It's exciting to research and find points of interest that can be adapted for the novel. Even though the book is set in Brisbane, I based the alleys and laneways on Melbourne where many prettily named lanes had dark and sinister goings-on. The fabric suppliers, Duncalfe & Co, owned by Edward and Thomas Duncalfe, were based in George Street, Brisbane – a street that became known for tailoring and fashion.

The two desserts that Mary prepared for Daniel's birthday – jam roly-poly and bread-and-butter pudding were served up on Australian dining tables in 1889. But no one made them like my grandmother, Mrs Dulcie Watson, did in the 1970s. Grandma was also an amazing seamstress, a skill many of us never acquire these days.

While choosing names can be tricky, the most popular birth names of past years are always helpful. A great resource available online is the British 1881 census, which ensures a good supply of genuine male and female names of the era.

The stories discussed by the ladies of the *Women's Journal* were real stories taken from the pages of newspapers in Queensland, Australia, in 1889, including whether women should have the right to propose. Today, I imagine many women do, but it is still very much the male bastion – most likely for the pure romance of it. Australia's first female doctor was Emma Constance Stone as mentioned and she did partner with her doctor sister, Clara Stone. What trailblazers! And Mr Grant Allen's letter on the risks to the population if society continues to educate and emancipate women when the focus should be on child rearing was very real. One can only imagine the struggle many women went through to gain us the independence, education and freedoms we take for granted today.

Coming next…

Thank you for reading and taking Matilda's journey with me. Look out for the pending adventures of the mortician, Miss Phoebe Astin, and her handsome brothers, in a soon-to-be-released series.

Sign up for my newsletter or follow me on Facebook or BookBub to be notified of new releases.

Also in the *Miss Hayward and the Detective* series…

Murder at the Freak Show

Matilda Hayward is determined to have a career; after all, it is 1888! While reporting for the *Women's Journal* newspaper, Matilda is sent to cover the visiting 'Freak Show' and to interview Mrs Anna Tufton, a giantess. During the interview, the giantess slips a note to Matilda begging for her help to escape from the show her husband forces her to do. But when the giantess's husband is found murdered, the giantess is a likely suspect.

Matilda enlists her lawyer brother, Amos, to help prove the giantess is no killer and to free her from a life of exploitation. But a close family friend, Detective Thomas Ashdown—who has feelings for Matilda, having known her since childhood—would prefer Matilda was nowhere near his murder case. There is mystery, danger, and love afoot!

The Artist's Missing Muse

Miss Matilda Hayward admits she is no art critic, but when she meets the artist, Mr Marlon Dominey, and his beautiful muse, Miss Sapphire Reubens, she can appreciate beauty on and off the canvas. Her brother and art gallery manager, Gideon, is to exhibit Mr Dominey's latest collection and Matilda and Miss Alice Doran—her fellow writer for the *Women's Journal*—get a preview of the inspired work featuring his muse illuminated and immersed in water.

But when the muse, Miss Reubens, can't be found, and two artists are found murdered and posed in the manner of their paintings, Matilda and her new beau, Detective Thomas Ashdown, fear the artwork might be a death portrait. There is mystery, passion and love afoot!

Mystery at the Asylum

Miss Matilda Hayward has a nose for a story that serves her well as a writer for the *Women's Journal* newspaper. Her beau, Detective Thomas Ashdown, is not quite as enthusiastic about her role. When Matilda's brother, Elijah, takes up a doctor's position at the Asylum for the Insane, she volunteers, seeking more life experience to improve her writing. Joined by her illustrator friend, Miss Georgina Urry, the two ladies are thrust into the mystery of several strange asylum deaths as patients believe they can fly. When Thomas is sent to investigate, their worlds collide. Now the race is on to find the sinister threat dwelling inside the dark and gloomy walls of the asylum.

There is secrecy, danger, and love afoot!

The Mortician's Clue

Miss Matilda Hayward has been assigned her first book review for the *Women's Journal* newspaper and she is very much enjoying Mr Linton Turner's novel, *The Pyjama Girl Mystery*, until it comes to life. When a young lady is found murdered and left on the church steps dressed only in blue satin pyjamas—just like in the plot of the novel—the author immediately comes under suspicion. But no one can identify the victim.

Matilda's beau, Detective Thomas Ashdown, is on the case, and with his partner, Detective Harry Dart, they hire a talented mortician, Miss Phoebe Astin, to illustrate the deceased lady for identification purposes. After Matilda and her friend, Miss Georgina Urry, make Phoebe's acquaintance, the three ladies find themselves unwillingly caught in a battle of words and hearts between an author and a poet with deadly intent. There is secrecy, danger, and love afoot!

Coming next... The Lady Mortician's Visions' series:

The Missing Brides

Miss Phoebe Astin and her brothers, Julius and Ambrose, lead an unconventional life working in the family funeral business – The Economic Undertaker. But Phoebe is not just a talented mortician, she is a medium for the spirit world, and often enjoys the company of her clients before they move on to the next world. When one gentleman begs her to investigate his murder, Phoebe contacts her brother's friend, Detective Harland Stone, and soon she finds there are several missing brides, feared murdered. For the Astin family, being dead is no excuse for letting crime go unpunished! *And... The Fake Child*

You might also enjoy by this author...

The Forgotten House (historical fiction):

"If you've ever been truly in love, you'll identify with Lexie and James." Judy Alter, Story Circle Book Reviews.

Once the grandest of homes, now deserted and ramshackle; Autumn Manor lies in ruins. But when Carrie Howell asks her granddaughter, Rachael, to stop awhile in front of the old mansion, Rachel decides to investigate the house's history. Behind the facade, she finds a love story interrupted by war. Who were these people her grandmother was remembering, and what was her connection?

Jesse Clarke series (cosy mysteries):

Death by Sugar:

"If you are a fan of Kathryn Ledson or Janet Evanovich you will love unravelling the mysteries in the Jesse Clarke series." Carol, Reading, Writing and Riesling.

Private investigator, Jesse Clarke, thought sugar was such a friendly substance until it appeared in two of her cases for all the wrong reasons. Traces of sugar were connected to a bomb that blew up her client's Mercedes. Was the bomb meant to kill or was it just a warning of what was to come? And could sugar have duped the immune system of a client's mother over thirty years ago, resulting in death?

Juggling the two cases—one in the present and one in the past—Jesse finds herself talking to the living and the dead to get results.

Death by Disguise:

"A fantastic read that had me laughing; it thoroughly surprised me!" Christine – Goodreads

The dead are walking and it is not even Halloween! Sassy private investigator Jesse Clarke knew it would not be a normal week when two dead people are spotted alive but their death certificates say otherwise, Spiderman steals a collection of costumes made for the next Comic-Con, and Batman drops in to warn her that all is not as it seems. Supported by her own man of steel—the tall, dark and handsome Dominic; business partner Ed; police contact Officer Jason who has more than a professional interest in Jesse; and, best friend Melanie, Jesse finds herself talking to witches, superheroes and morticians to solve her two cases and looking behind the disguises for answers!

Death by Reunion:

Jesse Clarke's 10-year school reunion boasted a few shocks – and that didn't include Jesse running a publicity and private investigator business. Rather, the talk of the reunion was

Alex Bryson, the overweight kid who transformed himself thanks to winning a place on the TV reality program, Lose it! But a week after the reunion, Alex is dead. That's not the only reunion that's taking up Jesse's time. At a family reunion and 80th birthday celebration for a family matriarch, a very expensive Titanic relic goes missing – a Titanic Mourning Bear. And now T-Bear, as he is known, is showing up all over the country! With support from her boyfriend, Dominic, along with her grumpy business partner Ed, Police Officer Jason, and Jesse's enthusiastic best friend, Melanie, Jesse is back solving mysteries while juggling publicity clients including Mona and her choir, again.

Special thanks to:

Penny Clarkson for proofreading, and to my supportive reading friends and family, especially Lisa, Bev, Jenny and Mary, thank you.

About the Author:

After studying English Literature and Communications at universities in Queensland, Australia, and obtaining a Counselling Diploma, Helen Goltz has worked as a journalist, producer and marketer in print, TV, radio and public relations. She was born in Toowoomba and has made her home in Brisbane.

Visit her website at: www.helengoltz.com

Or Facebook at: www.facebook.com/HelenGoltz.Author

Follow on Twitter at: https://twitter.com/HelenGwriter

Sign-up for Helen's newsletter for book discounts and specials, and to hear when the future titles are released, including the spin-off with the psychic mortician, Miss Phoebe Astin.

To hear of new releases and discount books, please follow Helen on BookBub.